RETURN TO ATLANTIS

DOMINO TAYLOR

VIVIENNE SAVAGE

CONTENTS

ISBN: 978-1-7335029-0-0

1

—————

THE SEA ANGEL

ON A TYPICAL SPRING EVENING, THE ROCKING motion of the waves would have comforted Kailani. She had the ocean breeze in her hair, the fading sun on her bare shoulders, and a glorious view of the Atlantic as water lapped against the *Sea Angel's* hull.

It would have been the end to a beautiful day, if not for the enormous whaling ship headed dead-on for their smaller vessel.

"I don't get it. Why did they change course? Don't they see us?" Rose asked. The young marine biology major had joined the environmentalist group earlier that year.

"Of course they see us. This boat is small, not microscopic. They *mean* to crash into us," Kai said. The poachers must have realized the *Sea Angel's* crew was there to film more of their illegal activities, which meant thousands in fines for hunting endangered creatures.

"But they'll wreck our boat!"

"Yeah. That's the point," Kai muttered, more furious than she was petrified by the events. "Dead people can't report crimes."

The twenty-five years Kai could recall of her life flashed before her eyes, the latter half a time peppered with accomplishments ranging from an honorable discharge from the U.S. Navy to earning a marine biology degree.

Every moment brought her to where she stood now, throwing her life away to save the whales.

No. Not throwing it away. *Sacrificing* it. If they were fortunate, their deaths wouldn't be in vain, and one of their choppers had a clear shot of the encounter. At least, she hoped the *Zeus* 2 had it all. The chopper didn't normally fly with them, but the benefactor of their organization had wanted to cover more ground.

They should have been two passing ships in the afternoon, the *Sea Angel* a smaller scouting boat designed strictly for surveillance, the *Cristóbal* sailed by poachers guilty of murdering the endangered North Atlantic right whale. At the last minute, the other ship had made a dramatic change, altering its course head on for them.

It had seemed like an intimidation tactic until Captain Johnson changed course and the *Cristóbal* adjusted to remain in their path.

"This is going to be hairy! Everyone hold on!" Johnson cried from the helm.

There wasn't enough time. No amount of evasive maneuvering or skill could pull them out of the monster ship's path. They'd realized their enemy's intentions too late, and the *Sea Angel*, while swift, wasn't fast enough to avoid the much larger whaling ship. They were David against Goliath.

The intentional ramming would leave every member of the *Sea Angel* stranded in the frigid open water of the Atlantic Ocean. If they survived at all.

Kai didn't have much hope.

While their captain made a hard right to evade the threat before them, Kai gripped the rail and braced for impact, staring down the illegal whaling vessel set on a direct course for their ship's bow.

The *Cristóbal's* crew must have reached peak desperation to attempt sinking them, perhaps tired of paying the enormous fines levied against them for poaching. Every member of the *Sea Angel's* crew volunteered as a member of Clear Shores, an organization devoted to monitoring the Atlantic and reporting crimes against ocean animals.

Kai's team had already gotten the other vessel into deep shit once.

Despite Johnson's attempt to remove the *Sea Angel* from their opponent's path, the other ship smashed into their stern. The deafening shriek of metal against metal punctuated the crash of ships coming together in a powerful collision. They rocked back and forth, and bits of the *Sea Angel* splintered into the water. As the stern split, a great wave of water lapped over the portside bow.

A woman's scream joined the tearing metal, drowned out by the screech made by shattering wood. The rocking ship capsized, sending the crew sliding to the starboard rail. Cries of pain filled the air and bodies toppled over the rail.

Everything after that moment happened quickly. Her body slapped against a wall of chilly water, and then waves engulfed her, surging up her nose, into her mouth and throat, and over her head.

But naval training kicked in along with instinct and she surfaced moments later, bobbing on the turbulent and choppy waves while desperately searching for any other survivors.

Their scouting vessel had been reduced to sheets of ruined metal and splintered wood. She swam to a nearby piece of debris as the *Cristóbal* left the *Sea Angel's* wreckage in its white-capped wake without concern for the injured, the stranded, or the dead.

Yards away, their undamaged lifeboat drifted out on the current created by the crash.

Thank goodness for small miracles, though that appeared to be the only godsend she spotted at a glance.

One of their researchers, a gentle man who had signed on due to his love of dolphins, floated face down beside her. Blood streamed from the back of his shattered skull in a frothy, pink river. When the waves tossed his corpse further away from her, she had no choice but to let him go.

Kai discovered another unconscious researcher among the ship's ruin while Collins recovered the lifeboat. The big and tanned Royal Marine was their muscle, but they'd never needed him for more than infrequent intimidation tactics.

Another volunteer heaved herself into the boat, then helped Kailani and Collins to get the unconscious man inside. Rose touched two fingers to his pulse point and sighed in relief. "He's alive and definitely breathing, but what if they come back to finish what they started?"

"Then we die. We have to hope that *Zeus* 2 captured it all on video, otherwise it's our word against theirs. All of our video footage of their illegal activities will be at the bottom of this fucking ocean by now."

Gods, they needed the chopper. Sooner, not later.

One by one, she and the other able-bodied survivors guided the injured to the life boat. It happened over the course of minutes but felt like hours before everyone but she and Collins huddled in the boat for safety. And warmth. But too much adrenaline pumped through Kai's body for the cold to affect her.

"Where's Franco?" Collins asked. "He's shite in the water...should have been wearing a vest from the bloody start. Do you see him? Franco!"

"Antonio!" Rose called. "Antonio, are you out there?" She turned to face Kai, who treaded water alongside the boat. Rose's lips were blue, and her teeth chattered. Thin strands of white-blonde hair stuck to her pale face. "How many are we missing?"

Collins glanced at her. "Too many." He found a

body, grimaced, and pushed his way through more of the wreckage.

A quick headcount determined more of them remained among the missing than found or alive, including Johnson. Shit.

"Keep looking," Kai said, sifting through debris. "We have nine men unaccounted for and—" Vibrations in the water churned the ocean beneath them. Though she saw nothing immediately below her in the twilight depths, she sensed something was there and dared to hope it was one of their people desperately struggling to swim to the surface.

It could be a shark attracted by the commotion or the blood in the water. Or some other fish hoping for a nibble. A school of them, perhaps. The moment those thoughts danced through her mind, a calm voice of reason and logic said otherwise, telling her to trust her instincts.

Heart slamming a frenetic drumbeat against her ribs, Kailani took the less sensible option. She dove under and searched the black water, leaving the oblong shape of the lifeboat behind as she delved yards below the surface. The Atlantic welcomed her with a sense of tranquil comfort, like soaking in a warm bath with a sweet glass of champagne. It invited her in, urging her to swim deeper.

The others shivered from the cold. She did not. Something told her she was different. That she could take what they couldn't. Her mother had always called her a water baby, a child born for swimming and more comfortable in a pool than on two legs.

Within seconds, she put yards between herself and the surface.

Where could they be?

Something disturbed the water to her left and sent micro-ripples toward her. She jerked that way and saw the silhouette of a man's motionless body drifting through the near pitch-black veil of the fathomless deep far below her. What little remained of the dwindling sun penetrated the ocean and cast diffuse silver ripples over Antonio's jacket. Kai curled an arm around his broad torso and kicked to the surface.

Moments later, when she'd dumped him with Collins and Rose, something told her if she returned to the deep, she'd find another.

Without questioning that tiny voice whispering in her subconscious, Kailani dove under again and resumed the search.

2

SURFACE BOUND

The Gift of the Sea glowed.

Manu had been a child when its light dimmed twenty-five years ago, signaling an end to the royal line of Atlantis. On that day, mers across the Atlantic Ocean mourned the loss of their compassionate monarchs, but more than that, Manu had grieved the death of his own mother.

Commander Malie had traveled as a guard in the king and queen's personal escort, but her body wasn't among the remains at the site of the ambush. Sea life was a cruel life, and any number of hungry scavengers could have taken her away.

That was the infinite nature of energy; one thing died and gave life to another.

But on today, the stone affixed to Queen Ianthe's scepter shone a deep golden-orange. It flashed, held its gleam, but then dulled anew.

Had he not been paying his respects at the memorial, it would have gone unseen. He stared at it for a time, convinced it had been a figment of his imagination or a trick of the light, but then it sparked one more time.

That stone hadn't so much as flickered in a quarter of a century.

Two guards were to stand watch over the Chamber of Heroes at all times, but their men had been stretched thin during the past season by the encroaching rise of the darkness. Recruitment was at an all-time low.

With no one present to send for the high priest, Manu went to fetch the man himself. He pushed up to his feet and launched himself toward the palace corridor, long legs crossing the marble floor at a fast clip. His footfalls echoed beneath the vaulted ceilings when he reached the entrance hall and the great stone doors. A pair of armed sentries stood watch, holding spears and shields they'd hopefully never need to use on the palace grounds.

Manu sent one to fetch the regent, then he hurried onto a lantern-lit, paved road leading to the temple devoted to their goddess. That was where he would find their high priest, as the man rarely left these days, having shut himself away in seclusion under a vow of silence, emerging for no one.

Now it was time to drag the hermit from his cave.

A literal cave.

The Temple of Thalassa stretched as tall as the royal palace, several stories of chiseled rock sculpted from the ocean floor into a place of worship able to house thousands of the citizens who dwelled within the city's protective glass walls.

Manu's gaze scanned upward to the colossal dome stretching far above Atlantis. The magic-imbued, nigh-indestructible barrier played two roles: it divided the dry streets of Atlantis from the ocean and protected their city from creatures of the Gloom. Though actual aberrations had not approached within a hundred leagues of Atlantis in centuries.

The temple claimed credit for the peace, basing the years of silence from the shadowlands as proof of Thalassa's love for her people. No one believed it. Many had lost their faith—lost their hope—since Queen Ianthe and King Neptune's deaths. What good was there in believing in deities of the earth, sky, and sea, when the people of their colonies and rural homesteads were slaughtered by the dozens each day?

He walked through the temple's tall arches, passed between marble pillars, and strode through cold and empty echoing caverns with polished floors gleaming silver beneath the gemstone torchlight. Though he visited rarely since his childhood, he knew his way around.

High Priest Hipponax knelt before a radiant statue of the goddess, all five meters carved from luminescent white stone. Some considered the sculpture to be one of the temple's greatest treasures, though the object of real value—according to the priest—was the gilded bowl at the base by her feet. That vessel held the purest, most pristine water in all the realm, a magical fluid that never evaporated and never moved.

Legends claimed the water was Thalassa's tears.

Manu snorted. And seahorses flew. He'd believed that nonsense when he was a child; now, as an adult, he knew better than to trust fairy tales. Their goddess, if she even existed, had long ago forsaken Atlantis and left them to be overtaken by the Gloom.

"Excuse me, Commander Manu," a young priestess said, intercepting him the moment he stepped into the chamber. "High Priest Hipponax has asked for privacy and—"

"I've come bearing important news." He gave her a tight smile, the kind that didn't reach his eyes. Happiness, or even pleasure for that matter, wasn't an expression Manu often wore.

"If you could tell me your news, I'll relay it to him—"

Manu thrust out one arm and pressed the woman aside, parting her from his path with the ease of opening a curtain. Gently. "High Priest, forgive my interruption, but your attention is needed at the palace."

Hipponax waved toward him with one hand in the universal gesture of "hold on a moment," but Manu had the patience of a ravenous mako shark.

"High Priest Hipponax is not permitted to speak," the priestess insisted, fighting her way between them. "I must ask again for your patience."

"He'll speak to me." Manu clenched his jaw. "I

understand he's taken a vow of silence, but does he not receive a half hour of respite each day?"

"He's used it. If you want a discussion, perhaps his assistant or I can grant you a moment—"

"A moment won't do." Manu raised his voice to be heard, letting it echo throughout the chamber. "I need you now, priest. Day after day, you kneel here praying for a miracle, hoping for some sign from Thalassa. Well. She's answered you. *Someone* has answered you. While I paid my respects to my mother in the Chamber of Heroes, Queen Ianthe's scepter glowed as if she were still among us. Several times."

The priestess fell back a step, staring at him with alarmed eyes. "Truly?"

While the woman's mouth fell open, Hipponax stared at him with the shrewd gaze of a man expecting to hear the punchline of a joke. When one didn't come, he rose to his feet with aid from his staff. "You speak the truth to me?"

"I wouldn't lie about this."

"Then we must return to the palace."

SOME MERS DISAGREED with placing a regent on the throne, but they'd little choice in the matter when Atlantis required formal leadership.

Twenty-five years of political conflict had boiled across the city, tearing families apart and turning brother against brother. One faction, the Loyalists, wanted to adopt a modern state of governance for their kingdom. They claimed to owe allegiance to the kingdom and capital city itself, not the highborn mers who controlled it. Others, the Royalists, longed to continue the monarchy and officially crown Regent Aegaeon and his wife as the new king and queen. After all, hadn't enough time passed without someone sitting on the throne?

Manu had yet to decide which camp he stood in, having little contact and no communication with their stand-in ruler. As the brother of King Neptune, Aegaeon had no royal claim to Atlantis's matrilineal throne, but he was a just high mer, and that was reason enough for Manu to serve in the Royal Army.

As hoped, Regent Aegaeon awaited them in the Chamber of Heroes, standing tall with both hands behind his back while he stared at the lit scepter. To Manu's relief, it hadn't yet dulled. Part of him had feared the light would dim before anyone arrived to witness it.

Its glow was truly magnificent, an amber light with a core bright as the sun. He stepped into the circular room and walked down one of the aisles between statues depicting deceased ancestors and fallen soldiers. The room held dozens of such monuments to the dead.

"It's beautiful, isn't it?" Aegaeon murmured. "I never thought I'd see it lit again. All this time, I wondered if another might ever wield it, and yet... here it is."

The scepter nestled in the hand of a marble

figure carved in Queen Ianthe's likeness. She and her king stood side by side in full armor, her husband wielding his trident. Both weapons were the real thing, treasures incorporated into their memorial stones by the artisan responsible for the chamber's upkeep.

Manu's presence no longer served a purpose. Realizing this, he bowed stiffly. "I will leave you both to discuss this, my lords. If you'll excuse me—"

"No." The scrawny old priest studied him. "Perhaps it is a blessing in disguise that you were the one to witness the light's return. I would not have you leave, Commander Manu. Surely this is a sign from Thalassa."

It took all of his control not to laugh in the man's face. A sign from the goddess? If the goddess wanted to send Atlantis a sign, there were better ways to do it than creating a pretty light show with a jewel. Manu would settle for her proving her existence by wiping out the Gloom so no more of his friends died in senseless battle.

That would be a sign.

What he wanted, what he truly desired, was to see Thalassa bitch slap Calypso to the darkest pit of Tartarus, never to be seen again, and saving more young mers on the brink of adulthood from dying in the never-ending war.

That would be a sign.

Flickering lights were *not* signs.

Actions were signs.

Aegaeon appeared to be every bit the heretic

Manu felt in recent days. He snorted and glanced away from the stone. "Forgotten goddesses aside, what do you suggest this means?"

A quiet smile came to Hipponax's face. "It means a member of the blood touched these waters. Somewhere, a mer of royal lineage swims in the Atlantic once more. That is what it means."

"Impossible. We found the remains of my brother and the queen many years ago. There were no survivors."

The priest glanced at the scepter again. "The child may have lived."

"Ah, I don't dare to have such hope and see it crushed, Hipponax. Wouldn't the Gift of the Sea have shone long before this eve if Princess Zephyrine survived the ambush?"

"Possibly. We cannot know for certain. It is an ancient relic, Aegaeon, and as such, it is unpredictable. Only the queen truly understood it, and we lack her wisdom. What I do know is the remains of Commander Manu's mother and our princess were never recovered. Our princess could be alive and awaiting a rescue. We could restore a queen to the throne."

A pregnant pause hung in the air between the two men, Manu the only spectator. Aegaeon's jaw worked a few times, clenching with tension. His gaze darted to the scepter and lingered.

"All right," the regent said in a quiet voice. "For a moment, I will humor your theory that my niece survived the ordeal that slew two dozen Myrmidon guards, my brother, *and* our queen. What do you suggest we do to find her?"

"It will take time to develop the proper ritual spells to trace her whereabouts, but it can be done. I require blood from you, as you and she are kin."

"I agree to this."

"We must move quickly. And quietly. For the Gift of the Sea to remain dormant all this time can only mean her powers have also been dormant. Now that they are awakened, she will be a target to all things creeping and dark in these seas. I propose we send Manu to safely retrieve her."

Manu jerked around to face the high priest. His mouth opened and closed in silent protest, but words never came. For High Priest Hipponax to recommend him for a surface mission was the highest honor, one he couldn't dismiss, no matter how much he dreaded leaving the water behind.

He swore internally. There were dozens of reasons he'd prefer not to go to the surface, chief among them that the mortals were unpredictable, barbaric creatures.

"Will you accept this appointment as our champion, Manu?" Regent Aegaeon asked.

Manu placed his forearm against his waist and dipped forward into a deep bow. "I would send no other in my place, my lord."

"I will contact one of our many agents among the humans." Hipponax stroked his waist-length white beard and gazed into the distance. "You can begin the search in a place called Texas."

"Why Texas?"

"When the king and queen left with their escort twenty-five years ago, they were to meet with a mortal dignitary there. If the princess lives, it is possible she washed ashore there."

"And what am I to do if I do find her?"

A low chuckle shook Hipponax's shoulders. "Return with her, of course."

GIRLS' NIGHT

Sunset shone over the Gulf of Mexico, turning thousands of waves into gold slivers beneath the darkening sky. Sitting on a towel printed with characters from *The Little Mermaid*, Kailani watched the gulls swoop and hunt for food.

Three months had passed since the afternoon from hell, the day she'd pulled three unresponsive bodies from the Atlantic Ocean. Johnson and Franco had recovered. Morris didn't. Despite their best efforts to revive him, the conservationist had been underwater too long for any amount of CPR to bring him back.

If only she'd realized they were in danger sooner. If she'd been quicker to act, all three could have survived the ordeal.

No matter how much logic told Kailani it wasn't her fault another ship decided to play chicken with their boat, she couldn't let it go. A minute might have been all the difference between Morris's death and survival.

Survivor's guilt was a fucking bitch, and it had curled its unrelenting hooks so hard into her psyche no amount of rationale would dislodge it, even when Morris's widow hugged her at the funeral and told her she'd done everything possible.

Kai heard the approach of her younger sister long before Sadie's shadow fell over her. Saying nothing, she plopped onto the sand and gazed into the turbulent water.

For a while, they sat together with the sunset behind them and foamy ocean waves crashing against the shell-speckled shore a few meters to their front. Gull cries and the roar of the surf made their own evening melody, filling the silence between them. This place, to the rear of their beachside property, was where Kailani went to do her best thinking. And her brooding. And any other verb requiring absolute peace and solitude from other human beings. Her mother and sister had learned long ago to leave her alone as long as her moods required.

"Hey. I know you came out for the quiet, but Mom sent three texts asking about dinner."

"Sorry. Tell her I had a snack. Not really hungry."

"Oh." A deliberate pause. Kai didn't have to glance at her sister to know Sadie was watching her. "What's up?"

"Thinking."

"About?"

Kailani didn't respond. They both knew the answer.

"Come on. Let's take a walk."

"Where?"

"Anywhere."

"Why?"

Sadie rolled her eyes. "You never go anywhere. You're always home, sitting here on the beach looking at nothing. Let's have some fun." Sadie took on a pleading expression, practically begging. "Please? When school starts, I'll never have time to hang out with you. These are my last two semesters. They'll be the most difficult. A few weeks from now, you'll wish you hung out with me when you had the chance."

"You'll manage. You always do."

"That's not the point," Sadie whined.

"Mm."

"I miss you, silly. You were gone for *years*, and now that you're back, it's like you're still not here with us."

Six years in the U.S. Navy satisfied Kai until the desire to study marine biology lured her back to civilian life. And that pursuit of knowledge afterward led her to joining Clear Shores, a charity founded by a Hollywood billionaire with way too much money on his hands and a desire to help ocean life after playing a conservationist in a movie.

Gods. She missed them. She missed them so badly it hurt. After the run-in with the *Cristóbal* claimed so many lives, their benefactor had backed down and declared the organization finished. They'd lost five men and women who would never again feel the ocean breeze or hear whale songs on a pleasant afternoon.

It didn't help that their murderers were still tied up in court. *Zeus 2* hadn't been close enough to capture clear footage after all, so it was one crew's word against another.

"I just want to spend time with you again. I miss having a sister."

That one plea snapped Kai out of her pity party. Her gaze lifted from the sand to Sadie's worried face. They may not have been flesh and blood, but she'd known from the moment the social worker arrived with little Sadie in her arms that they were meant to be sisters.

"All right. We'll go out." The words tasted like impending regret. How long would it take to contemplate slitting her own throat to escape the party scene?

"Yaaaas, Queen."

Kai rolled her eyes at the inside joke. Their last name was Queen. The instant they were inside the house, Sadie wasted no time dragging Kai upstairs and rummaging through her wardrobe. While Kai was four inches taller, her sister was plumper and liked to steal the stretchy, elastane minidresses from her closet. In some cases, the twenty-one-year-old nursing student actually put them *back*.

Those were rare moments indeed. Kai rarely counted on seeing anything again once it disappeared into Sadie's room.

"You have thirty minutes to get ready, but I'm doing your makeup."

"I don't need makeup."

"Everyone needs eyeshadow and brows. Besides, I have a new green and a gold that will look *amazing* on you."

"I don't—"

"Thirty minutes." Sadie whisked one of Kai's sarongs from the closet and swept from the room, leaving her to stare into the vast space of pretty things acquired during her Navy career but never worn.

What a waste. Studying her reflection in the mirror hanging from her closet doors, she wondered if her carefree younger sibling was right and if abrupt change was what she needed to shift her depressing life on its axis. Something had to change.

And there was nowhere better to start than visiting a beachside club.

OF ALL THE missions Manu undertook through the years, infiltrating human society irritated him the most. Other members of the Royal Army would have seen a visit to the surface world as an honor. He saw it as punishment.

Less than a day ago, when Manu arrived in Atlantian armor, his contact had outfitted him in board shorts to blend in with the locals. He already missed his sharkskin, also longing for pristine water and the beauty of a city unspoiled by humans. Homesickness would have to be the motivation to find Princess Zephyrine sooner than later, as he couldn't imagine spending more than another day in this dismal hell.

Manu maneuvered around a cluster of scantily clad teens. The boardwalk was nothing more than a narrow strip of cement running parallel to a dirty little beach crowded by too many people. He must have arrived during the height of the tourist season, but nothing excused the state of the sand. The filth. The litter.

Did humans care nothing for their world?

Of course not. The bits of trash that came to Atlantis from the surface were proof of that, as humans treated the entire world as their refuse pile. It infuriated him that they enjoyed carefree, safe lives while his people fought against the Gloom. The only wars the humans faced were those of their own making, wars caused by greed, corruption, and hatred of their fellow man over little more than which figure to worship in the sky.

He snorted. Humans. They didn't deserve the protection they received from Atlantis or any of the *other* worlds.

Dragging his attention back to the present, he noticed a pair of women in bikinis passing by on his left, whispering to each other while sneaking glances at him. "Check out the tattoos on that one," tickled his hearing along with the words, "Forget the tatts. Look at those abs."

Ah.

Humans were always good for a little ego stroke, at least. They'd been his attentive admirers during his last visit a decade ago, when he'd escorted a dignitary from Atlantis to visit a human lawmaker in Orlando. The small handful of humans aware of their world served an important purpose, keeping the secrecy while also fighting for a healthier Earth.

Ignoring the ladies devouring him with lustful gazes, he changed direction and gauged the reaction of the bloodstone in his pocket. Since his arrival on the shore, it pulsed like a homing beacon. The closer he came to her, the faster the single drop of ruby blood throbbed in the translucent gemstone's center. When Manu neared five girls by a seaside bar, the bloodstone practically hummed.

One of them was bound to be the princess, and yet none appeared stately or regal. Except for...

There was a *woman* among the group. She stood tall and lean, built like a warrior goddess with athletic thighs exposed by a sarong knotted at her left hip. Like the others, she wore next to nothing, with her stomach exposed, but she towered above them like a giantess.

His heart raced just looking at her. Dark violet hair spilled over her shoulders, blacker toward her roots—and her skin glowed golden bronze in what little remained of the sun.

This woman couldn't be human. He scanned her arms, strong limbs that were defined but not overly muscular, certainly capable of wielding a spear or a trident in battle. Her top consisted of two triangles and string, but those barely covered her breasts on account of their design, not her size. They'd have filled his palms if he cupped them, but just barely. She dressed like the embodiment of desire but everything about her said Atlantian, from the proud carriage of her shoulders to the color of her hair. She'd inherited Queen Ianthe's deep violet shade.

"You got to get laid tonight, girl. You just have to," reached his hearing.

"Sex is the only solution to your problem."

"You need a guy who will beat it up and put it on you right."

Beat it up? He pondered the unusual words, raking them in context over his brain a few times until understanding dawned with skyrocketing disgust.

There was no mortal among all the kingdoms of Earth worthy of their future queen.

He had to take her away from here at once.

A SCIENTIFIC NIGHTMARE

THREE OF SADIE'S COLLEGE FRIENDS HAD JOINED them. As the night dwindled, so did Kai's hopes of getting home at a reasonable hour and crawling into bed with a damned good book. She had a new paranormal romance to enjoy, and a pile of romantic comedies by her favorite hockey romance author, novels she'd set aside for when her mood improved and life felt worth living again.

Now she was shackled to four college sorority girls as their designated driver, and the likelihood of returning home before last call seemed a distant impossibility. Kai sloshed the ice around in her third cranberry, lime, and soda while watching the girls groove together to some popular summer rap song the world would forget about before winter.

Earlier in the night, they'd tried to coax her into picking up a man, swearing they'd catch an Uber if she did. A one-night stand didn't hold appeal, something she hadn't indulged in since her days in the military, when the selection of men had been some-what plentiful during three deployments aboard naval ships.

Years later, she realized she must have screwed herself into the mother of dry spells.

Not a dry spell. A goddamned sexual drought.

Six years, going on seven. That's how long it had been since she'd had a man. At one point in her life, she'd considered a week to be a long while. What a naïve child she'd been.

Sadie nudged her ribs, appearing like a magical imp to her left. "Hot guy at four o'clock. He's been watching you."

The moment Kai twisted for a look, Sadie pinched her. "Don't turn around to *look* at him. Geez. Way to be a novice."

"Short of growing eyes in the back of my head, there's no other way to look at him," Kai hissed, rubbing her hip. In no mood for playing coy, she turned and made eye contact with the king of all surfer hunks, a guy with a body women would feign drowning for if it meant he'd possibly apply some mouth-to-mouth action.

He had muscles for days and an athletic physique built by work and labor, not machines and leg days at the gym. Her nameless admirer reminded her of the Marines stationed aboard her old ship, though he was tall, dark, and bronze under the sun with shoulder-length black, almost-blue hair that definitely didn't fit military regulations.

Professional model, maybe? Surfer? No one

would call him beautiful, his features too rugged, too masculine for that. A strong jaw and high cheekbones gave him a chiseled look. Kai's adopted mother would call him classically handsome, like an old portrait drawn in a forgotten style no artist dared use in modern day sculpture.

"Looks sort of like...um, one of your people, you know?" came Sadie's whisper in her ear. "Hawaiian maybe? Hm, no. Samoan?"

"Maybe. Doubt it though."

"He definitely has the body of one. Check out those muscles. Maori, maybe? No? Doesn't matter. Whatever he is, he's hot. And *enormous*. What do you think? Six foot five maybe?"

"Maybe." Kai shook her head again while silently agreeing with her sister's lecherous observations. Looking at him made her knees weak. And that was not acceptable. She tore her gaze away, faced the bar, and slammed her drink, only to mourn that she was the designated driver sipping virgin cocktails.

"He's hot. Seriously. If you want to go hit that, we'll grab another ride."

"I don't," she lied between her teeth.

"Is this any way for a Queen to behave?"

Kai snorted. Their mother had been born with the unfortunate, yet legitimate and legal, name of Sunshine Queen, which meant when the two girls were adopted, the ambitious surname became theirs as well. Sunshine always joked that her parents had been born into the hippie lifestyle a few decades too early.

When she stole another look behind her, the sexy Pacific Islander-looking guy had vanished into the throng of dancers. Regret swirled through her stomach for many reasons, none of them having anything to do with her dire need to get laid for the first time in almost a decade. The longer she thought about it, the worse it seemed.

Kai belonged to a culture she didn't know, didn't remember her parents, and certainly hadn't ever made friends with another person who resembled her in appearance. While Sunshine had done an admirable job of teaching her about the many different island cultures of the Pacific, none had ever resonated with her as being the people with whom she belonged. This guy was the first, and she'd foolishly allowed him to slip away.

An hour later, it was a little after two in the morning, with her sister safe in bed but doomed to awaken to a massive, skull-splitting hangover. Kai finally had what remained of the night to herself. By then, neither her bed nor the intriguing romance novel she'd looked forward to called to her. The ocean did, though, so she headed outside barefoot onto the sand and stood beneath the silver moon shining above her.

The silent beach should have brought her peace, visiting it prior to bed part of her nighttime ritual and more relaxing than a few milligrams of melatonin. Her skin crawled instead, and a creeping sensation tickled the back of her neck, not unlike the feeling of being watched. Kai glanced at her surroundings but saw nothing out of place. The private strip of beach belonged to her mother, and tourists rarely passed by.

A little voice told her to run. Flee.

And because she wasn't the heroine of a teenage slasher flick, she obeyed that tiny voice urging her to haul ass toward the house. Kai bolted, but it was much too late to get away from the danger, because the danger had surrounded her. Huge crabs larger than Labradors burst from the sand and advanced on her, boxing her in toward the ocean. Something that could have been a cross between a lobster and a scorpion scuttled toward her from the left. To her right, a new nightmarish creature surfed in on a foamy wave, glossy black and clicking its pincers, while venom dripped from a barbed tail dragging behind it.

No matter which direction she turned, a monster closed in on her. Some wore thick shells that glistened beneath the night sky and others scuttled on multiple appendages, though they resembled nothing she'd ever studied. The ebony waves shimmering off them appeared to suck in the moonlight, darkening their surroundings and casting the beach in semi-shadow.

Kailani dashed across the sand toward a small opening, unable to believe what was in front of her. These creatures didn't exist. They *couldn't* exist, yet everything she'd ever learned over the duration of earning her degree in marine biology—and the years of research that followed—told her there were vast places beneath the ocean scientists hadn't explored.

Anything could technically exist, even sea monsters belonging in a cheesy B-movie.

They were both a scientific miracle and a nightmare.

Scuttling crabs raced along the shore behind her, closing in with surprising speed. Before she made it to the grass, a grayish-pink tentacle shot out and caught her in the midsection. Successfully clothes-lined, she lost all the air from her lungs at once and would have crumpled if the slimy limb didn't spiral around her body.

Screams left her in soft wheezes. The tentacle was like rubber. She'd never seen an octopus of this size in all of her life, though she'd cared for several at the aquarium and many more while with Clear Shores. This thing was the Godzilla of cephalopods, a beast that immobilized her entire body with *one* arm.

She'd thought she was staring down death when the *Cristóbal* rammed them. This was death in the flesh, rotten and foul-smelling like the stench of an abandoned fish market left steaming beneath a noon sun.

The monster secured her legs together and held both arms against her sides. A suction cup covered her entire face, smothering her with its foulness. Death, decay, and illness.

It shrieked, and the unbearable force constricting her torso let go. Something shiny flashed in the night beneath the starlit sky, and her attacker retreated toward the ocean, streaming dark blue blood. A crab jumped on her and knocked her down, then the swarm flooded over her body, tearing her clothes and pinching her.

Screaming out in pain, Kai grabbed a rock and desperately bashed the largest crab until its shell split open and cool goo spilled over her hands. Bludgeoning the second labracrab bruised her fingernails and her knuckles, but it freed her bleeding arm from the stunned creature. Not missing her chance, she jumped to her feet and sprinted away, shaking off the smallest crustaceans.

Kai didn't make it far. Less than a yard from the grass, something struck her from behind and she tumbled face first into the sand.

SOMEONE HAD TRIED to crack Kai's head open with a chisel. A low, methodical sort of whirring noise filled her hearing, and she was lying in a bucket seat lined with soft ash-gray leather. When she tilted her head left, she saw the profile of the sexiest man alive —the hot guy from the beachside bar who had undressed her with his eyes.

What a hell of a dream she'd had. Sea monsters on Galveston beach. Ha!

"Who the fuck are you? Where am I?" The blues and gorgeous silvers of the ocean bottom passed her by in a blur, with the occasional flash of a silver fish.

"I am Manu of Clan Ghostfin, Myrmidon Commander of the Royal Army's Artillery Forces. I am taking you back to Atlantis where you belong."

Kailani waited a beat for the laughter. If Sadie was behind this prank, she'd gone through some serious trouble to set it up. Professional lengths maybe, like that show *Candid Camera* or one of those videos always circulating around Facebook where people were chased by a guy in a clown outfit or a dog in a spider costume. There was probably a green screen or a projector involved and a film crew videoing the entire thing, waiting for her to freak.

"Atlantis, huh? Like...the mythical city of Atlantis?"

"It isn't mythical."

"Right. Okay, this is hilarious and all, but how do I get out of this thing? Sadie? Are you out there?"

He didn't laugh. His solemn features remained unchanged, stern gaze fixed on her face.

"This isn't funny anymore. Let me out of this thing."

The stranger shook his head. "We won't reach our destination for several hours. Perhaps another day. It would be unwise to stop now when the Gloombeasts have already gained your scent."

"The Gloombeasts," she repeated, staring at the hot guy piloting the craft. What little bit of amusement he'd given her dried up.

"Yes. The creatures that assaulted you on the shore. Did you forget?" The man's mouth flattened into a thin line, and dark eyes darted to her. "Are you okay?"

No. But she wanted to forget. She clawed at the seatbelt and twisted in the seat, desperate to release herself from the contraption. Kai just knew the moment the phony submersible vessel opened, she'd see theatrical lighting, a director, maybe even a show host beside her laughing sister. The guy beside her? He had to be a model or an actor. He was too good-looking, both rugged and pretty at the same time. "No, I'm not fucking okay. Those...things—they're real?"

"Those were Gloombeasts, monsters born from the dark gods of the sea."

Right. This dude was an amazing actor. She wondered why she didn't recognize his face from any Hollywood blockbusters, because his current performance blew the summer hits she'd recently seen with her friends out of the water.

And he was hot.

"We have several hours before we reach Atlantis."

Another lapse into awkward silence. The man just kept driving, steering them through coral reefs and rock formations of indescribable beauty. Sea life skittered out of their way.

It felt real. She felt the turns, the micro-adjustments as he steered, and yet she couldn't possibly be in an underwater vehicle traveling the ocean floor, because that was impossible.

It had to be some sort of 3-D ride, like one of the attractions she'd enjoyed in Universal Studios one summer with her mother and sister. Either the viewing window in the front of the phony vehicle hid the theater screen or it was an LCD panel.

Kai leaned forward and touched it, stroking cool glass with her fingers. "Ha ha ha. Okay, you're an amazing actor, and I really respect your ability to keep a straight face. Seriously, though. Can you let me out? I kind of need to pee." She was a damn liar, but she figured that would bring an end to the charade.

"No. I've spoken only the truth to you. I came seeking Princess Zephyrine, lost scion of Atlantis, and you are she."

"I'll humor you for a second. Let's pretend I believe a word about this shit. What makes you think I'm this lost princess?"

Manu glanced at her. "You're the image of your mother. In fact, you could be her, if I didn't know better."

"I look nothing like my mother. My mother is a tiny little blonde hippie named Sunshine who lives in Galveston. I'm six foot one and dark-haired."

He snorted. "I don't mean that woman. I speak of your true mother."

And then anything that could have been funny about this predicament disintegrated. Both hands fisted on her lap, nails biting into her palms hard enough to not only leave crescent indentations but also draw blood. "All right. Fuck this joke. Let. Me. Out."

"Though it was the resemblance that identified you for certain, the bloodstone carrying your uncle's blood led me to you." While she stared at him, he removed a pendant from around his neck and held it out to her. In the pale lights dotting the interior of the underwater cruiser, she saw a translucent stone with a blood-red pulsing center that picked up speed the closer it came to her until it rested on her palm.

If it was a prank—if this dude was still fucking with her—it was the most elaborate and sick prank in the history of practical jokes.

It was not a prank.

It couldn't be a prank, because no one in their right mind would have taken a joke this far when she was clearly losing it.

"Oh gods. You're not fucking crazy."

"I'm not."

"We're really... We are really underwater."

The corner of his mouth ticked up. "And now you're beginning to understand."

Her pulse beat harder, faster. The thundering of it echoed between her ears and drowned out the gentle whooshing noise accompanying their underwater excursion. She wanted to panic and scream.

She also wanted to punch this asshole in his nose for stealing her off a beach, but common sense told her not to lay hands on the man piloting a mysterious underwater craft at the bottom of the ocean. Certain choices were hazardous for a girl's health and not worth the consequences. "What about my family?"

He glanced at her again, brown eyes warm with unconcealed compassion. "Queen Ianthe and King Neptune died years ago, Your Highness."

"No. My mother and my little sister live in the

house not far from where those…things came from the water. Are they safe?"

He snorted and glanced away from her, out the viewing window. "Ah, the mortals. They were of no interest to the Gloombeasts, as they don't carry your royal blood. I drove them off and doubt they'll return. You're fortunate I arrived when I did to rescue you."

"Fortunate?" Her voice raised an octave and cracked on the last syllable. "You abducted me!"

"Saved your life."

Her heart slammed harder until she thought it would burst through her ribcage, dooming her to death by cardiac eruption. This was real, and there was nothing she could do to escape the craft if she didn't want to be crushed by the immense pressure of the ocean. Or drown. "My family will worry. They'll call the police."

"What?" This time he huffed out a hard laugh. "Your mortal law enforcement has an aquatics division now? An underwater sea force?"

He had her there. "What part of 'my family will be worried' don't you get?"

"Not my problem. I was tasked with two things: find our princess and return to Atlantis with her. I've accomplished the first. At our current speed, the other will happen by tomorrow evening."

"You're a dick," she spit out, hating him.

He shrugged. "I've heard that before."

She slumped against the curved wall to her left and sank down in the leather seat again. Losing her shit and attacking the driver wasn't going to get her to the surface because hell if she knew how to pilot the thing. Or their current position at the bottom of the ocean.

Shit. The longer she let her rational brain comb over the current evidence, the more apparent it became that she wouldn't be returning to Galveston any time soon.

This fucker had taken her to the bottom of the ocean.

The *bottom* of the *ocean*.

Kai pinched her thigh. Instead of awakening from one hell of a ridiculous nightmare, she left a red mark below the hem of her shredded cover-up.

Manu glanced at her, cocking one dark brow. "What in the name of Tartarus are you doing?"

"Trying to wake up," she muttered.

Silence fell between them again. She let it remain and stared out the viewing window.

Crying wasn't in her nature. Neither was giving up.

Instead, she'd plot and find a way back home.

LACKING any sense of passing time without the sun overhead or a watch on her arm, Kai drifted in and out of sleep, because snoozing was better than having claustrophobic panic attacks every few minutes. She always woke to the same surroundings and somber mood, endless ocean and a solemn companion.

Manu of Few Words, as she'd dubbed him in her

head, said nothing unprompted, remaining so silent she wondered if speaking hurt the bastard. Or maybe he avoided speaking because of her smell. The octopus stench had soaked into her skin and clothes. She could taste the nastiness when she opened her mouth. No wonder Manu had nothing to say to her.

It seemed they traveled for hours before they reached an unusual rock formation jutting from the ocean floor, its bleak mass barely visible in the light emitted by the vehicle's lamps. It blocked the path ahead of them, but that wouldn't have disturbed her if they weren't hurtling toward it.

"Manu?"

In lieu of a verbal response, he shifted his gaze toward her.

"There's a wall."

He didn't veer from their course. "I'm aware."

"You're taking us toward a wall—Manu, there's a wall!"

She screamed and yanked her belt, pushing with her feet against the craft's floorboard, though nothing, no amount of wiggling, could save her from the impact.

Torn between diving for the wheel, or whatever one would call the steering column he clutched in his hand, she watched in horror as he sailed toward the obstacle...until the moment they melded into the rock formation and appeared on the other side.

Kai stared at her surroundings. They had broken the surface beside a dock despite being thousands of feet underwater. A pair of sentries stood guard, each one armed with a spear longer than they were tall. Their armor shone dark blue and green, resembling a crustacean's algae-covered shell.

"I know what I'm doing. A little patience, please."

Sweat beaded against her brow. They'd survived somehow, but all it did was make her want to throttle him more. "What...? Is this Atlantis?"

"No. An outpost. We've traveled for several hours and require a new energy cell for the coral glider. There are many cities across the oceans, way stations for travelers and homes for our soldiers. Without them, we could not stand against the Gloom or protect the surface from the spreading evil."

At last. Answers. Though her heart was still in her throat.

The hatch opened and fresh, warm air scented by salt rushed inside. Manu stepped onto the dock with ease then turned and offered her a hand. As he helped her out, another man came striding toward them, dressed like the others but with glossy symbols across his armored chest she couldn't read. They tickled her memory with familiarity, like a dream she'd had long ago and forgotten upon waking.

Part of her still expected to awaken at any moment. The rational part of her, however, realized she'd slept for quite some time and this was no figment of her imagination.

The decorated soldier stepped forward between his two sentries and spoke in a robust, booming voice that echoed against the dome above them. "Welcome to Port Bermuda, Princess Zephyrine." In unison, her greeter and the other two crossed their forearms across their chests in an X pattern and dipped forward into deep bows. "I am Lieutenant Noro, and my men are at your service. Whatever you need, we'll provide."

They knew her name, and the moment struck her as so surreal she fought back tears. She'd spent her entire life answering to the name Kailani, but Zephyrine didn't *feel* wrong. Not like she'd thought it would. Instead, it stirred something in her chest, like a key fitting into an old lock rusted from years of disuse, its mechanisms finally oiled and loosened again.

The place had the look and feel of an underwater research center out of a science fiction movie. No matter which direction she turned, everything was sleek metal, glass, or rock, the three materials merging to create a work of beauty beneath the ocean. A larger replica of their coral glider bobbed on the gentle current on the other side of the pier, and it was joined by at least a hundred more of varying sizes.

"I can't believe the size of this place."

"Bermuda is the largest outpost in this region of the Atlantic Ocean." His chest puffed out with pride.

She swallowed the dryness in her throat. "How did you recognize who I was? Did someone send out an oceanwide bulletin? 'Beware: lost princess, soon to drop by your neck of the sea'?"

Noro had a warm chuckle that crinkled his eyes and deepened the laugh lines around his mouth. "No,

Your Highness, I'd recognize you anywhere. You resemble your mother."

Her birth mother. She'd known for years that she'd been taken in by her foster mother at a young age, but she couldn't remember the time before she'd come into the Queen family.

When she wasn't fucking petrified, the irony would be hilarious.

"Certainly, the princess would like to stretch her legs for a while. The journey from Texas must have been long indeed."

Manu frowned. "We're only here for a energy cell. She—"

"Yes, she would," Kai cut in. "The princess hasn't eaten in hours, has been planted in the same seat just as long, and she lacks a bladder made of iron. It's about to burst. What can you do to remedy those problems, Lieutenant Noro?"

The man laughed. "I'll take our princess for a tour. Someone will see to your coral glider, Commander."

"Pardon me, Lieutenant, but—"

Noro stepped up to Manu and said something to him in another language, voice in the low and confidential tone of someone sharing a secret. Their tongue also struck Kai as familiar, the words invoking a sense of melancholy that she could no longer understand their speech. Whatever was said, Manu stiffened straighter than a metal beam.

He replied. Something told her the response was

something like, "Did he?" because Noro nodded soon after.

Funny. A nod was the same in any language and culture.

"I leave you in Lieutenant Noro's care, Princess." He bowed to her, spun on his heels, and left.

"What was that about?" Kai asked.

"Nothing worthy of your concern, Your Highness. Please. You must be exhausted from your travel and in need of rest and..." He glanced over her bikini and ripped cover-up, gaze too brief to feel lascivious, but long enough to set in her mind that her attire stood out. "Proper garments. We have quite a bit to show you, but first, allow me to take you to the royal chambers."

PORT BERMUDA

Proper garments turned out to be tight-fitting leggings and a thigh-length, fitted tunic sewn from sharkskin leather. The boots reached her calves, lacked heels, and were lighter than they looked but attractive in both form and function.

He'd given her green and violet, the latter the same shade as her hair.

Kai admired her reflection for a while longer in what had to be the equivalent of a bathroom. She'd been concerned for a while, wondering how people who dwelled under the sea used the facilities, disturbed by bad memories of having to evacuate pools as a child.

Thank the gods for small miracles. The people had actual bathrooms: commodes, sinks, and running water that didn't taste like salt. Later, she knew the scientist in her would need to learn everything she could about their society. For now, she let the magic of it all carry her away, too exhausted to fight it or ask a million questions.

Kai emerged from the restroom to find a young woman with a waist-length, cotton candy-pink braid, kneeling on the floor. "What are you doing?"

"Awaiting your commands, Your Highness."

"Down there?"

She didn't raise her head. "Such is the proper way to greet royalty. I'm your handmaiden."

Oh no. "Please stand up."

"But—"

"Let's pretend I ordered you to stand. Please get up. I can't do this right now."

The bewildered woman stood, blinking at her. "Please, if I've done something to offend, I beg your forgiveness. Whatever mistake I made—"

"You haven't made any mistakes. It's just..." Kai inhaled a deep breath, letting it fill her lungs. In and out, counts of three and five. *Focus.* Staying calm was the only way to get through it, because losing her shit like a psycho wasn't going to change that everything she'd ever known had turned around overnight. Adaptation was her only option.

"I only found out today that I'm a princess," she said in a quiet voice, infusing all the patience she could muster into her tone. "This is all very new to me. I don't want to be bowed at and knelt to or whatever else you were told to do. I just...want to have something to eat and lie down to rest. Please."

"Oh."

"And I want to know your name, too."

The maid tucked her chin. "Amerin."

"Call me Kai."

Fair brows knit together in obvious confusion. "Kai? But you're—"

"Please. All of my friends call me Kai, and it would really help me a lot right now."

Amerin tucked her chin. "Princess Kai it is then."

Kai sighed. Better than nothing.

"I am to take you to the dining hall. Commander Manu and Lieutenant Noro await your company there."

"I'd rather not—" She cut herself off, wondering about the mysterious message relayed to Manu that had turned his features rigid with fury. There was a story there, and focusing on someone else's business meant a distraction from her worries. "Lead the way."

Amerin led her along a corridor chiseled from the rock and down a flight of stairs decorated with a scarlet strip of carpet down its center. Lanterns with glowing, pale-yellow orbs shone all around them, spaced at equal intervals. Standing near one felt like sunlight had been captured and imbued into a glass jar.

"This is beautiful," Kai said, passing beneath a sea glass chandelier hanging within a grand passageway decorated by silk tapestries depicting Grecian mythology and marble busts in lantern-lit alcoves.

"Bermuda Post pales when compared to Atlantis, Your Highness. You will not be disappointed once Commander Manu takes you home."

Kai's home was a two-story beach house on Galveston's coast where a twenty-one-year-old nursing student and a sixty-three-year-old sculptor waited for her. By now, they would have called the police to report her missing, especially if any signs of a struggle remained on the beach bordering their rear yard. She wondered if the police were dragging the ocean right now for her body, her family fearing the worst.

Their path continued into a grand dining hall where each of the long, polished stone tables seated a dozen armored warriors beneath a curved glass ceiling revealing the ocean above them. Silence fell over the chamber when they saw her.

To say she was intimidated would be an understatement as she stood before over a hundred armored men. And every set of eyes in the room was on her. Dining stopped, and two-pronged tines were lowered to plates.

A table at the head of the chamber seated Noro and Manu opposite two other decorated men and a lone woman. All five rose from their chairs when Amerin guided Kai to the empty seat at the table's head. She didn't leave after that, kneeling on a pillow beside Kai's chair with her eyes downcast. When the sole woman among them didn't react to Amerin's submissive behavior, Kai tried to shake off the strange feeling burning through her gut.

"Your Highness," five voices greeted in unison, complete with identical ninety-degree bows.

"It is an honor," Noro said, pulling out her seat, "to host you at our table this eve."

"An honor," another man echoed. This one was older than Noro, with a healthy sprinkle of silver hair, but his features retained their youth.

"Thank you for having me," she murmured, positive she'd humiliate herself or break decorum before the dinner ended. Then again, eating like a savage surface-lander was the least of her concerns.

"We are blessed to have you among us again, Princess Zephyrine," said the only female officer.

Kai didn't bother to correct the lieutenant, though she wondered how long it would take for the name Zepyrhine to feel like hers.

"I am Lieutenant Vaissa," she said.

"And I am Lieutenant Akamu," said a black-haired man with massive biceps tattooed with images of sea turtles and manta rays, competing with Manu for largest dude at the table.

One by one, the remaining officers gave their names and bowed again. After Kai sat, they retook their chairs. They kept her entertained with small talk about the port, asking what she thought of her chambers and the glider ride from Texas. A few minutes passed before a young man arrived carrying an enormous silver platter covered in an array of colorful slivers in unusual shapes and several dipping dishes with black, inky liquid.

No one moved, all eyes on her. Kai also froze.

Catching on, Noro chuckled first. "Etiquette

states we wait for you to take the first bite, Your Highness."

"Oh." At least they hadn't expected Amerin to take the first bite as her poison taster. She followed their lead and speared a piece, dipped it, and placed it in her mouth.

Don't ask what it is. Don't ask what it is. The tender morsel filled her mouth with salt and sweetness from the inky dip and released a creamy, succulent center when she chewed. She pretended she was dining with Hannibal Lecter, reminding herself if she knew what it was, she'd likely not want it. When they were down to the final sliver of meat, all forks retreated to their linen napkins.

Kai took the hint that this, too, the last piece, was meant for her. When she claimed it, Noro nodded in approval.

Afterward, a leafy green seaweed salad arrived for each of them, not looking too different from an appetizer at her favorite Japanese grill. Maybe it was because she was starved and hadn't eaten in a day, but she choked it all down in record time.

"Did you not find it necessary to feed our future queen, Commander Manu?" Vaissa asked. Her gray eyes twinkled with mirth, and though she appeared to be the youngest of the officers at the table, her hair gleamed silver with lavender streaks. It had been bound in several plaits and pinned with starfish no larger than Kai's thumb.

"She slept during most of the journey," Manu

muttered. "As she had been injured by a Gloombeast, I thought it prudent to let her rest."

"Good fortune led you to her at the onset of the attack," Lieutenant Akamu said. "Tell us, Your Highness, of your time spent on the surface. Many of us have never visited dry land."

"Ah, I wouldn't know where to begin." She reached for her drink and reluctantly sipped her wine. It tasted no different from surface wine, full-bodied and sweet in her mouth.

"What occupied you? Were the humans kind?" he persisted.

"You must have made a difference there," Vaissa said, eyes alight with curiosity.

A difference? Her thoughts turned to Clear Shores: the whales saved over the years, the slaughters they'd stopped, and the abrupt but grisly end of their fight against the callous poachers.

Had she made a difference?

She liked to think she did.

"Sometimes they weren't," she replied. "And sometimes I did."

While she had their rapt attention, she told them a little of her surface life in the U.S. Navy, her time at school, and the three years she'd worked with Clear Shores protecting the whales. It wasn't until she reached the end of her tale that she realized another hush had fallen over the entire dining hall, and that the eyes of every single Atlantian were watching *her* and listening to the tale with obvious reverence in their eyes and unconcealed curiosity. In this strange room, her voice carried and magnified.

Hunger, and a dire need to fill her stomach, made it easier to ignore the staring when the next course arrived. They ate seared fish, and crisp grilled vegetables that crunched when she chewed them. She didn't recognize a single thing, not even the fish they dined on. By the time some unusual, unrecognizable desserts of dried fruits came out that melted like candy in her mouth, she could barely stuff in another bite.

"I am sure Princess Zephyrine would appreciate a moment of rest," Noro said, rising when she lowered her fork. Shit. Had she signaled the end of the meal? Everyone else lowered their forks too. "Amerin, please guide Her Highness back to the royal suite."

"With pleasure, Commander Noro."

A round of farewells preceded her departure, and minutes later Amerin delivered her back to the spacious room where she would sleep that night.

Too exhausted to strip out of her suit, she sprawled across a fluffy, hanging bed, and knew nothing else.

THE NEXT MORNING, or night—or whatever hour it was when Kai finally stirred after falling comatose in the world's most comfortable bed—Amerin arrived to show her how to dress as a proper

Atlantian lady. What she received to wear under the suit was barely a thong. Of all the things taken from her, she hadn't thought her Fruit of the Loom bikini briefs and T-shirt bras would be yet another sacrifice.

Between her frustration with the undergarments, lingering exhaustion, and too many years of communal showers in the military, all her modesty had been stripped away and she allowed the young maid to dress her.

"Thank you. This is lovely," Kai said when Amerin finished taming her tangled hair into neat braids and pinning them with tiny white starfish. "But can I ask you a question?"

Amerin paused. "You may ask me anything you desire, Your Highness. Serving you is my only purpose."

Kai frowned. "Why is it your only purpose? What did you do prior to my return? Were you the servant of another person?"

"No. Never. I was born to be your maid. Your uncle, the acting regent, sent me here days ago to await your arrival. He knew Commander Manu would deliver you to this post once you were found."

Another one of those awkward, deafening silences passed between them. Kai wondered how long it would be before she grew accustomed to the changes. "Surely you don't mean that in the literal sense?"

"Oh, but I do. You are forty-six years old, and I am forty-four. My parents conceived me to serve as your lady's maid and gifted me to the royal family once I left infancy."

Slowly, Kai turned to face Amerin. There were so many things wrong with every part of the woman's statement, but the one that stood out the most, were the words "forty-six." *Forty*-six.

No, she couldn't be that old. Unless Atlantians calculated their math differently, nothing about that age made sense to her. She'd seen photographs of herself shortly after a social worker delivered her to Sunshine's door as a ward of the state needing foster care, a confused child no older than eight; nine at the most. They'd taken a guess at her age, and those days were cloudy, a hazy memory she could barely recall. It hadn't been much later, when all efforts failed to find her parents, that Sunshine adopted her.

"Please repeat that," she spoke in a quiet voice, barely holding it together. "I'm how old?"

Amerin repeated herself, blinking in bewilderment. "Is something the matter, Your Highness?"

"I...thought I was no older than thirty-three. I've been told my entire life strangers found me on the beach at the age of eight or nine. I don't understand."

"We of Atlantis age differently than humans, Your Highness. We do not reach adulthood until our thirtieth year, and from that point forward, age much slower. You were an adolescent of twenty-one at the time of your parents' death."

No. Everything she'd ever known came crashing down around her, her life a flimsy house of cards built from unintentional lies. The world around her swam in and out of focus. It couldn't be possible, and yet, a magical outpost in the middle of the Bermuda Triangle should have been equally impossible. Her shoulders shook, and the tears she'd been tenaciously holding at bay since the previous evening came streaming down her cheeks in hot trails.

Suddenly lightheaded, Kai stumbled toward a nearby chair. She didn't make it. When the floor rushed up to meet her face, Amerin caught her instead with surprisingly strong hands and held her upright in her arms. It was then Kai realized her lady's maid stood only two inches shorter.

Amerin guided her to the same chair, left the room, and returned quickly with a cup of green-tinged tea that smelled like grass.

Kai held the warm vessel on her lap until her hands steadied, then she sipped it. It tasted like sweet memories, though she couldn't place why.

"Please rest a moment. This has been a difficult day for you, Princess Kai."

"Difficult is an understatement. There are...so many things I do not understand. How do you understand me? Do all Atlantians know English?"

"Atlantians know every language," she replied.

"I don't, but I'm supposedly one of you."

"You've forgotten the magic and how to be one of us, but it will come back in time. You need only remember who you are, I'm sure."

Kai's shoulders shook with a peal of hysterical laughter. "Magic. Now you're telling me I know *magic*?"

"We all do to some degree, though some of us better than others. You are a high mer, and your ability surpasses any amount of sorcery I could ever perform."

"What's...what's a high mer? If you're not a high mer, what are you?"

"The rest of us commoners are descended from the Oceanids and their trysts with humans, but high mer were crafted in the sea goddess's image, her creations who weren't born of her, but made. Designed to lead the city."

"And me?"

Amerin's smile widened. "*You* are born from the direct descendants of Thalassa and Pontus, the goddess and god of the seas. And you are the fifth in their royal line."

HOME IS WHERE THE HEART IS

Kai became aware of three facts when they departed Bermuda Post. First, Manu appeared incapable of stringing together more than four words in a sentence to her. Most of his responses consisted of "Yes, Your Highness," "No, Your Highness," and "Of course, Your Highness," all of which pissed her off even more. Second, an escort of six additional gliders had been ordered to accompany them to Atlantis, one of which carried Amerin. And third, Manu no longer zipped along the ocean bottom faster than light, the glider cruising at a dramatically slower speed. She wondered if the ocean had speed limits, and if he'd been guilty of breaking them before.

Though Manu had previously predicted they would reach Atlantis, they stopped that evening at another outpost for a refuel, sleeping overnight and resuming travel the next day. During those hours of confinement in the glider with him, Kai wished for Amerin's conversation again. What a pity that

Manu's glider only seated two people. She'd seen the others, especially the one carrying Amerin, and it held six men. Noro had assigned a damned army to protect her. Considering the tale of her parents' deaths, it made sense—in a morbid way—that they wouldn't risk losing their last link to the royal family a second time.

"How much longer until we reach Atlantis?"

Dark eyes shifted toward her. "Soon, Your Highness. We are closing in on the city now." His gaze lingered with the weight of an iron bar, studying her so long she wondered what he thought of her and what he saw when he looked at their admittedly awkward princess. She couldn't speak their language, didn't know their ways, and didn't have a hope of living up to the stories she'd heard about her warrior-queen mother.

The aquatic craft descended into cloudier depths toward the sand bed at an alarming rate that made her squeeze both armrests and tense in the chair.

Manu laughed at her, and it was the most genuine reaction she'd seen in him since he shrugged off her calling him a dick. "That isn't the true ocean floor."

"It *looks* like it," she muttered. But then she remembered the last illusion.

"Trust me." He reached for the dash and flipped a few switches before pressing a button. A gentle red glow lit the display. He uttered a brief phrase in his gorgeous language, and a voice replied, equally brief. The light dimmed.

They coasted through the illusory sea floor, no different than a plane breaking through a cloud bank. Before she could question it, Atlantis came into view, and she realized her imagination, as well as Amerin's descriptions, hadn't done the place justice. The city stretched beyond her sight, as large as any American metropolis but contained beneath an immense glass dome. What was inside reminded her of Bermuda Post. Rocky spires reminiscent of city skyscrapers rose from the actual seabed, the windows of each glowing with blue light. Some of the structures resembled coral growths and others glowed brighter than jellyfish.

The city's exterior was a different matter. Green plant life populated the ocean bottom, though there wasn't an ounce of sun to sustain them. Their verdant boughs still swayed in the current like clusters of aquatic weeping willows lining manicured paths lit by yellow lanterns.

"What do you think?"

"It's breathtaking."

"Better than Bermuda?"

"If you'd asked me yesterday about the most magnificent sight I've ever seen, I would have told you Bermuda. Now..." She said nothing more, fixated on the city ahead of them.

Manu led the procession of underwater vehicles to a gate. They passed through a flooded tunnel beyond the glass shield and emerged on the other side to an enormous port rivaling the docks at Norfolk where her last ship had been stationed.

Dozens upon dozens of vessels of varying sizes and shapes floated on the surface—small coral gliders, medium-sized skippers, and enormous things sporting huge guns that reminded her of destroyers. The vast number of them put what she'd seen in Bermuda Post to shame. Noro had been kind enough to describe most of their vehicles and their purposes.

The assortment of weaponry fascinated her so much it took a while for Kai to notice the welcoming party. A dozen men and women waited on the adjacent pier, clad in attire studded with jewels, shells, and metal embellishments. Most pieces were form-fitting, though a few of the ladies wore flowing lace trains in bold colors attached to their tight bodices or draped from their shoulders like capes.

A familiar man with hair the warm, rich shade of golden toffee stood at the forefront of the group beside a woman with electric blue braids beneath a jeweled tiara. Something about him stirred her memory, and their body language implied they were together—a couple or possibly even married. Of the entire group, he appeared the most regal, his smile jovial and kind. He spoke to her, though the words were nothing more than beautiful sounds and syllables that all rolled together in a lyrical cadence.

Manu cleared his throat. "Pardon me, Regent Aegaeon, but she no longer speaks the tongue."

Bewilderment spread across the regent's face. "No longer?"

"I believe she has spent too long on the surface to

recall her high mer roots, my lord. She recalls nothing, as mentioned in my report."

"Ah, then you must accept my apologies. We will all speak your surface language until such a time comes that you speak as we do."

Low murmurs of agreement rumbled behind him.

"It is my deep and profound honor to welcome your return to Atlantis, Zephyrine." He passed his trident to a retainer standing at his side then stepped forward and offered her both hands to her. "I am Aegaeon."

Petrified of making the wrong move, Kai took them. "My uncle?"

He nodded, gaze never leaving her face. "I can't believe you stand here now. For years, we thought the royal line had been severed. Yet you're here, alive and strong. But enough of this. You must be exhausted, and there is much work to do now that you've been recovered. Please come with me."

Lost, Kai allowed Aegaeon to lead her from the pier, leaving Manu and the other arriving gliders behind. She glanced over her shoulder and saw the mer watching from the pier, standing among the many soldiers disembarking from their craft.

Their gazes held until her uncle took her beyond his line of sight.

FROM THE MOMENT of her arrival, Kai didn't receive

a second of time to herself aside from a few stolen minutes of freedom in the palace baths once Aegaeon declared her travel garb unfit for meeting with the nobility. After a servant guided her to her private quarters, she soaked for an hour in fragrant water. Then Amerin returned and took a seat on a nearby marble bench, chatting with her about trivial things but reminding Kai too much of Sadie for her to take offense to the intrusion.

Afterward, she met people. A lot of people. Names blurred in her mind, and faces all began to look the same, no one mer standing apart from the next noble lord and high mer lady. The same questions were on everyone's tongues: how had the mortals treated her, had she missed home, how had she survived so long on land?

Hours later, she wanted nothing more than to be left alone after relaying the story of her life on the surface to no fewer than three dozen people and touring the palace.

She felt like a zoo specimen, an animal to be stared and gawked at, but protected for the sake of conservation behind a glass wall. No one cared that she'd been taken away from a happy life on the surface and people she'd loved very much.

Lying across the divan in her new quarters, Kai wondered if she'd ever have freedom again. Tomorrow, she was to attend a welcome home feast in her honor organized by Lady Nammu, but no one asked if she wanted it. They assumed, and Amerin had implied it would be unwise to refuse anything offered by Aegaeon's wife.

"Princess?" Amerin called from the antechamber.

Instead of feigning sleep, Kai sighed. "Yes?"

Amerin paused. "I sense all is not well with you. What may I do to ease your transition?"

"Nothing."

"There must be something."

Short of pulling a magical road to Galveston out of her pocket, there wasn't shit Amerin could do for her. "Nothing's wrong."

Amerin's bare feet made no noise against the marble floor as she crossed the room. Like Kai, she wore leather leggings beneath a fitted bodice with a flowing lace train, though her garb was far less intricate and had little embroidery, making it plain by comparison. "You lie as poorly now as you did when we were girls."

"I don't remember when we were girls."

"I do." She perched on the edge of the seat. "What was it like on the surface? No—not that shit you told Regent Aegaeon, or the lies you repeated over and over to the Council of Lords. What was it truly like to be with the humans?"

Kai blinked.

"What?"

Curiosity piqued, Kai leaned up on one elbow. "You know swears in English?"

"Magic is a wonderful thing. Similar words of the same meaning exist in the Atlantian tongue. Besides,

I may or may not have met a mortal or two over the years. I've traveled and visited the surface."

"Then you don't need me to tell you what humans are like."

"Ah, but you are wrong there, Princess Kai. I don't want to know what all humans are like. I want to know about *yours*. Will you please tell me about the family who raised you?"

An immediate answer didn't come. Kai lay there, gazing at the high ceiling and the colorful crystals dangling from the ornate chandelier. Everything about her personal suite resembled a work of art, from the hanging, hammock-style bed supported by gilded chains, to the balcony overlooking the city below. "They were good to me," she finally said. "And I miss them so much it hurts."

So she told Amerin about Sadie, about the day their mother arrived on the doorstep with this younger child in her arms, with matted brown curls and heat blisters on her feet from walking barefoot on the scorching Texas ground. She'd had bed bug bites all over her arms, legs, and face, some of them infected. Kai had been fourteen then, or so she'd thought, but she'd loved her new little sister on sight and asked how long Sadie would stay with them.

"Children only stayed with you for a short while?"

"We were all her foster children once. I was her first, but others always came and went. Sometimes they returned to their mothers and fathers, and sometimes they went to their grandparents or other relatives. We were the two she kept. She has this... enormous and loving heart. There wasn't a child she didn't care about and want to save."

"She sounds wonderful."

Kai eased to a sitting position. "She's 'Mom' to me. She'll be worried sick about me now and wondering what happened."

"I am sorry for your loss. And for theirs."

"It isn't your fault."

"Just the same, I am sorry for you, and the mortals who will mourn your disappearance." Amerin rose and trailed to the door, lingering long enough to bow. "No one will trouble you for the rest of the day, Princess. If you need anything, there is a resonating crystal atop the nightstand table. A tap will summon me to you at once, no matter the hour. Rest well."

"Thank you."

Amerin shut the door behind her and left the chamber, leaving Kai with deafening silence and heavy thoughts.

7

OF SACRIFICE AND WAR

AMERIN LED KAI DOWN IMMACULATE PALACE corridors carved from stone to meet her uncle in his personal study. Despite his warm and welcoming greeting three days prior, they hadn't spoken more than a few words since the grand welcome home feast his wife had thrown, reintroducing Kai to the high mer of the royal court and the Council of Lords.

He took care of her in other ways, she supposed, by tasking a team of servants with her care. She never went hungry, and Amerin had no shortage of lovely garments in which to dress her. She felt like a pampered doll and missed doing things for herself such as brushing her hair, microwaving a damned pepperoni Hot Pocket on a whim, eating cold Pop Tarts, and picking out her own clothing. She would have killed for denim cut-offs or a tank top that couldn't pass for studded leather armor.

"Did he mention what he wants with me?" Kai asked.

Amerin shook her head. "Only that he and General Lago need to speak with you regarding a matter of supreme importance."

General Lago had been absent from the dog and pony show Nammu and the other "esteemed" ladies of the high mer court put together for Kai's benefit.

When she entered the room, Aegaeon glanced up from the parchment spread across his desk. Manu stood on one side, and a man of equally impressive shoulder breadth stood on the other, like an older, blonder, and more distinguished model of Manu, with fine silver strands in his blue-streaked hair and beard. Unlike his son, the general was fair-skinned and gray-eyed, but she could see Manu had inherited some of the man's best traits. It shamed her that she noticed they both had a mouth that looked absolutely kissable.

Both bowed to her and murmured low welcomes. "Greetings, Princess."

Ah, to be sandwiched between those two fine men. Quick as the filthy fantasy came to mind, she banished it from her thoughts, praying no one could secretly read minds. "Hello."

Aegaeon smiled. "Good day, Zephyrine. Thank you, Amerin. You're dismissed."

Once Amerin was gone, her uncle gestured with a hand toward the empty seat opposite him, a high-backed chair with ruby velvet stretched over the plump cushion. The rest of his study was pure opulence, not so different from a 1930s British gentleman's study.

"Thank you for joining us, Zephyrine. I apologize for how little interaction we've had since your arrival." A tiny tension knot in her chest loosened. "You returned to us during a trying, difficult time for Atlantis. Our forces are overwhelmed, and I've been away since your celebration."

The rest of her unease faded. His ambivalence toward her hadn't been caused by resentment after all. "Because of the Gloom?"

"Yes. You spoke of being a warrior for the surface in the American Navy. How well do you fight?"

"I can hold my own." Manu glanced at her, brow raised in unspoken judgment. The Gloombeasts had kicked her ass. Had he not arrived when he did, they would have killed her. "Against humans. I've never fought anything like the monsters that came for me on the shore."

"Some combat experience is better than none. It is something we can build upon. After all, none of us are born with a weapon in hand," Aegaeon said, gesturing toward the trident propped against his desk. "But we learn and do what we must to protect this world."

The general cleared his throat. When he spoke, it was with a deep timbre that practically rumbled through the room. "Perhaps we should tell her *why*, my lord. To bring the matter of her training and its importance into perspective."

Aegaeon leaned back in his seat and rubbed the bridge of his nose, looking stressed and more tired than she remembered during their initial meeting.

"You're right, as usual. There are many things no one has told you, Zephyrine. We hoped to give you a brief period to adapt to the Atlantian way of life following your years apart from our traditions, but we find ourselves without the luxury. As I said, you arrived during a difficult time. We are a kingdom divided, and your presence may have exacerbated the issue."

"I don't understand. How so?" So far, everyone she'd met, with the exception of Lady Nammu, appeared thrilled by the idea of her potentially claiming the throne.

"There are mers who do not want a strong and thriving monarchy. They want a government similar to those of the surface world, with your Congress, ministries, branches, and divisions of power. They want votes."

Kai raised one brow. "It's a sensible system. It works for most of us on the surface."

"It does; yet during the days of your mother and father we had peace in Atlantis, as well as safety. Queen Ianthe and my dear brother were as much our protectors from the Gloom as they were our monarchs." He shrugged. "Why should we change a good thing for an unknown governmental structure that may not be to our benefit? High Priest Hipponax believes you are the answer to our problems. If you return to the throne and lead our forces against the Gloom, the people will understand you are not only worthy of their love, but you are also the only one with the power to defend them from evil and rule this kingdom."

"Isn't that why the Myrmidons exist? They're the top-dog soldiers of the Royal Army, right?" She'd come to understand them to be supercharged Marines, like Navy SEALs on magic steroids. "Why do you need *me*?"

General Lago glanced at her. "No one else can wield the Gift of the Sea. Only a mer of her bloodline can use it to abolish the Gloom. When agents of Calypso killed your mother and father, they knew they would be casting the ocean into vast, unending darkness. In the meantime, we can only halt the spread of their evil and slay individual monsters. We cannot destroy them as a whole or reverse the damage she's caused."

"Calypso?"

Aegaeon answered in a curt nod. "The queen of deception herself."

Kai scoured her memory for everything she knew about Greek mythology. "She's a nymph, isn't she?"

"*Was* a nymph," he replied. "Now, I fear she is something different. What do you know of her?"

"There are stories on the surface, but the one I'm familiar with is that she abducted Odysseus for seven years and forced him to live on her island, refusing to let him leave until Zeus intervened."

Her uncle grimaced. Rising from his seat, Aegaeon crossed the room and retrieved a book from a shelf fashioned from polished whale bones. It struck her as both terrible and beautiful at once, an odd juxtaposition to what she'd believed as a conservationist fighting against the slaughter of whales.

"That tale is similar to the truth as we know it, though centuries have passed. Calypso has a taste for men who do not belong to her, and once coveted your ancestor."

"In the story I know, she claimed the gods despised goddesses having affairs with mortals."

Lago crossed both beefy arms against his chest. "Not so. Had she not always chosen men claimed by other goddesses, her efforts to take a lover would have gone unimpeded. Her downfall occurred when she turned her attention to Pontus, our patron god of the sea and husband to Thalassa. Her sorcery drove a wedge between them until Thalassa discovered the truth and realized her husband was under an enchantment. Then a bitter rivalry began."

"None of us know for certain what happened," Aegaeon said, "and the mers who lived during those days are long dead. But the legends claim when Thalassa sought to reclaim her husband, she struck Calypso down in battle and cast her to the depths of the darkest sea to die for her crime."

"But she didn't die," Lago continued. "We believe she struck a pact with Phorkys and Keto, for only they possess power equal to Thalassa and Pontus."

"Phorkys and Keto?" The only keto she knew about was the extremist diet her sister had tried out for a couple weeks before succumbing to her addiction to sugar and subsequently gorging on a pound of chocolate cake late one night.

Aegaeon passed the weathered book to her and tapped the center of an illustrated page featuring a man with a fish tail and slimy crab claws, his skin the mottled gray of a crustacean. "The cruel god and goddess of sea monsters and dangers, progenitors of every evil beast to ever haunt the ocean."

"If that's the case, why don't Thalassa and Pontus do something about it? Why wouldn't gods fight gods?"

Aegaeon shook his head. "When Pontus returned to his senses and realized he had been unfaithful to his wife, he withdrew from this world and Thalassa fell silent. Perhaps he even ceased to exist. We do not know. What we do know is that no priest has heard Thalassa's words of wisdom in centuries, and both of our patron gods may be gone forever. What we have are the gifts left to us from them."

"The scepter," Kai said.

"And my brother Neptune's trident. It was a gift from Pontus, a weapon of power equal to her scepter passed to each new king."

Her gaze darted to Manu and found the silent mer watching her. He hadn't added anything to the conversation yet, but she wondered what he thought of it all. He'd seen her at her worst, running panicked from the Gloombeasts and screaming her fool head off.

"War is coming, Zephyrine. We need you. If you fail to regain your gifts and wield the scepter, every city within the kingdom of Atlantis is doomed. And, quite possibly, the world beyond. The kingdom of Pacifica has their own battles to fight, and what happens in this sea is our responsibility. We don't have a chance without you. I've done all I can to protect our world since your mother and father's deaths, but I'm not enough. Neptune's trident won't accept me, and it's also missing the pearl blessed by Pontus. Without that, I fear it's worthless."

Her shoulders sank, and with them, her hopes of returning to the family who loved her. No matter how much she longed for the surface and lazy days sprawled on the beach, these people needed her more.

"Will you accept?"

"I will. I don't know if I can be what you want me to be, but I'll try."

"That's all we ask," Lago said, granting her a brief smile. "Manu will begin your instruction at once."

Manu started, blinking at the commander. "General—"

"He teaches well, and he has patience with the youngest mers," Lago spoke over his son's attempted objection. "She will be safe in his hands, my lord."

"Wonderful. Since we've settled that, General Lago and I have much to discuss about the security of the Western Sand Belt. Alohi has been told to expect your arrival for an armor fitting. If you should need anything, my office is open to you always, Zephyrine."

Once again, no one asked what she wanted. Kai shuffled from the room with Manu on her heels, and moments later they stood in the corridor alone.

"Come with me, Princess Zephyrine."

"Kailani."

He paused, a puzzled expression coming to his rugged face. "What?"

Kai clenched her jaw. "Please don't call me Zephyrine."

"But it is your name."

"It's... It's a pretty name, but I don't actually know it, do I? It isn't the name I've used for the last twenty-five years of my life. It's a dead name from a time I may never remember, and when I hear it, it still doesn't *feel* like me. The Zephyrine from then is gone. I'm not her."

Something like understanding dawned on his handsome features. She actually saw the lightbulb switch on and his dark eyes fill with compassion. He nodded. "All right. Princess Kailani it is." He bowed before her, crossing both arms over his chest and dipping low enough that his dark hair swung down over his shoulders. "It is my honor to meet you, and you have my deepest apologies for the circumstances surrounding your arrival. I *am* sorry."

A relieved breath deflated her lungs, then her shoulders sagged. "Thank you."

"It is the least I can do for the difficult introduction you've had to my world. Or should I say, reintroduction to *our* world." Manu led her through the palace and down two levels, pausing at the bottom landing. "Have you learned your way around the palace yet?"

She shook her head. "No. It's a maze in here. Amerin or some guard has had to practically lead me around by the hand because every time I think I've got it figured out, I learn there's another wing I haven't explored."

"It is a large castle. I grew up within these walls, so I know it by heart." He paused. "As did you. If I may offer a bit of advice?"

"Feel free. I'm willing to try anything at this point."

"The main corridors wind counterclockwise in the likeness of a nautilus, though there are smaller halls and passages along the way. Each upper level has one less than the floor below it. If you remember that, you'll never become lost. Retrace your steps back to the main corridor."

"Counterclockwise," she repeated, feeling dumb for failing to notice the place was built in a spiral. "Are you serious?"

"Yes. It's a subtle incline. Easy to overlook when overwhelmed. There are also three lifts, the main one just off the entrance hall. One goes directly to the royal residences."

He took her to the armorer, who made a mold of her torso, took the rest of her measurements, and told them to return in three days for a suit. Alohi's no-nonsense and brusque manner was a pleasant change of pace. She didn't shoot the shit with them or waste their time with small talk. Afterward, they approached the training arena, a place she only recognized because Amerin had shown her the Myrmidon recruits during their evening training. It wasn't far from the palace, its shape reminding her of a coliseum beneath a glass dome.

"Now. There is one last thing we must do before we begin your training."

"Yeah?"

"I need to see how well you swim."

Kai tilted her head. "Shouldn't we be going outside first?"

"This will be sufficient." He glanced toward the doors where two guards stood watch. "Roll the waves."

"Wha—" Before she could finish the word, semi-translucent bubbles covered the exits and a flood of water rolled across the arena, slamming into her. It was a tidal wave of epic proportions, and it swept her away with its force. She tumbled with it, screaming from both cold shock and surprise. Eventually she rolled to a stop.

The frigid water continued rising at an impossible speed. A couple of inches became feet as she scrambled off of her ass and stood, then it was suddenly to her waist. To her chest, rising to her neck. Her feet no longer touched the ground, and then the next wave rose like a small tsunami, and she braced herself for impact.

Under the water, she saw Manu weathering the turbulence with ease. She hated him for failing to warn her.

Her previous assessment of him had been accurate. The guy was a *dick*.

"The water is rising toward the ceiling."

He surfaced. "Yes, it is."

The arena floor was no longer a few feet beneath

them, gone from being six feet away to twenty. Deeper. They bobbed on the choppy waves.

"I can swim good, dude, but this is ridiculous. What if that wave had knocked me unconscious before this place filled up?"

"You can breathe underwater," Manu said, shrugging.

"You're fucking crazy."

"I'm not. I brought you here to show you that you're different."

"The only different thing about me is that I can swim faster than most people. Big deal. Phelps can do better. I would have never made the Olympics."

"I know nothing of this Phelps person or your mortals' Olympics, but you're faster than any mortal. You just don't realize it."

"You're fucking insane. You just don't realize *that.*"

Another wild wave tossed her, and a contained whirlpool sucked her into its current. Water surged up her nose and into her mouth as she kicked toward the surface again. She held her breath to no avail, because Manu dragged her deeper despite her kicking. The man had the strength of a weightlifter twice his size, and then suddenly the tiny air bubble at the top of the arena dome was fifty feet away and Manu was still dragging her toward the bottom.

8

SINK OR SWIM

Twenty-five years of mediocrity had passed before Kai's vision when a crash on the Atlantic Ocean reduced the *Sea Angel* to toothpicks. This time, she saw nothing but red-hot fury.

This asshole had a lot of nerve.

She managed to catch his nose with her free heel, taking him by surprise. The brief moment that he released her wasn't enough of a reprieve to reach the surface. Manu caught her again, but she scratched at him and raked her fingers down his chest. All that did was snap a nail when his leather breastplate resisted her efforts. Desperation turned her into a wildcat beneath the water, and she no longer knew how much time had passed since the chamber filled.

She fought against the current to reach the pocket of air at the top, but he pulled her down again with inhuman strength. Her lungs burned for the air he'd denied her. Minutes had passed.

"You won't drown, Princess. Trust me." The

words reached her ears as clearly as if they were spoken above the water, but all the logic in the world wasn't enough to overpower natural instinct. And natural instinct told her it was a bad idea to inhale a mouthful of water into her lungs.

This time, she snuck a fist past his guard and cuffed him in the jaw, though he turned his head in time for the blow to roll past his cheek almost harmlessly. Almost.

"Would I be speaking to you under the water if we were going to *drown*? Drowning is a thing humans do, Your Highness. You are a high mer. You are a descendent of Thalassa, war goddess of the seas. You. Won't. Drown," he enunciated each word before wrapping his powerful arms around her body and trapping her to his chest. The effect was no different from a straitjacket, for all the good her struggles did then.

God, his torso was so hard, biceps like steel cables instead of muscles. Then it pissed her off that she noticed his spectacular body at a time like this, when he was already pissing her off by trying to drown her in a nightmarish coliseum with its own hurricane system.

"Breathe," he commanded.

Kai dared to hope he was right and inhaled. Water flew into her lungs and filled them. Instead of choking, she coughed a few times until she reached a point of equilibrium. The godawful burning sensation in her chest eased like she'd gulped in a deep breath of air. Seconds later, the discomfort vanished altogether. She took another breath, letting water move in and out of her lungs, the oxygen exchange resuming by some strange act of sorcery.

"I'm breathing."

"Yes."

"I'm really breathing underwater. I'm breathing *and* talking underwater."

Manu smiled. And it was such a beautiful, gorgeous smile that it made her angry because she didn't want to find the asshole sexy at *all*. The ridiculously buff arms encircling her body finally lowered, releasing her from his embrace. She floated back from him a foot and marveled at herself. At the magic of the moment. At realizing she could breathe underwater all this time.

Then she hauled back and drove her fist into Manu's face with all of her might. The force snapped his head backward.

"I deserved that." He rubbed his jaw. "I apologize for the abrupt lesson, Your Highness."

"Forgiven, I guess. Since, you know, I didn't drown."

"You have one hell of a right hook. Impressive. I'd had doubts, considering what happened on the beach, but no longer."

"All of that from one punch?"

"You're strong. Tell me, have you ever lost a fight?"

"Hell no." Before her high school growth spurt, she'd been picked on in school by bigger, meaner students who taunted her about having no parents, but she'd always come out of every scrap on top. When puberty hit, there'd been no more fights at all, and everyone knew better than to mess with the six-foot-tall Glamazon. If they spoke about her at all, they did it behind her back.

"Ever been sick?"

She shook her head. "Rarely."

"Even the frailest artisan of Atlantis is stronger than a mere mortal," he explained. "That was easily one of the best hits I've ever taken."

"I can't be too strong if you're still running your damn mouth."

He grimaced. "Trust me. It hurt like a bitch, but pain is a weakness Myrmidons can't display."

Can't. The connotation differed greatly from *won't.* "That so?"

"It is."

It must have been difficult to thrive under the weight of so much damned masculinity that he had to shrug off taking a hit that had broken a man's jaw before.

"You prepared for one more surprise?"

"Sure. Why not? Nothing can be more shocking than discovering I can breathe water. Let's have it."

That rare smile returned to his face. "I under-stand mortals have a fascination with mermaids."

"They do. My favorite movie when growing up was *Splash.* I used to dream about being Darryl Hannah's mermaid character."

Manu lazily drifted around her in a circle. "I do not know that movie, but I can tell you those weren't dreams. Maybe they were suppressed memories, but they weren't dreams."

"You're shitting me."

"No."

Kai glanced down at her legs. They were long and strong, her thighs powerful from years of jogging, swimming, and weight lifting during her spare time, but there were definitely two distinct limbs. "How does it work?"

"Ah, this time you believe me."

"You haven't lied yet. So far, you've told me about terrifying Gloombeasts, hidden cities, and spiteful homewrecker goddesses. You may be a dick, but you aren't a liar."

This time he chuckled again. "High mers draw strength from the skins they wear. In your case, you wear the scales of the Gigas fish."

She glanced down at her golden leggings. Light glittered off the scales as she floated in place, occasionally fluttering her feet. "And my boots?"

"The same. Your transformation and the quality of it requires practice as well as mental conditioning. See yourself gliding through the water. Envision the transformation you need to take, and it will happen."

Skeptical, she eyed him and gave it a try.

Ten minutes later, she felt like an idiot. "I'm not entirely sure you aren't fucking with me now."

"I'm not fucking with you." He rolled his eyes. "A little focus would be appreciated, Princess Kailani. I'd like to have supper at some point today."

"Asshole."

"I preferred dick. At least that's used for pleasure and makes two people happy."

Kai jerked around to stare at him.

Manu could make jokes? He'd been a solemn companion during *days* of travel across the ocean, a grumpy guy who barely glanced at her until they reached their destination.

"I didn't think you had a sense of humor."

"I've been known to have my moments. Now focus, please. The sooner you grasp this, the sooner we'll be able to proceed to the next lesson."

Despite wanting desperately to know what the hell followed learning to turn two legs into a fish tail, she nodded and drifted away from him to close her eyes. A few Myrmidon guards watched from outside, viewing through the semi-translucent barrier. She didn't want to look like a fool in front of them.

Whatever she did here, whether it was success or failure, would be retold in gossip across the city. She had to do it. Manu said nothing to rush her. She noticed that now. He'd only teased and encouraged her when she expressed doubt. Keeping that in mind, she blocked out her surroundings. Forgot the spectators. Ignored the sexy-as-hell Commander of the guard waiting for her to pull off a miracle.

A few more minutes passed of floating aimlessly in place. It began as a tingle in her toes, and then it became a tickle in her bones. Kai glanced down. When her legs spontaneously fused together, she screamed, startled by the reaction rippling down her body, beginning at the hips and flooding downward in a rapid reaction that ended at the tips of her toes.

Toes that were no longer toes elongated into a thick, opaque fin the color of clotted cream. Her lower body became long and sinuous, a lithe and flexible ribbon that moved in an effortless dolphin kick.

"I'm a mermaid."

"You are."

Manu was most handsome when he smiled. He didn't do it often, and that was a shame. Damn near criminal, really. After snapping out of her appreciative daze, she twirled in a loop and tested her new lower body, mesmerized by how it had returned to her at last.

"Now reverse it," he murmured.

The sensation wasn't unlike pulling a resistant Band-Aid off skin. It didn't *hurt*, but the discomfort almost discouraged her from continuing. By the end, her legs had been restored to two distinct limbs and were no longer the svelte, gorgeous length of mermaid tail that had propelled her through the water.

She blinked a few times and stared at her own legs in amusement. "Why didn't you do the same?" It didn't take much from her imagination to envision Manu cruising through the waves with a powerful tail whipping through the water. She'd never gone through a merman phase as a teen, but she definitely rated the vision an 11 on the Austin Powers to David Gandy scale of sex appeal.

It had to be seen.

"I'm not a high mer. Such tricks are a talent belonging only to the highborn."

"Oh." Damn. "That must suck."

"But I wouldn't need a tail to keep up with you, Princess." He grinned and swam around her in a lazy circle, long hair drifting in the gentle current. "How did it feel?"

"It felt..." She paused, considering the initial terror as well as the exhilaration. "Kinda bad-ass."

"Yes?"

"Like something I'd done a thousand times before, could do a thousand times more. Really natural."

"Show me."

She did. Her legs melded together once more into a sleek fishtail, sparkling gold scales glittering beneath the coliseum lights. "So, if I wore sharkskin?"

"Shark tail. Now that you've mastered the basics we learn as babies—"

Damn him. Her feeling of accomplishment dwindled.

"—we'll move on to the elementary lessons."

"What are elementary lessons?"

He grinned. "Evasive maneuvers, Your Highness. I've been ordered to make you battle-ready, and I don't intend to fail."

9

PERPETUAL FAILURE

Helike had fallen to the Gloom.

It surprised no one, least of all Manu, that one of their distant cities to the south had been crushed by the spreading darkness. What did surprise him was that there were so few survivors to tell the tale.

Of course, he had to be the bearer of bad news.

Commander Lago slammed a fist against the war table's desk. "Unnecessary. What a hopeless, unnecessary fucking loss. We told them to evacuate."

"We did, but they believed their fortifications could withstand a round of attacks from the Gloombeasts. Had they obeyed Regent Aegaeon's official decree, they would still be among the living. This is no fault of ours nor a reflection on your leadership. They chose to break apart from the monarchy." Helike had been one of the first cities to claim independence from Atlantis, seceding to become their own sovereign Loyalist state.

They'd claimed they could protect themselves.

And they had for a time, building up an impressive military that could never rival Atlantis, but had certainly stood against the forces of the dark for a decade on its own.

Now the proud Helicians were dead, their corpses food for the ocean scavengers, and any survivors used as shock troops for the never-ending tide of Gloombeasts.

Lago grunted, kneading his temples with one hand. "Some good news would be appreciated. Tell me, Commander, how goes your training with the princess?"

"She learns, but progress is slow and difficult, General." Manu couldn't recall the last time he'd called his sire "Father," as Lago hadn't been much of a father at all over the past few years. He'd been a teacher, a mentor, and certainly a leader, but he'd not been a father to Manu at all. "I have my doubts that she will ever be prepared to lead the army as Queen Ianthe once did. In fact, I—"

"Then you aren't trying hard enough."

The sharp words sliced through Manu with the force of a harpoon. He blinked a few times, squared his shoulders, and took in a careful breath through his nose. "I do my best, as does she, but there are twenty-five years of surface living to unravel. What you and Regent Aegaeon expect of her is impossible. It will take *years* to make her into a warrior-queen."

And while Kai *did* try her best, he struggled to see her as anything more than a stunted adult, albeit a sexy, desirable one with legs that went on for miles and a mouth his traitorous imagination pictured wrapped around his cock.

Yeah. Training sessions with her were hell, and he didn't foresee that changing in the near future. Putting professionalism first in the training arena didn't mean his body understood and heeded the command.

Thank the gods for Atlantian codsarmor and the protection it offered—both from damaging assaults and revealing spontaneous, future queen-induced erections. Popping a hard-on in front of their princess wasn't part of the training regimen.

"Perhaps I should have tasked Commander Cosmas with this honor, as he would have no doubt achieved results."

Manu's back stiffened tight and tension drew across his shoulder blades. "If you find my methods unsatisfactory and prefer Commander Cosmas to step in as the princess's trainer, you won't receive any objections from me."

Lago leaned back in his seat and studied him. "Is that so?"

"It is, sir. It is also my personal opinion that Commander Cosmas will encounter the same difficulties. Neither her intelligence nor my methods are at fault. However, I find myself unable to dedicate adequate time to both my duties and our princess. My fellow commander is far more deserving of the distinction as her royal tutor."

Kai was putting everything she had into learning basic self-defense, but she struggled with it. In the two weeks since he'd taken up the role of her instructor, he'd sacrificed valuable evenings of free time between sleep and duties as Commander of the Myrmidon Artillery Units.

But he couldn't make her learn faster.

His father stared at him, stoic features unchanging and perpetually unimpressed.

Had he ever in his life made this man proud of him? Manu thought back to the day Regent Aegaeon named him leader of the coral glider units, passing the coveted position of cavalry commander to Cosmas, his wife's nephew. Lago had merely glanced at his son, shaking his head. "A mediocre promotion. You could have done better."

Better indeed. Acquiring either position should have been seen as a tremendous accomplishment at his age, but his father had wanted him to follow in his footsteps, riding into battle upon a shark. Though sharks were preferred for their maneuverability and the bond that often grew between a rider and his beast, Regent Aegaeon chose Manu to lead their artillery for his unparalleled talent behind the wheel. No one piloted a glider better than him.

Lago, however, saw it as a failure.

The general saw *everything* as a failure when it didn't align with his plans for Manu.

"No," Lago growled. "It's your task."

All right then. "Then am I dismissed, sir?"

Lago waved him off.

Free from further judgment, Manu strode from the war room where his father planned out the kingdom's protection and met with his subordinates. He loathed that room as much as he loathed the man who commanded from it.

"Manu! There you are."

Manu froze when Cosmas's voice echoed down the corridor. He ground his teeth and slowly turned to face the high mer son of Lady Nammu's oldest sister, his childhood friend and greatest rival, the man against whom his father always measured him, though his opponent couldn't be more oblivious. The other commander had no time for conflicts and jealousy, and whenever one of his peers attained some small advancement—especially Manu—Cosmas was among the first to offer genuine, heartfelt congratulations.

The man didn't possess an envious bone in his body and did in fact live for doing the best for Atlantis, one among few high mer who voluntarily served his kingdom's military and set an example for all other members of the nobility.

He'd deserved his title as Commander of the Cavalry. And Manu had deserved his promotion to artillery commander. It was only a shame Lago would never be satisfied with any of his professional accomplishments and saw him as a perpetual failure.

"Greetings, Cosmas. What may I do for you?"

Cosmas halted in his tracks and arched a dark brow. "What happened?"

Wondering if it was his expression that gave him away, Manu's gaze darted toward the polished wall.

His tense posture, tight shoulders, and grimacing face told a story of frustration. "Nothing."

"You're an awful liar. What happened? General Twat at it again? Have you told him to shove it in his blowhole yet?"

Manu failed to snort back a laugh. The chuckle escaped him despite his effort to remain stone-faced. "He is, and no, I haven't. My training with the princess isn't to his satisfaction, so I offered the task to you."

A deep furrow slashed across his friend's brow. "I've seen your training with her. She's flourishing."

"She is. Of course, I would prefer if she grasped some concepts sooner rather than later, but..."

"But what?" Cosmas crossed his tattooed arms. "You have an idea. I can tell from the devious expression on your face."

"I do. I think she'll need a little more pushing. Much like the new trainees, our princess requires a different kind of encouragement."

"What are you suggesting?"

Manu grinned. "She seems to respond best to being told what she can't do. Perhaps I'll appeal to her anger."

And if she was furious with him, it'd be easier to push her away and not fantasize about her lovely thighs wrapped around his waist.

10

LOVE IS WAR

KAI HATED MANU'S SMUG FACE.

His absurdly handsome, perpetually gloating, smug face that seemed all the more gleeful whenever he knocked the water out of her lungs. Manu struck her so hard she spun in the current and saw stars.

"Isn't it illegal to strike royalty?" Kai demanded at last, voice rising with frustration.

"Not when it's in the name of training. I'm allowed to strike you as many times as I want then." He cocked a brow, and then his smarmy grin returned, making her want to strangle him.

All those weeks of underwater aerobics and yoga suddenly didn't seem like wasted time anymore, though she wished most of all that she could write home to tell Sadie she'd been right. That one day, she'd be glad of all those hours spent at the group workout sessions.

Today, Manu proved he was more of a bastard than any fitness instructor on the surface. Her body was screaming for rest, every muscle from her abs to her—Kai's exhausted mind couldn't even recall the name of the muscle connecting her caudal fin to her piscine half—ached like she'd swum a thousand miles.

Maybe she had. A thousand miles would be an understatement however, since Manu made her swim the same exercise over and over from day to day without any rest in between. In the real world, a physical trainer would have let her rest a day, allowing her muscles to recuperate, but Commander Taskmaster didn't believe in breaks.

The moment she acquired mastery of one skill, he ran through another until she wanted to cry. Under his instruction, she twisted into loops and performed spirals, also learning to bolt from a stand-still. Yet he always caught her and wrestled her to the sandy ocean floor. For more than a fortnight, they'd maintained a pace of training four hours each morning no fewer than three or four days a week. The rest of the time, Kai attended classes with stoic scholars who drilled Atlantian history, law, and reli-gion into her head. The tales of Thalassa's blessings never ended.

Exhausted, Kai settled across a patch of sea grass and sprawled on her back. For the day's lesson, he'd taken her to the city outskirts beyond the dome, intro-ducing her to the discovery that mers weren't affected by sea pressure.

Manu stood over her. "It isn't yet time to rest, Your Highness."

"I'm going to rest anyway. Everything *hurts*."

He settled opposite her in a relaxed, cross-legged pose, resting both hands on his knees. "You'll heal. Besides, it wouldn't hurt so much if you didn't let me pummel you. You kind of stand there and take these ass-beatings."

She jerked up into a sitting position. "*Let* you?" Feeling petulant, she flicked him with her tail then swept it again, stirring a cloud of sand into his face.

He coughed a few times and waited until the dust settled before replying. "Very mature."

"You bring out the child in me."

"How unfortunate that I haven't brought out the child in you during our practice, since we teach children these maneuvers and they seem capable of comprehending the skills."

"Eat a dick."

"Such words from a princess. Is this what the mortals taught you during your land-bound years?"

God, there wasn't another man in the world she wanted to punch more than she yearned to strike Manu, and that one love tap in the coliseum seemed years ago. "My language isn't any worse than yours! Besides, I'm barely a princess. I don't remember anything about being one." Then she muttered, "I wish I wasn't."

"Ah, wishing it were not so does not change the facts. You *are* a princess, and until you grasp the importance of this exercise, we will remain here."

Fucker.

For this lesson, they had the roles of aggressor and

prey. His aim was to disable her, and her goal was to thwart him and escape. Thus far, she'd only broken free from the initial grapple once, and was caught on the escape route. The man swam faster than a fucking harpoon bolt.

"Ready?"

"Ready when you are."

When he came at her, she twisted into position and slapped him with her caudal fin hard enough to bloody a normal man's nose. Then she bolted toward the east.

Manu caught her again by her dorsal fin—appearing at her rear as if summoned by magic—and slammed her beneath him in the sand. He trapped her body beneath him and caged her with his muscular forearms. "This should be performed in one motion, Princess Kailani. Time and time again, I watch you waste precious seconds. It needs to be fluid, without time between the flick and dash. One second can be the difference between life and death for a child. That is why we teach them the importance of fleeing an attack."

"I thought the Gloom never comes this far? A hundred leagues or something like that?"

"A rough three-hundred-mile radius has been safe, but it was once larger. Besides, it never hurts to be prepared. If it isn't the Gloom, it could be a hungry predator. There are dangers everywhere."

Kai quieted. She'd discovered only high mer and specially trained Myrmidon guards developed the technique to command sea life. It was not a gift all shared, and thus traveling too far from the city could prove dangerous at any moment. For high mer, it came easily. For common mer, they had to fight for every milestone.

The way she had to fight for improvement as Manu's student.

Head in the game, Kai reminded herself. She had to do it. Had to.

Ignoring the pain in her ribs and the ache throbbing in her belly each time she flexed or bent, she assumed her defensive position again.

He came at her fast, a blur of muscle and man, hard fists and a grip tighter than a locking vice. If the youngest children of Atlantis could learn to evade a predator, then so too could she. She twisted to the side and let his palm strike glance past her torso, barely skimming her, but the motion synchronized with the curve of her lower body.

Kai imagined herself driving Manu's balls into his throat and making him choke on them along with all his taunts. She snapped her tail, simultaneously striking him in the junk and propelling herself away from her phony assailant at the speed of light.

It felt like the speed of light, anyway. Probably nothing close to it, but what mattered most was that she heard his grunt of pain when the blow folded him in half and dropped him like a stone to the ocean floor. Another whip of her tail jettisoned her away, so fast she probably left a streak through the water. He didn't have a prayer of grabbing her, too busy cupping both hands to his abused genitals.

When Manu caught up, he squinted at her through a haze of unconcealed pain. He'd probably have tears in his eyes if they weren't underwater. By then, Kai reclined on a bed of algae and feigned interest in examining the little hermit crab rummaging through it beside her. She aimed a satisfied grin at him.

"Looks like I managed. How was it?"

"Acceptable," he grunted.

"Thank you."

"Let's never speak of this again."

"Oh no, let's. I think my accomplishment should be shouted from the tallest rooftops of Atlantis. But I'll begin with the barracks as we pass by, en route for the palace. How are the boys? Recovering well? Pain is a weakness foreign to Myrmidon, so you must certainly be all right by now."

He glowered at her and opened this mouth, only to snap it shut when Amerin approached on a sandskipper. The little buggers were as nonaggressive as sharks came, a bottom-dwelling carnivore that only hunted small fish and crustaceans. In the weeks since her arrival, she'd noticed children of wealthier Atlantians sometimes kept them as pets, no different than human kids riding ponies. Merchildren rode everything from magical sharks to giant seahorses.

A Royal Guard swam alongside Amerin. As a member of the domestic caste, she had little experience in combat, trained no further than the lessons Kai struggled to comprehend.

Well, *had* struggled to comprehend.

The guard bowed to Kai and spoke a polite greeting before he fell back and went silent.

Amerin bowed courteously from astride her beast. "Excuse the interruption, Your Highness and Commander, but I come bearing a message from Regent Aegaeon."

Still flushed and clenching both fists, Manu gritted between his teeth. "Of course."

"Is something wrong?" Kai asked.

Amerin shook her head. "No. Your uncle would like to see you in private before dinner. It's not urgent, he says, but important."

"Thank you. Tell him I'll—"

"She'll be with him shortly. Our lesson is finished," Manu said tersely before he strode away. After a few steps, he pushed off the sand and swam away quicker than a mer pursued by a megalodon.

Served him right. Maybe he'd be a little less cocky next time.

⚊⚏⚊

THEY MET on a stone bridge curving above the palace's aqua garden, overlooking a field of flourishing soft coral interspersed with clusters of rock. Practically every stone featured some living creature, hermit crab, or striped feather duster wobbling in the gentle current.

Kai loved this corner of Atlantis. Here, despite the bubble surrounding the entire city, they were submerged beneath yards of pristine water.

"And how has your training progressed with Commander Manu?"

"As well as can be expected, I guess. He *is* a good teacher." Aside from a few immature quibbles, she had no true complaints. The mer pushed her frequently, and he urged her always to do her best, to outperform her previous achievements and grow as a warrior.

"Excellent. I'm glad to hear it. And how are you adapting to the rest of life in Atlantis?"

"It's...different."

"And you're happy here?"

If he wasn't both her uncle and an authority figure, she would have shrugged. Happiness could be considered subjective. Was she cared for? Yes. Did they provide for her needs? Yes. Had she made friends and new acquaintances? Certainly.

But she wasn't happy. She missed Sadie and Sunshine and wondered if they thought of her as frequently as they crossed through her mind.

"Not yet," she answered truthfully. "But I will be."

Aegaeon leaned forward, resting his elbows against the rail. "I appreciate your honesty. Ianthe and Neptune raised a wise girl. Brave and smart." Before the frown could even tug her lips down, he added, "As did your mortal surrogate mother. But I didn't call you here to kiss your tail. Tell me, what can I do to improve your outlook toward the city?"

She shook her head. "It isn't anything concrete. I miss elements of my old life and how things used to be, but I understand I'm needed here and it isn't about my happiness now. It's about the safety of Atlantis." All her life, she'd wanted to *belong*, and now that she'd finally found home, that sense of inclusion was still missing.

He nodded. "You may have guessed, but I called you to discuss a particularly sensitive matter, and I hope you do not take offense to my prying. Your... relationship status. Are you unmated?"

"Definitely."

The stunned look in his eyes faded after a moment. "I imagined you would have at least taken a companion. I worried for some time that you were forced to leave them behind."

"No." She shook her head. "Never came close," she uttered, gut clenching with dread.

His shoulders dipped with relief. "Despite how much we've needed to talk, I didn't want to over-whelm you with too much, too soon."

The implication stretched tension down her spine. No good could ever come from the words "we need to talk" regardless of how they were phrased. "What have I done wrong?"

"Done? Nothing. Please, it isn't anything you've done wrong; it's what I hope you will do."

She arched a brow. "What can I do to help?"

"I won't pretend I wouldn't prefer to remain regent of Atlantis, but it isn't my role to keep. The responsibility belongs to you. Until you are capable of leading the city, I will do my best to maintain the peace in your stead."

"Thank you. I think. I'm definitely not ready, but I'll do everything I can to prepare for when I will take my place as queen. It's...surreal, though. Little girls above the surface dream about being princesses and queens. I never did."

"Perhaps deep down in your subconscious, you knew you already were." He smiled. "Now I am afraid I must get to the heart of the matter. The general visited me to voice a concern. I've neglected to teach you the extent of your duties. Much of what I do day-to-day in the name of preserving this kingdom can be accomplished with you by my side. Will you attend court with me each day? How else are you to learn your responsibilities if I do not share them with you, right?"

"Of course."

"Thank you. There is one other thing. The reason for my question regarding your personal life."

She watched his expression change, a solemn mask sliding into place where warmth had been seconds prior. "I'm not going to like this, am I?"

"Probably not," he admitted sadly. "I need you to consider taking a husband from among the high mer."

Her belly dropped to the floor, and nausea rippled through her chest until she thought she'd puke. "A husband?"

"No ruler can lead Atlantis alone. Your mother, the most powerful queen to lead our kingdom, took a husband as her equal to pick her up in times of sorrow, to guard her during times of weakness, and... to conceive you."

"How the hell am I expected to lead an army if I'm pregnant?" she blurted out.

Aegaeon chuckled. "I don't mean for it to happen right this moment."

"I hope not this moment," she deadpanned, hoping to diffuse the awkward situation with a little humor. "They have terms for that kind of thing on the surface, Aegaeon."

When she cocked a brow, he grinned. "We have similar words for it here in Atlantis, I assure you. What I meant is, it doesn't need to happen in the immediate future. Your parents were wed for centuries before they chose to have you."

"Oh." She nibbled her lower lip. She liked Aegaeon. Compared to most people she'd known on the surface, he was real and honest. He held nothing back from her.

And she liked that the mer had an actual sense of humor, not at all some stuffy dictator compelling her to fall into line or else. He'd given her nothing but choices since her arrival.

"The most important thing, however, was that the possibility of your birth existed. Our people waited anxiously for more than four hundred years to see a child born from their two beloved rulers."

Four hundred years. The idea of being married to anyone so long churned her stomach and flooded her mouth again with sour bile. She couldn't even find a man to date on Tinder, and this guy wanted her to *marry* someone.

"There is no need to make your decision now. I

merely ask you to consider it. If so, there are ample young mers of quality from outstanding noble clans eager to meet you."

"And I'll have the final choice? There aren't any unusual traditions or rules I need to know about before I agree to this, are there?" She shuddered, imagination running wild with the worst-case scenario—her uncle marrying her to a bloated, ancient, and graying old noble with a whale paunch and nothing in common with her.

She'd swim back to Galveston before she agreed to that, no matter how much she liked Aegaeon.

A wrinkle notched between his brows. "Unusual traditions?"

After she explained everything she'd ever read about the old traditions of medieval England and their predisposition for marrying young girls to ancient rulers and doddering lords old enough to have fathered them, her uncle snorted back a laugh. His shoulders shook with amusement, and then he took her hand, squeezing it.

"No. Certainly not, Kai. Ultimately, the final choice will always be yours. My duty is merely to facilitate the meetings and ensure you've met our best and brightest. You're free to deny or accept whomever you desire, and of course, to court as many as you'd like at once."

"As many as I want?"

"Romantic exploration is standard in our culture. Young mers often go through a period of courtship with many potential mates until they choose to enter an engagement with one partner. A little competition is good for them." Aegaeon grinned. "I was one of seven pursuing Nammu."

Kai found that difficult to believe, but maybe mers were gluttons for punishment, masochists who liked to be sneered at and talked down to. "So, a bunch of guys may fight over me? What happens when I make a choice?"

"As you dismiss them, a good sport will take it in stride and thank you for your time. Once you're down to your final pick, however, monogamy becomes expected, much like what you're accustomed to seeing on the surface. Will this be acceptable?"

Dating a lot of hot guys and potentially watering the sexual desert? It sounded too good to be true. "I'm down for it. When does it begin?"

"Tomorrow."

THE SUITABLE SUITOR

A TRIO OF ENTERTAINERS PLAYED ON A LOW stage at the edge of the restaurant's dining floor. Kai sat opposite Lord Fridericus, a handsome mer with the features of an Italian runway model. His dark violet hair fell beyond his shoulders and skimmed the small of his back, woven with dozens of pearls and polished gemstones.

If there was one thing she liked about Atlantis, it was that sexism and racism didn't exist, though those had been replaced by another evil—classism. Mers like Amerin didn't have the same rights as high mers, all because she'd been born into a family of servants.

Kai loathed the system.

It wasn't fair that parentage dictated their entire future. At least in America, a person born into unfortunate circumstances could claw their way to the top after running a startup business out of their garage. In Atlantis, a housekeeper would always be a housekeeper.

"Princess Kai, you honor me by accepting my invitation to dinner this evening."

It wasn't like I had much of a choice.

At least the view was nice, even if the guy wasn't her type, beyond his incredible physical looks. Fridericus's dolphin-leather suit hugged his muscular body like a second skin. When Amerin had offered her similar, she'd balked at it, distressed by the sentient creatures she once swam alongside dying to provide clothing—but Atlantis was not a vegetarian society, and they put every scrap of the creatures to use, including their teeth. So she stuffed her judgment where it belonged.

"I... Your leggings are nice," she muttered. "It's dolphin, isn't it?"

He brightened. "It is. Thank you for noticing, Your Highness."

On the third week of her arranged dates with the noble sons of Atlantis, Kai recognized one shortcoming among her suiters: noble-born men were ridiculously pretty, and pretty was not a favorable physical trait for her.

Though it wasn't their prettiness and fair features that turned her off, as she'd spent hours drooling over the elf lord Thranduil while watching *The Hobbit* last year. What bothered her was that prettiness was the only defining feature among them. They had nothing else. No substance.

By the end of dinner with Fridericus, she couldn't claw her way out of his company fast enough.

"Is the companionship not to your liking?" Aegaeon asked when she joined him for court the next day in the reception chamber. Soon, the Council of Lords would be meeting for their seasonal review of Atlantis law. As they were the kingdom's royal advisors, he was obligated to *listen* to their advice, though he'd already told her he rarely took it. She looked forward to attending the meeting and discovering why.

Kai did not, however look forward to answering Aegaeon's questions about her string of failed dates. She blinked at him. "That was a random question."

"Not so random, my dear. Now answer the question."

She wondered what he'd been told and by whom but sighed as she settled into the throne beside him. "They're fine men, but not my type. Perhaps someone more..." She gestured, searching for words, hating to sound shallow but unable to bond herself to a man who spent more time in front of his mirror than she did. "Someone more masculine. Rugged."

"I hadn't known that to be your taste. How big and rugged are we talking?"

Her cheeks warmed a bit. "I don't know. Like... broad shoulders and taller than me."

"Larger than I?"

Her face flamed hotter than a torch. Talking to her uncle, with whom she was still developing a relationship, about what she found visually pleasing in men was not her idea of fun. "Quite a bit larger, please." She and Aegaeon were only about eye to eye.

As the corner of his mouth tipped up, she got the feeling that he was restraining a bigger grin. "Of course. So you're into whales instead of dolphins. Got it."

"*Uncle.*"

"What?" he asked innocently.

"If you set me up with some blubbery man—"

Laughter shuddered through his shoulders. "Sharks then? I'm only teasing. I think I have an idea of what you're looking for. I'll *flesh* out your pool of suitors with some variety. A little from all three fields, perhaps?"

"Haha," she said dryly, though her shoulders sagged in relief. "I'm not against, uh, larger men, as long as they take care of themselves." She couldn't imagine another dinner or evening stroll with a man worried about chipping his nails or getting algae on his fine clothes. To her, nothing could beat going for an evening swim through the cultivated wilderness.

It seemed quite a sad waste, their noble-born men gifted with such a beautiful talent for transforming yet unwilling to use it for anything but fashion.

"Thank you, Aegaeon. Perhaps someone with an interest in aquatic animals, too?"

His brows jumped up, and then a big grin crossed his face. "I know just the mer to send to you next. Have no worries."

"Something tells me I should be even more worried."

"Don't. Trust me."

Nearly two days later, Aegaeon summoned Kai to the palace courtyard to meet her next suitor.

Her uncle stood beside a man of impressive stature, shorter than Manu—weren't all of them shorter than him?—but tall enough she didn't have to hunch over to speak with him. He was the finest specimen to don a military uniform, with Manu as an exception once again, the ruler against which she measured all mers. That man was just sin in sharkskin.

Unlike the others with their waist-length tresses, this man wore his green-black hair cropped to his shoulders. Friendly turquoise eyes crinkled at the corners when he saw her.

"It is my honor to meet you this fine eve, Princess Kailani." Dipping forward into a low bow sent his dark hair coursing forward to frame his handsome face. "I am Commander Cosmas."

Kai's gaze darted from Cosmas to her uncle. "Uh. Hello." Then she searched the yard for her actual date. The man in front of her looked like he chewed up whale bones and spit them out.

"Kailani, Cosmas is the youngest nephew of my dear wife's sister."

"Wouldn't that make him...?"

"My nephew by marriage, but of no blood relation to you. I consider him among the finest of the mers in my acquaintance." The corner of Aegaeon's mouth quirked. "And should he prove otherwise or do anything to contradict my fine opinion of him, I certainly don't mind seeking a replacement to lead our cavalry units. As he will be shark bait."

"*He's* my date?" she blurted out at the same time Cosmas gave him an alarmed look.

"Yes."

"Are you serious?"

"Yes. I did promise to do better by you, didn't I? There couldn't possibly be a better match. Cosmas is the most suitable of all suitors to whom I could present you. Thank me later." Aegaeon looked so damned proud, his chest puffed out, that she didn't have the heart to shatter his hopes and point out this handsome mountain of man-muscle didn't fit the job description.

The moment Aegaeon left earshot, Cosmas gave a low, nervous chuckle. "I hope he's joking about making me shark bait. I promise to have impeccable manners."

"If I've learned anything about my uncle, it's that he has a healthy sense of humor. I imagine that's why you're here today."

Cosmas blinked. "What do you mean?"

"You. Me. This arrangement. I think he's having a joke at my expense."

The Myrmidon commander's mouth flattened into a tense line. "You seem startled, Your Highness. Am I not to your expectations?"

"It isn't that. I hadn't expected a military man. Aegaeon led me to believe I'd only be courted by nobles. Uh, high mer."

"I *am* a high mer."

Her attention darted to the insignia on his shoulders. "But you're a Myrmidon."

"That I am. There are some among us high mer who voluntarily enlist in the corps, Your Highness. While we are few, we do exist." His quiet smile soothed her raw nerves and eased the twisting sensation in her gut.

"Oh. A rare breed then." She nibbled her lower lip, thankful her darker skin rarely showed a blush. "It's nice to meet you. Uh, so, what are our plans?"

Was it going to be another boring dinner during which her companion strove to impress her with his knowledge of fine dining etiquette and art?

"I don't know yet. I thought I'd play it by ear a little and see what trouble we can get into." Cosmas offered her his arm. "Shall we?"

Kai sucked in a breath. *Here goes nothing.*

If it came down to it, she could always pretend the Atlantian food didn't agree with her again and sprint away to the nearest restroom.

"I can touch it?" Kai asked, reaching out.

"You certainly can," Cosmas said, looking keenly smug.

"I can't believe it's so big."

"Things are different in Atlantis."

"But is it supposed to be so soft and squishy? I can barely grip it."

Cosmas rolled his eyes. "Be gentler."

"I *am* being gentle."

The baby octopus resting on the palms of her submerged hands had to be the cutest *and* the weirdest aquatic animal she'd ever held. It was absolutely adorable, dusky purple and blue, and a creature she'd have never touched if the merman hadn't passed it to her and promised it was safe.

As Atlantis wasn't anywhere near Australia, the land where anything colorful and aquatic had to be poisonous, she took his word for it.

"Are you sure that they enjoy being held?"

"They do. Now, they're a little too young to be on their own, so they're socialized to enjoy physical contact."

"I've never seen this species before."

"There are many species accustomed to the depths and bred to withstand the change of pressure, that you won't find in the rest of the world. Thousands of years of magic and selective breeding have produced these little ones." Cosmas reached into the shallow pool. One of the octopus babies wrapped around his wrist and clung to him, forcing him to withdraw it from the water. "Hello there, darling. No, we aren't going for a swim today."

Kai grinned. "You talk to them, huh?"

"Of course."

"Are they pets?"

"Other species serve as ideal pets, though these are trained to accompany our keeper patrol units. They're..." He paused and tilted his head, eyes briefly closed. "Many years have passed since my last visit to the surface, but I seem to recall your mortal law officers traveling with dogs."

"Not all of them do. They're called K-9 officers. Or drug hounds for locating narcotics at airports..." Cosmas's brows jumped up, eyes glowing with unconcealed interest. Assured he didn't find her rambling dull, she continued. "And the military uses explosive sniffing hounds in regions where terrorists hide bombs. Police officers train them, too, for the same purpose and to assist them with tracking or taking down criminals."

"Our worlds are more similar than I originally believed. Some time has passed since my last visit to the surface, but from what you say, our beasts perform similar duties. The creatures detect the Gloom and notify their handlers of approaching dangers. As their sense of smell is leagues above our own, they're also used during criminal investigations by our keepers."

"What kinds of crimes happen in Atlantis? I've yet to hear of anything." She'd also never seen one of their patrolmer keepers with an octopus, and the promise of spying one at some point thrilled her. His octopus reached for her, extending a glistening tentacle. She let him grab her and coil around her forearm.

"You wouldn't. Aegaeon is going to coddle you because he wants you to see the best of Atlantis. He's under the mistaken belief that if you see it isn't superior to the surface, you'll swim screaming back to the humans."

"I wouldn't!"

"We've tried telling him."

She pursed her lips, eyeing him suspiciously. "Who is 'we'?"

"Manu and myself, of course. He calls you stubborn." At her frown, Cosmas only laughed. "Stubborn isn't the worst quality in a princess and future ruler."

"About that..." Kai tried to release her new friend back to the observation pool, but he refused. As Cosmas explained it, the hatchlings were kept until survival was guaranteed a few weeks later. "You do realize he means for us to like one another enough to marry, right?"

"I realized as much, yes."

"And you're all right with that?" She paused. Of course he'd be all right with that. It was a shot at becoming king of their entire underwater kingdom, though whether he wouldn't morph into an egotistical asshole remained to be seen.

"I know what you're thinking."

Her brows rose. She straightened, folding her arms against her chest, tucked just beneath her breasts. The octopus clinging to her forearm nuzzled against the sharkskin body suit. "You're a mind reader then?"

"No, but you're a smart woman, and I know if I were in your place, I'd have suspicions about anyone courting me." He shrugged, appearing more casual than his predecessors. "From what I've seen of your training—"

"You've seen my training?"

"I may have watched one or two sessions unbeknownst to you." His grin widened, flashing pearly teeth in the dim room. Only a few blue lights glowed above them along the ceiling. "And I liked what I saw. You're intelligent. You don't whine. You speak your mind, and I hope in time we can become friends. There's no rush."

Kai scrunched her nose. "Aegaeon made it sound like time was of the essence and that the sooner I marry, the sooner I can restore peace to the kingdom."

"Uncle is very melodramatic. More so than his wife at times."

"Your aunt, melodramatic? Never."

Cosmas had a jolly laugh. He chuckled so hard his shoulders shook. "I like your company. I like *you*, and I'm absolutely all right with doing this again."

"All right. I'm willing to give this a shot. This isn't official or anything, right? Not to sound mean, but if someone else comes along that—"

"You're not tied to me. High mers court many among the peerage at a time when the need arises."

Relief loosened the knot between her shoulder blades. "Then I'm down for seeing where this might go."

He wasn't her tall, dark, and quiet Manu, but he had a charm all his own.

12

———

DISTRESSED

MANU BARELY SPOKE DURING TRAINING THE next day. For three sessions, Kai received her instruction from a curt yet professionally aloof mer with an altered personality. Each morning, she wondered if she'd unintentionally offended him and lost his favor.

As they'd attained sufficient progress in evasive maneuvers, Manu was now teaching her to wield the preferred weapons of the realm, though she found the spear less awkward than the trident. They both wore armored plate and Corinthian helms with red fin crests, but she despised how much it interfered with her hearing. A true warrior, Manu said, did not require sight or sound to know his enemy approached. He demonstrated this fact twice by having her attack him from behind and the side, always anticipating her moves, always disarming her.

The ripples were what gave her away. Whether on dry land or in the water—but *especially* in the water—an Atlantian had a keen sense of awareness. It was a gift from the gods who had created them, a gift that made them superhuman. He told her battle training for a Myrmidon was about muscle memory and repetition, performing the same strikes over and over until her body took charge and reflexes acted for her. Fighting had to be instinctual.

They trained in and out of the water in the coliseum, the space far advanced beyond anything she'd ever encountered on the surface. Water filled and drained from it on the whim of an unseen guardsman who pulled a lever to roll the waves. According to Manu, a true warrior could go from land to sea without missing beat.

Afterward, he strode in silence alongside her to the barracks where they stored their tridents in the armory.

"I think I like the spear more. Thank you for the—"

"Good day, my princess."

"Good—" She was already speaking to his backside.

Staring at his rather fine ass, she tried to recall some sort of law related to turning one's back on royalty, until she realized she was remembering random etiquette facts she'd learned about Queen Elizabeth of England.

Later that afternoon, once Kai concluded her evening tutorial sessions with the rest of her teachers, she excused herself from the castle and made her way toward the barracks. Her head hurt from the attempt to cram too much knowledge into it at once. College had been different, an environment filled with other students on equal footing.

In Atlantis, she sat at a desk in an opulent office before a stern tutor who lectured about their history, from the time when the goddess sank their world beneath the sea to the many dynasties of the different queens who ruled before Ianthe.

"Excuse me," she spoke to the first guard to cross her path. The young mer snapped to attention, taken by surprise it seemed, since she'd never until that moment had a reason to prowl around their barracks outside of her usual training hours.

"Princess Kailani. Forgive me, I didn't notice you were—"

She waved him off. "No need to apologize. Where can I find Commander Manu?"

"His office, I believe. You go down this corridor and swing a left up the stairs to the second floor. His is the second door on the right."

"Thank you."

Other soldiers bowed along the way and gave humble greetings.

Kai smiled back and wondered how they were treated compared to people on the surface in the human militaries. Did Atlantian citizens thank them for their service? Did they purchase their meals and drinks at the bars, offer them discounts at vendors in the market squares and malls?

When she reached the door to Manu's office, she found the glossy panel shut, but knew it belonged to him as his name had been scribed on the gilded faceplate with gorgeous penmanship. It wasn't English, yet each loop and straight line looked eerily familiar the longer she stared at them until the word made sense to her.

Strange. She'd always had an easier time in foreign language classes than most other students, picking up enough Spanish to have above-average grades when she applied herself, but this had never happened. Kai filed it away as another example of the unusual evolution that began on the day of the *Sea Angel's* scuttling.

Kai knocked. "Manu?" When no one answered, she knocked again.

The door opened a moment later to frame a female Myrmidon with golden-red hair pinned in a tight bun. The young woman promptly dipped into a bow. She moved aside with a nimble step, permitting Kai inside. "Greetings, Your Highness. I'll return at another time, Ma—Commander."

Manu rose from behind his desk. "No, Elpis. Have a seat. I'd prefer to conclude our...business now."

The two exchanged a silent gaze, the look charged with enough palpable energy for Kai to feel uncomfortable sharing a room with them. And since she was all about helping out her fellow woman, Kai smiled and said, "I'm sure Elpis would be glad to return at another time. I'd like a word with you. In private."

"Perhaps a little later, Your Highness. If you wouldn't mind. I'm currently on duty, and Elpis—"

"Thank you, Your Highness. Good eve to you both." Elpis shut the door behind her, leaving Kai alone in the small office. It had only a pair of windows overlooking the narrow street outside, the lamplight golden through the thick panes.

"It won't take much of your time."

He nodded. "As you wish. How may I be of service, Princess?" He gestured to a seat, still standing behind his desk. Kai didn't take it.

"You've been different for days now. The moment our lessons are over, you bolt off like someone's lit a fire under your tail."

"Technically, I don't have a tail, Your Highness. You do."

"You know what I mean. Don't be a smartass with me."

"Better than being a dumbass, I would think."

He'd sassed her again. It took a moment for it to set in that he was behaving in a surprisingly obstinate way, unlike the Manu she'd always known—then again, how well did she truly know the man who had brought her to Atlantis and spent the last weeks teaching her the basics of survival?

"You're behaving like an asshole because I beat you, aren't you?"

He flinched back, blinking at her. "What?"

"That's it. Everything changed on the day I went for your balls. Now you're always cold to me."

"That isn't it."

"Then what is it? Manu, please. If it changes anything, I'm sorry that I took the low blow. It was childish, and if I hurt you more seriously than intended, I apologize."

When Manu didn't reply, she stood taller and squared her shoulders, refusing to back down from his stare. "What. Is. It? If I've done something to offend you, I'd like to know."

"It wasn't the attack. For the record, my armor absorbed most of the force and redistributed it appropriately. No lasting damage occurred."

"Oh. What is it then?"

"With all due respect, Your Highness, it's no business of yours. My reasons are my own."

Chills. An icy prickle touched her spine and lingered, blanketing her body beneath a cold sheet of dread. "I really did do something, didn't I?"

"As I said, it's nothing *you* have done. The fault lies with me. Regardless of my recommendations, my father insists I remain as your teacher."

She blinked at him. "You tried to quit?"

"I did more than try, but found my offer refused. It seems you and I are stuck together until I have produced the warrior queen they desire."

"Oh." He disliked her that much—enough to feel trapped. A vice tightened around her heart, squeezing on every breath she took. "I had not realized that...." She paused, wetting her lips. Her mouth had gone drier than chalk, juxtaposing her stinging eyes. "I hadn't realized you despised me so much, Commander Manu. My apologies. I will speak with Aegaeon at once and personally request a new trainer."

Manu crossed the room in a few long steps. "Princess, wait. I believe you misunderstood me."

She paused, her back to him. "What else is there to understand?" She wouldn't look at him, wishing they were surrounded by water to hide the tears blurring her vision.

"I don't despise you. I despise the situation."

"I *am* the situation."

"No." The moment his warm hand took her by the bicep, sensation zipped down her nerves and lit her with heat she hadn't known she was missing, coupled with an indescribable yearning to throw herself into his arms. To be in *anyone's* arms for at least a while.

At times, she loathed Atlantis. She hated that they'd taken her from home, and she hated the mountain of responsibility they'd thrust on her. She wanted to sob and crawl into her room to throw the mother of all pity parties, but an entire kingdom depended on her being an adult committed to self-sacrifice. Despite all of the things she hated, she didn't hate Manu nearly as much as she wanted to for being the one to take her away from the only home she recalled. The fingers on her arm felt too nice.

"Please. Give me just one moment to explain."

"All right."

When she didn't turn, his quiet sigh stirred her hair. "Will you at least look at me?"

Debating whether or not she wanted to risk making a fool of herself, she turned and gazed up at him. The tears didn't fall, and her dignity remained intact after all.

"I talked out my ass just now, Princess, and I'm sorry."

The candor took her by surprise, and her emotions took a direct 180, going from depression to hysterical laughter. "You did. Yes. I'm glad you're finally able to 'fess up to it."

He sighed. "My father and your uncle aren't pleased with the rate of your growth and feel I haven't yet encouraged you to reach your full potential. So yes, I did offer to step down. I've offered twice."

"Oh."

His reasons had everything and nothing to do with her at all—it wasn't her behavior or any offense taken to her presence, but her inability to become an overnight sensation with a trident.

"Well. Just the same, I'm sorry that I haven't been enough."

"You've done well. The fault lies with them."

"You've made it abundantly clear that Atlantian children master these techniques faster than I can."

"I was wrong to say that. I'd hoped goading would motivate you."

"Which it did."

"It did."

His gaze remained locked on hers, the fairest shade of brown she'd seen yet beneath the sea. Brighter than honey. Before she could stick her foot in her mouth and make a regrettably stupid compliment, a shrill whistle pierced the air. Seconds later, a fist hammered on the door.

"Commander! It's a distress signal from Fare."

"We'll finish this discussion later," Manu said, turning away from her to yank open the door. "Notify General Lago."

"Fare?" Kai asked.

"A smaller village to the south, one of the many colonies established by Pharae," he explained, gesturing her ahead of him through the office door. It shut behind them.

"Right, right. I remember this from my history lesson. Pharae had fallen under siege from Rome and become one of their colonies. Then Thalassa answered their prayers and sank it into the sea."

"Correct. Pharae became the second of three great cities in the Atlantian Empire, though Atlantis remains the largest of them."

Kai fell into step behind Manu. As he paused in the corridor and glanced back at her, she quirked a brow. "What?"

"This is military business."

"Yes, it is," she agreed, squaring her shoulders and raising her chin to gaze up at him. "And as the future queen of Atlantis, that makes it my business."

13

FARE GAME

Manu didn't expect Kailani to join them. He also didn't expect his father to permit it, given the importance they'd placed upon her eventually claiming the throne. It seemed reckless to him that they would order him to take the princess into a potential skirmish.

Within an hour of the distress call reaching Atlantis, he led a battery of coral gliders to the south, with Kai sitting in his passenger seat. Her golden armor shone over the layer of sharkskin, a necessary precaution in the event that they saw battle beyond their glider. He'd never lost one in a fight, though he liked to prepare for the worst. An artilleryman always came prepared, ready to fall back on a martial weapon when necessary. For that reason, his trident and her spear had been strapped overhead behind them, though she barely knew how to use the thing aside from artlessly lunging, stabbing with it while leaving herself exposed to attack.

What training she'd received from her parents and General Lago had been forgotten over the years of living on the surface, lost to time and therefore useless.

So much for muscle memory, though Kai couldn't be blamed. He placed all the blame on her damn uncle and his incorrigible father, because the two were too impatient to grant him the time required to hone and refine her skills. Like a raw gemstone, she needed months, if not years of polishing before she'd shine in battle the way they wanted.

And like a beautiful rare jewel, they risked ruining the final product by rushing and chipping at her before she was ready. He hated it, but what more could he do? As an officer under his father's command, he had no choice but to accept their orders, though it killed him. Four hours of training each morn would no longer be enough, though he suspected she would protest him requesting her from bed even earlier each day, considering the amount of lessons she endured from stuffy aristocrats and historians.

Had she been raised among her own people for the second half of her life, she'd have known it all. But that, too, was not Kai's fault.

"Do you think we'll make it in time?" she asked, breaking her prolonged silence.

"Hopefully."

"That doesn't answer my question."

"I wish I knew, Princess." As of the last report to reach them by comms, Fare's defenses were holding the Gloom at the main gate. Other artillery forces had also been deployed, and a few units from the cavalry of a nearby village had been sent to help drive back the darkness.

Over the course of the next seven hours, they received intermittent updates, though they tapered, growing fewer and farther between, until at last the dome of Fare arose from the obscuring mist. Dozens of coral glider headlamps reflected off the glass surface in the far distance.

The underwater craft traveled swiftly when Manu didn't obey the usual speed limits set forth by the Council of Lords. Few did when a true emergency arose, but he'd called only their best and most experienced pilots to cruise in their forward formation. Exceptional reflexes and talent were needed to not only avoid dangers and obstructions in their path while shooting along at over one hundred miles an hour, but to also avoid striking each other.

"Commander Manu Ghostfin to Fare. What is your current status?" Silence greeted him. "Fare, what is your current status?" He heard Kai suck in her breath, and the sound of his own racing heart pulsed a nervous drumbeat between his ears. Radio silence was never what one wanted when rushing to an ally's aid. "Fare, report," he barked out. Again, no one responded. A deep weight centered in the middle of his chest when he considered the possibilities.

"Are there any reasons why they wouldn't

respond less than thirty minutes after their last check-in?" Kai asked in a quiet voice.

"They could have evacuated or taken refuge deeper in the city. Comms could have been taken down during a fight. Numerous reasons." None of what he said alleviated the unrelenting pressure around his heart.

"Worst case scenario?"

"Everyone is already dead."

Kai sucked in a sharp breath between her teeth. "They can't be. Not an entire city, right?"

"I wouldn't be so sure. Helike was utterly destroyed, though they were less prepared for danger than Fare." He bit his lip, staring ahead while decelerating. If anyone had evacuated, they would have seen evidence of refugees fleeing from the battle. At least, the Gloom was already dispersing, its bleak veil of darkness thinning.

They found devastation moments later along with the first corpses and a few crushed gliders. The dome hadn't ruptured, unlike Helike's barrier. Instead, the guards and all defenses at the forefront of the city had been obliterated. Kai twisted in her seat to stare at their surroundings through the rear viewport, a window intended for a second gunner.

"These men can't have been dead for long. Look. There's no scavengers. Not even a few hermit crabs."

"You're right." Manu tapped a button on the comm. "Daedalus."

"Yes, Commander?"

"We're going in on foot. Fall back and maintain a defensive perimeter."

"Roger that, Commander."

Kai glanced at him, raising a brow. "We're going in on foot?"

He raised a skeptical brow. "You understood that?" He'd spoken in Atlantian at all times unless addressing her directly.

"You weren't speaking English?"

"No."

He sailed into the city's port, followed by a platoon of gliders, though it took precious minutes for the six squads to disembark from their craft into a crowded bay and await his orders. He didn't miss the number of eyes shooting curious glances at Kai as they fell into formation, their officers at the lead of each group.

Captain Daedalus's voice reached him through the comm pinned to the collar of his suit. "Commander."

"What do you see?"

"We've found what remains of Gailshark Battery. Bits of their gliders are littered around the southwestern perimeter of Fare."

"And their pilots?" His gaze snapped to the men before them. Some were related to mers serving in Fare's Myrmidon force.

Daedalus exhaled a slow breath. "Shark bait."

"I copy. Resume your mission," Manu said before raising his voice to address the squads before him.

"Keep aware. This is no longer a defensive mission. We now search for survivors."

KAI'S ANXIETY levels rose each time they made a new discovery of corpses in the overrun city, though it was more of a large township than anything, home to five thousand mers. According to Manu, Fare was only large enough to keep a single battery of gliders, approximately one hundred and fifteen vessels, each manned by a pilot and a gunner. All appeared to have been destroyed during the fight, along with their only whale thumper. She'd yet to see a whale thumper in action, only in passing, as Manu hadn't opted for one of the enormous underwater tanks to join their mission.

That was what she compared them to at least: heavily armored marine tanks designed to crawl on the ocean floor, though they possessed glider jets and propellers.

"Are you nervous?" Manu asked suddenly.

"No."

He studied her for a moment then squeezed her shoulder. "The Gloom sweeps in and often sweeps out. If there are any straggling beasts, there won't be many."

"I'm not worried about that."

He arched a brow, but he didn't question it. As pleasant as she found his touch, she shrugged out from under his hand and proceeded forward on the path. Fare didn't differ much from Atlantis with its paved roads and neatly manicured grounds, enchanted lanterns casting captive sunlight over their underwater realm.

Mers liked wisteria and fig trees, incorporating a lot of Greco-Roman plant life into their city designs, as well as homes resembling the stone structures she saw in gladiator flicks and historical movies. When the squads broke into pairs to cover more ground, Manu and Kai moved together down one side of a bloodstained lane. Her belly twisted every time they passed some piece of a dismembered citizen. The place had been reduced to a ghost town.

Gods. She swallowed down the bile rising in her throat and tried to hide her rising panic when they crossed near a graying, half-blackened corpse. Manu gestured for her to go ahead and drew a blade as long as her forearm from his belt.

"What are you doing?"

"Making sure this one doesn't rise from the Gloom."

"What?"

"As I said, Your Highness, I am guaranteeing this one does not rise from the Gloom."

She didn't linger. He stopped multiple times after that, whenever they crossed a forgotten body stiffening in a road or some shelter. Maybe she wasn't strong enough for this after all.

They searched homes with vacant bedrooms, shattered furnishings, and empty cribs.

Empty cribs.

Her heart constricted in her chest at the sight. Better empty than to see Manu putting an infected child out of its misery. Kai didn't know if her heart could take that.

She swallowed sour bile without any relief and hastily wiped the back of her hand across her face, furious and hurting, inundated by more emotions at once than she thought possible. And still they encountered no beasts, only the carnage left in their wake.

"Commander, Daedalus reporting."

Manu paused, eyes narrowing as he tapped the button on his collar. "Good news?"

"Survivors found northwest of the city. It appears some citizens tried to evacuate while Gailshark Battery threw themselves at the Gloom. We're escorting them to meet the rescue vessel en route."

Manu hung back to speak a moment longer with his captain. During that time, Kai proceeded forward into another home. The door had been bashed in off its hinges, and the stink of the Gloom permeated the air when she stepped inside. Furnishings had been tossed aside and squid ink splattered the walls.

Shallow breaths didn't help against the sharp tang. She already held a white-knuckled grip on her spear. Then something scuttled against the wall, and she picked up the sound of many legs clicking against stone. Kai whirled with her spear at the ready to see a giant bristle worm emerging from a crack in the wall, though there was a putrid essence leaking from raw, open cankers in its fractured crimson shell. There seemed to be no end to it, the creature as long as she was tall. Perhaps more.

It rushed at Kai, darting forward like a lance. She rolled to the side without losing her spear and was on her feet again, stabbing with it. The noise of her spearhead striking the hard, chitinous shell echoed through the small space.

"Princess?" Manu called, alarm in his voice.

The second time it lunged at Kai, she fended it off with the spear's long shaft, screaming, "Gloombeast!"

By then, Manu was already barreling inside with a curved blade in his hand, silver glinting in the dim light. He swore at the sight of it. Then it raced toward her like a furious serpent. "Shield out!"

She whipped the shield from her back, heart slamming faster than a snare drum in her chest. Terror made her lightheaded. This was the kind of moment he'd trained her to survive. While it was only one Gloombeast, she fought against her body seizing in fear when it flew at her. Then muscle memory and instinct led the way as she bashed the worm with her shield.

The worm struck metal hard enough for Kai to stumble back a step, unprepared for its strength. When it bounced away, Manu intercepted it with his blade and sliced it clean across the middle. Both halves flopped to the ground, one squealing and thrashing, while blue-green ichor flooded from the severed ends. Before the half with its mouth could go for her again, Kai reversed her spear and drove it down through the worm's head.

Kai stared at it for a long while after, until it stopped moving and was only a dead thing leaking on the living room floor.

"Are you all right?" Manu stepped in behind her. One of his hands curved around her upper arm, chafing up and down. Without caring if it was appropriate, she leaned back against him.

"I'm fine, I think. Just shaken up."

"I shouldn't have let you go on alone like that. I'm sorry."

"Not your fault. I walked off." She swallowed, hating when he let go and put a step of distance between them. She twisted around to look up at him. "How could so much damage be done here in so little time?"

He smiled bitterly. "Numbers. The Gloom is ever growing, and their army is *always* open to conscription. Once a mer or sea creature is infected with Calypso's vile sickness, they become part of it."

"I know that, but...is there no defending against it? No recovery?"

"Once infected? No. It's death once one of them pierces your heart with its toxic barb."

"When one of our own falls—"

"We put them out of their misery if they survive the initial injury. Were I sick, I'd want the same done for me."

"That's awful."

"That is life in Atlantis, Princess. Until the

Gloom is pushed back, until Calypso and her masters are defeated, it's the reality of our underwater realm. This is why the general and your uncle are desperate for you to learn."

Kai gripped her spear so tightly her hand hurt. "Then I'll learn. Whatever you need me to learn, I'll do."

"It'll require more hours than you already give."

"I don't care."

"It won't be like the training plan we've made for you. What Regent Aegaeon and General Lago want will require more than anyone could safely give. I'm against it, because I don't want to break you."

"It won't break me."

"Are you sure about that, Your Highness?"

"I'm positive. Fuck the history, fuck the lessons. Teach me everything you'd teach a mer entering your army. Make me a Myrmidon. Treat me to everything I need to know to fight this. Put me through hell if you have to, because whatever you do to me can't be worse than what happened to these people."

14

LEILEI

EVERY TIME MANU MADE HIS MIND UP ABOUT the princess, she turned his preconceptions about her inside out. A week ago, she'd been a clumsy woman-child with a weak understanding of their society. Yesterday, Kai held her own against a Gloombeast and showed the first signs of the fearless leader she'd one day become.

Manu stared at his bedroom ceiling, cursing both the hour and the unfortunate circumstances that wouldn't grant him even a few hours of reprieve from fantasizing about her. With a dream about Kai haunting his sleeping mind, he'd awakened harder than whalebone.

And now he had to dedicate eight hours of his day to her personal instruction. He groaned and rubbed his tired face.

Fuck. The gods hated him.

As a mer of the warrior class, he wasn't permitted to mate any female—or male, for that matter—of a caste higher than two ranks above his own. As much as Atlantis prized its Myrmidons, they didn't fancy warriors rising to the royal class. Beyond that, servants were the only members of the rigid caste system unable to elevate via marriage. A servant was always a servant, as were their children, committing mers like Amerin to a lifetime of domestic slavery.

Pacifica operated differently from her sister kingdom in the Atlantic Ocean, lacking antiquated social systems designed to oppress segments of its population. Had Manu not already devoted too many decades of his life to service in Atlantis, he would have immigrated to the neighboring ocean and tested his luck in the nation of his mother's people, a place where hard work and dedication determined futures —not birthright. He'd heard Queen Laka was a just and fair merwoman, as compassionate as she was strong despite her royal blood.

Sometimes, he wished he'd followed Calanthe. Life could have been good there for them both.

Despite the temptation to burrow deeper under the covers and shirk his responsibilities, Manu dragged himself from between the sheets and trudged into the bathroom. Without waiting for the fire crystals to heat the water to his preferred temperature, he eased under the shower spray and prayed the cold withered his arousal.

It didn't. Nothing washed away the sordid fantasies that had haunted his dreams of Kailani in her tiny swimsuit, those indecent and impractical cloth triangles leaving almost nothing to his imagination. And in those dreams, he plucked the delicate strings and pulled it away from her flawless skin, baring her to his mouth. In those dreams, the schism between warrior class and royalty didn't exist and he was free to touch and taste and kiss her to his heart's content.

As Manu took his cock in hand and stroked down to the base, his unrelenting subconscious tortured him with a new fantasy, a memory of the previous day he'd replayed over and over during the return trip home from Fare while Kai slept in the copilot's chair. In that fantasy, she stood over the corpse of another Gloombeast they'd encountered during an intended rendezvous with the squad, a disturbing chimera of squid and lobster with lethal claws, shooting vile ink while lunging at them from the shadows between two residences. As it was still developing a stinger, she'd been in no true danger, allowing Manu to stand back and watch her take it on.

When he tested her, she passed with flying colors, radiating confidence. She was no longer the same scared girl who shrieked while fleeing monsters from the Gloom on Galveston Beach.

Funny how the most arousing sight of Kai wasn't her in skimpy beach attire, practically naked under the setting sun, her hair wild around her shoulders and spilling down her back.

The most attractive he'd ever seen the princess had been her standing in triumph over her enemy with squid ink on her shield and blue blood on her spear. The sexiest he'd ever seen her, the hottest she could ever be, had been the moment their eyes met and he saw a glimpse of a powerful queen destined to rule their kingdom and restore light to the underwater realm.

That was the Kai he craved.

Cursing himself for dwelling on it, he continued to stroke, remembering the way she'd turned to him with pride dancing in her eyes, seeking approval he'd been eager to give.

Now, she was his student. Soon, she'd be his queen. To make matters worse, he had every reason to believe Kai planned to pick his best friend for her mate and future king.

Stop thinking of her.

If only it were that easy.

He'd hit rock bottom, stroking off to a merwoman he could never have.

WITH AN HOUR TO spare before Kai was due to join him at the barracks, Manu leaned into the neighboring office and rapped on the door. Cosmas was already behind the desk, kneading his temples with one hand and reading the morning edition of the *Daily Atlantic.* As the most recent suitor to be seen with Princess Kailani in public, Cosmas made regular appearances in the gossip section, his every move dissected.

All of the legitimate counting houses had started taking bets, giving Cosmas favorable odds at becoming the next king. Lord Fridericus, on the other hand, was last calculated at having a 25-1 chance at winning the princess's approval. From what Manu had overheard between Kai and Amerin, the mer had a *zero* percent chance. That made Manu childishly gleeful.

"You have a free moment?" Manu asked. "Or are you too busy admiring the newest photo of you?"

"The photo is shit, and I always have a free moment for you, my friend. What can I do?"

"I may have done something stupid—"

"*You* do something stupid?" Cosmas leaned back in his seat and crossed both arms over his armored chest.

"Shut up."

"You definitely have my attention now. What did you do and how bad a mess am I going to help you clean up? Are we hiding bodies, paying off mistresses...?"

"It's nothing that damned dramatic." At Cosmas's inquisitively raised eyebrow, he sighed and continued. "I may have chosen a shark for our princess from the riding program without considering whether or not she might be into riding. As you've been spending time with her recently, I wondered if you'd have any insight into it. And whether...this animal may be to her liking at all."

Cosmas stared at him, mouth falling slack with surprise.

"Don't look at me what way."

"You chose a shark for her? Really?"

"If you're going to make a big deal of this—"

"I'm not. Just a little startled that you're asking my opinion when you're as well-versed in riding sharks as I am."

"You're the Commander of the Cavalry."

"We both also know the title was stolen from you, Manu. This should have been your job, your honor. Uncle tossed it to me because—"

"Because you're unbeatable in the saddle and could outmaneuver a Gloom-infected squid while you were riding a dying blue whale."

"Everything I know was learned from you."

A companionable silence fell between them during the brisk walk from the barracks to the southern stables. They entered a building designed to resemble an elegant rock formation, cut into the side of the Atlantian dome near one of the city's trading ports. A young mer named Sophos approached them from the offices with a clipboard in his hand.

"Good day, Commanders. May I be of service?"

"We're here to see Leilei." Again, Manu saw Cosmas shooting him an inquisitive side-eye.

"Would you like her corralled, or will you be visiting her in the stall today?" Sophos asked.

"Corral is fine."

"Head up to level five. We'll have her out to you in just a few."

The multi-level stable designated for the Royal Army kept over five hundred beasts at any given time, each of them belonging to members of the Myrmidon cavalry or used in their personal breeding program.

They didn't lose an animal often, but as their cavalry was ever-growing, so too did their need for more creatures. With a corral on each level, the guys had plenty of space to train the young sharks entering the program in a safe, contained environment. Manu had been working with sharks since he was a toddler, introduced to his first sandskipper when he was no more than four years old and still wobbling on his young legs.

Manu and Cosmas took a spiral staircase to the fifth floor, arriving just as Leilei shot down the chute from her stall into the corral. A thousand pounds of energetic filly glided faster than a cross between a dolphin and a mako shark. Her svelte, navy blue body turned in the water, lights sparkling off the dappled pink and glittering purple on her flank. Her fins resembled a nebula, a replica of the Milky Way painted on sharkskin.

Cosmas sucked air between his teeth. "She's fast. A lot of energy. Gorgeous to look at, though. Is she the one that Anatolius failed out of the rider program?"

"Maybe." Desperate to avoid the conversation looming ahead, Manu stepped over the barrier separating them from the water-filled corral and dropped down into forty feet of water. Leilei twisted and rolled toward him, massive mouth open. She skimmed by his side and turned again, brushing past him several times until he stroked beneath her fins. "Hey there, girl. Told you I'd be back to see you soon."

"Already in love with her, aren't you?"

Of all the sharks Manu could have chosen, he'd picked the most energetic and eager for attention.

"She's sweet," Manu said, shrugging. "What do you think of her?"

"She may be too much shark for Kailani. I don't know." Cosmas rubbed his chin and observed the young filly at play. "She's cute and has a lot of spunk."

"Reminded me of the princess."

"Me too," Cosmas agreed, much to Manu's surprise. "You picked well. She can't ride yet, but if she attacks sharksmanship with the same dedication she devotes to all the other aspects of her training, it won't take long to develop her talents. I would have chosen a mellow older male for her. One settled, with some years in the saddle. Leilei is untrained, enthusiastic and...honestly, I doubt I'm telling you anything you don't already know. It'll either be a match made in Elysium, or an awful, regrettable idea. Have you gotten her under saddle yet, or is she *completely* green?"

"Greener than sea lettuce."

"Let's get it done then."

15

DIVINE PRIVILEGE

On the seventh day of Myrmidon training, Kai decided she hated life. Her bed, warm and comforting, invited her to remain between the sheets. She wondered how long it would take before Manu stomped inside and dragged her out.

Her body ached, her hamstrings protested straightening her knees to leave the fetal position, and she loathed the idea of going anywhere before the sun ever rose in their region of the world. One glance outside into the streets revealed dim lanterns lit by subtle blue and silver lights. The enchantments reflected the skies above the Atlantic Ocean.

"Princess?" Amerin whispered from the door.

"I'm awake."

"Commander Manu is here."

"Tell him I'm coming."

"He told me he knew you would say that, and that if you do not present yourself at the barracks' training ground within the next five minutes, he is doubling the distance you must swim and adding fifty pounds of weight."

Kai's belly roiled with nausea at the mere threat. "That's inhumane."

Amerin chuckled and shut the door. "I'll tell him you're on the way."

There hadn't been time since her arrival to get to know Amerin the way she wanted, but she enjoyed the merwoman's company. This evening, as a reward for surviving the first week of Myrmidon training, they were to go to a show in the city together in hopes of bonding and renewing the friendship they'd had as children.

But first, Kai had to survive eight grueling hours of hell. If Manu could complete his normal duties each day on top of training her, the least she could do was show up for it.

All right. You can do this. You got this, girl. It's just pain. Pain is just weakness leaving the body. Pain is just failure becoming success. Pain is temporary. Pain was also crippling her and making it impossible to swing her legs out from beneath the sheets. She tossed them off, but her back screamed and every muscle from her neck down to her hips stretched taut as unconditioned leather.

Prior to bed, she'd stretched, soaked in a hot tub with salts, and then stretched again before crawling under the blankets. Her treacherous body didn't care.

Manu had spent the week introducing her to a whole theme park of torture devices masquerading as training equipment, most of which she'd seen during movies like *Gladiator* or the show *Spartacus*. At least each episode of the latter had been sixty minutes of glorious abs, steamy sex scenes, and hunks like the delicious Andy Whitman and Manu Bennett fighting in a bloody, fictionalized Ancient Rome.

No wonder she liked Manu so much. He shared a name with one of her favorite actors. And realizing he shared a name with one of her favorite actors made her wonder about the many other Atlantians she'd met with names belonging to Pacific Islanders instead of the Greco-Roman names popular with most high mers. Her own father had been named for a Roman god, her mother a Greek ocean nymph.

Interesting, she thought.

Amerin returned to help her into her suit. Eventually, her body loosened enough to leave the room. She found Manu in the entrance hall instead of the barracks. The mer stood with his arms crossed, watching her descend at a hermit crab's pace.

"I've seen starfish move faster," he remarked.

"Blow me."

"Such words from a princess." A hint of a smile touched his lips.

"We've had this talk before. Besides, I don't feel like a princess today. I'm stiffer than driftwood."

Manu's dark brows popped up, then a big grin spread across his face. She scowled until he said, "You're picking up our euphemisms."

She was. Imagine that.

"I take it you haven't eaten?"

Kai shook her head. "Overslept. Sorry. I know. I know."

"No need to apologize. I may tease, but I'm not so much of a blowhole to expect improvement overnight, Your Highness." He nodded toward the corridor that would take them not to the courtyard, but to the dining hall. "You can't train on an empty stomach."

He stood by while she ate, patient as ever despite the waste of his time. She guzzled a glass of water afterward, then their path to the training grounds resumed.

There, she dragged heavy things, lifted other objects, and pushed an enormous wheel that required all her strength. In another room, he made her clutch a hundred-pound weight to her chest and run under-water. She discovered strength she hadn't known she possessed when it turned into a race, him urging her to shed her long legs in favor of a tail to keep pace alongside him.

One thing she liked about Manu was that he often participated in the exercises with her instead of standing by like a grim-faced fitness instructor. It wasn't like her time in the military where someone had always shouted for her to move it and hustle and go, go, go.

In small leaps, she made progress that week. It still wasn't enough. "Decent," he said at the end, clicking his stopwatch. She'd been overjoyed weeks ago to discover such technologies still existed in their realm.

"What's my time?" she asked him.

"Don't worry about your time."

"What's my time, Manu? I want to know it."

He sighed and led her from the racetrack to the armory. They each claimed a trident before entering a vacant sparring room. The barracks had several, built for training in focus groups as needed. "One minute, thirty-nine seconds."

"Thirty-nine seconds of failure," she concluded, deflating.

"It isn't failure."

"It is until I beat the requirement," she muttered, rubbing her neck.

"Princess." She glanced up into compassionate brown eyes, so very expressive and open it startled her into silence. He took her by the shoulders and squeezed with both strong hands. For that moment, she was captivated. Lost. Those eyes were all that mattered. "You've made greater improvement within seven *days* of training than you have in the weeks since your arrival. There is only so much a mer can be expected to master in limited time. You're harder on yourself than you must be."

"I want to succeed."

"I understand that. But even our Myrmidon recruits receive a year of training."

"I don't have a year to do this."

He sighed and dropped both hands, the loss of their warmth distracting her. "Please put those back." When he blinked, heat surged to her face and she hastily added, "If you don't mind. My shoulders are tight from all of the weapons training and that kind of helped."

"Ah."

And then, without asking anything more, Manu maneuvered behind her and returned both hands to her shoulders. He squeezed lightly at first, introducing her to a blend of pleasure and pain. "Ow, ow, ow. A little left with this hand," she muttered, tapping his fingers with her right.

"Here?" His thumb kneaded into the juncture of her shoulder and neck.

And it was magical. Within a few seconds, one of the worst kinks loosened.

"Fuck yes," she murmured, rolling her neck to one side and sighing. The man's hands were absolute bliss. The last time she'd received a massage as good, she'd been dating a hot machinist's mate during a naval deployment, a sailor with hands strong enough to tighten nuts and bolts without tools. But he'd still known exactly how much pressure to use, never hurting her.

And at that moment, her brain decided to recall that her body owned a vagina. It wasn't the most convenient moment to remember such things, but her imagination decided to wander from the platonic act of him kneading her shoulders to wondering how his fingers would feel in other places.

Between her legs. Skimming her naked skin. Squeezing her breasts. *Inside* her.

His breath stirred her hair, sending goosebumps prickling over her arms every time she imagined his lips touching the nape of her neck. Not for the first time, she wondered what it would be like to sit on his face instead of trying to punch him in it. Her nipples tightened harder than glass beads.

God. She must have been seriously hard up for a lay to fantasize about Manu of all people. The man didn't have an ounce of interest in her. And from what she'd once interrupted, she thought he had a woman. To distract from the flourishing, unwelcome thoughts flooding her body with need, she cleared her throat. "Manu?"

"Hm?"

"There's something I've been wondering. My true name is Zephyrine. It's Greek." She peered at him through the reflection in the wall.

"Yes?" Though he canted his head and gave her a look that suggested he thought she'd gone crazy. Maybe she had.

"And yours is Manu. That isn't Greek. How does a mer from Atlantis end up with a name belonging to another culture?"

"Many of our people have close ties to Pacifica," he explained. "Though their gods are different."

Her brows rose a mile.

"The limited number of high mer required many of our ancestors to broaden the gene pool by inviting nobles of the other underwater kingdom to our city. My mother's family hails from their region and emigrated from Pacifica as part of your grandfather Maui's royal retinue. He was a prince among her people. Our people."

"Maui. As in the god Maui?"

"He was a great mer, but not the actual god Maui. A descendent."

"A descendent of the actual god Maui, who married my grandmother, a descendent of the goddess Thalassa."

Manu shrugged. "We can't choose who we love," he muttered, the comment sounding like a loaded statement.

"This means I have a god's blood in me twice over." Nothing should have shocked her anymore at this point, but somehow, he'd still taken her by surprise.

"It does."

And it also meant she had to try twice as hard to succeed. With that kind of divine genetic privilege, failure wasn't an option.

GIVING Princess Kai a rubdown in the sparring chamber had been a mistake. Manu knew it from the moment Elpis stepped into the sparring room with her shield and spear, followed by three wide-eyed, impressionable recruits.

Fuck me. It looked bad in every kind of away, because it *was* bad.

Elpis stared, jaw working, violet eyes narrowed into tight slits. "My mistake. This room appears to be occupied. Forgive us, Your Highness." She bowed, as did her students. "Fellow Commander."

And from the room she strode, her back as rigid as the weapon she carried.

He turned to find Kai studying him with apologetic eyes. "I got you into trouble with your girlfriend, didn't I?"

"She isn't my girlfriend."

Kai leaned back and crossed both arms against her chest. "Does she know that?"

"She does."

"I dunno, man...that look she gave you said volumes. Do you know what it said?"

He didn't answer.

"It said, 'Fuck you, Manu. Eat whaleshit.' That look, my dude, was the look of a woman spurned."

He grunted. "It's no concern of yours, Your Highness."

"Yeah, yeah, yeah. No concern of mine. But you jumped back and took your hands off my shoulders like you did something wrong."

Or like he'd been busted giving his future queen an intimate shoulder rub while sporting the most painful erection of his life, by the comrade he'd shared a one-night stand with only a few short weeks ago. "I did." He licked his lips, once again thankful for his choice of armor.

"Which was?"

"I shouldn't be so familiar with you. It's one thing to touch you during training when it is necessary, but another—"

"What? Are you serious? I *asked* you to touch me. If you can put your hands on me to pummel me, why the hell aren't you allowed to fix it all at the end?" She rolled her right shoulder and gave a euphoric sigh. "That really did help."

Manu smiled tightly. "You are royalty, and you are spoken for. That's all that matters."

"Spoken for?" Her voice elevated and she took a step toward him. "I went out *twice* with Cosmas. He doesn't have any claim over me."

"In our society, mers of my caste—"

"Our society can fuck off. *I* make the rules about what I want to do with my body, and if I want my friend—my trainer—to rub the kinks out my damned shoulders so that I can hit the workout again, that's what I want done." She paused a moment, chest heaving, fire in her eyes. "That sounded really spoiled. Kind of diva."

"A little." He paused. She'd called him a friend. He let the words bounce around in his head a few times before deciding to address it. "You consider me a friend?"

Laughing, she rolled her other shoulder then plucked her trident from the floor. "Well, yeah. I guess I do." Her brown eyes twinkled when she smiled. "You believe in me."

"I do."

"You spend time with me. You make me laugh. When you're not doing the stern and disapproving teacher thing, you're a funny guy. And you make me strive to be better. Where I come from, that's a friend." She rapped the end of her trident against the floor then moved into her on-guard position, feet perfectly distanced, stance impeccable. "Ready when you are."

Manu stepped on the blunt end of his trident, popping it up from the floor and into his hand. "Let's get it done. Amerin tells me you both have a long evening ahead of you, and I'd hate for you to be late."

LOYALTY TO NONE

A NIGHT ON THE TOWN IN ATLANTIS DIFFERED only a little from a night on the town in Galveston. In the surface world, she would have tossed on a pretty summer dress, caught a movie at a theater, met someone for a bite to eat, or hit up an evening event at a local book store. Events were one of her favorite activities, and she'd even gone to a public hexing hosted by witches at an occult book store once in New York. That had been fascinating to watch.

The underwater kingdom had its own flourishing entertainment sector, complete with bars, exclusive clubs, and what she supposed were their equivalent to Michelin-rated restaurants. Atlantis had its own diners and dives, and it also had places that received glowing recommendations.

Wearing yet another garment from her mother's closet, Kai strode down an Atlantian street with Amerin at her side and a small retinue of Myrmidons trailing behind them. The teal silk hugged her curves, and its measurements hadn't needed to be taken in much to fit her. Beneath it, she wore sharkskin leggings, heeding Manu's advice *and* taking a lesson from one of her favorite television show heroines—always be prepared to run. And no woman could be expected to run with her ass cheeks hanging in the open for everyone to see. The dress enhanced what little cleavage she had with its fitted bodice, but it flared at the hips and split up the thigh on each side for maximum flexibility.

Since coming to Atlantis, she'd learned she and her mother shared the same shoe size—off by a centimeter, but close enough for Kai to raid the late queen's closet and adopt some of her fashions. Dressing like Ianthe made her feel closer to the woman she could no longer remember.

"I can't believe how busy it is in the city at night." Kai craned her neck, glancing up at the tall buildings glittering with dark blue lights. The lanterns glowed silver at this hour, no longer the warm yellow they emitted during morning and afternoon. Supposedly, light across the underwater kingdom had been a gift from the children of Hyperion and Theia to Thalassa, as real as the sun in the sky over the surface world.

While she didn't miss blue, cloud-speckled days or midnight stars, she wondered about life without a transition between points of the year. Sure, Texas only had two real seasons—sweltering heat or cold, cold rain—but she'd been able to watch golden leaves drop from oak boughs and grass go brown and dry in winter. Here, she didn't suspect anything would change.

Millions of humans lived in tropical or chilly climates without seasons. *People in the islands thrive without discernible differences in temperature all the time,* she told herself as they passed beneath a wisteria with branches hanging above one of the sidewalks. Atlantis had sidewalks. She liked that about the place, how much it resembled and differed from a surface city.

Even the traffic reminded her of Houston's afternoon gridlock. Atlantian citizens drove skippers—land-adapted coral gliders—down the city streets and residential lanes. In lieu of gasoline, magical stones powered them. A magical society made for a very green society, apparently.

If only the humans had access to such designs, though she suspected they would view the contraptions with suspicion and shun them, instead preferring their oil.

Still, she enjoyed walking the city on foot with her new friend. They ambled along at a sedate pace, arm in arm. Citizens didn't trouble her. One thing she'd learned was that Atlantis treated their royalty differently, approaching only when invited. For them, it was a matter of deep, profound respect. In the two months since she'd come to the kingdom, she'd made five public appearances, attended numerous dinners with her peers, and even given a speech to the military regarding her time spent on the surface in the service of the United States.

"How much farther until we reach the playhouse?" Kai asked Amerin.

"Not much longer. If you're tired, we can wait and summon a carriage—"

"No. It's been an enjoyable walk."

Though she had to wonder about the Myrmidon convoy marching behind her in plain sight, with yet more hidden from view. For some reason, her uncle thought it necessary for an armed escort to travel with her. They'd been hand-picked by Manu and Cosmas, each man chosen for his loyalty to her.

Loyalty. A shiver tickled across her shoulders and sent ice cubes down her spine.

It wasn't until they reached the Rose Shell Playhouse that the warmth returned to her limbs. It rose above them, a gorgeous structure built from multiple pink conch shells.

She and Amerin took seats in her uncle's private box, where they were served crab-cakes made with sweet algae flour, stuffed prawns, and other finger foods. Though the story was told in Atlantian, she found herself understanding more than mere snatches of conversation. Entire lines of dialogue made sense to her.

Afterward, she met with the cast backstage, at the request of the playhouse management. She never saw anyone glow so brightly or flush with pleasure for having met her. The men bowed, absolute gentlemen. The women gave her gifts, though after their performance, she thought she owed *them* trinkets of appreciation.

She'd have to send them something as a token of thanks.

"It was an amazing performance. I truly enjoyed every minute."

As they were leaving, Kai leaned into Amerin and hugged her. "Thank you for suggesting this."

"I'm glad I did. Are you ready for dinner? I don't know about you, Your Highness, but those little snacks did nothing for my appetite. I am *starved*."

"You're not the only one. Trust me. I'm hungry enough to eat a whale."

"I know the best place for that."

Kai stared at her. "Of course you do."

Amerin only grinned. "Trust me?"

⚜

TRUSTING AMERIN WAS A *GOOD* THING. Two hours later, Kai wandered out of an upscale Atlantian restaurant with a belly full of shark steak and the most delicious wine to ever touch her lips. According to their server, the vintage had been imported from Italy and infused with flowers grown only in Atlantian gardens. The end result: ambrosia.

"I'm confused about something," Kai muttered during their stroll down the sidewalk She thought back to the six types of oyster they sampled, from raw to baked and stuffed with cheese.

"Yes, Your Highness?"

"There are no cows here. How were those stuffed

with cheese? Does Atlantis import it from the surface?"

"We do import, but those particular oysters were prepared with Atlantian made cheese."

"Huh? Weird. Then what do you...?" When Amerin grinned at her, a terrible realization dawned over Kai. "Tell me that wasn't dolphin cheese."

"Whale, to be exact."

"I pity the mer tasked with milking whales. I don't know whether to be horrified or fascinated."

"Both. You can be both. Your expression right now is amazing."

Someone to the rear of them snickered, indicating their escort had also heard.

Damn them.

Fortunately, the appetizers had been too delicious for the horror to linger with her for long.

"Whale milk and crazy discoveries aside, I have another very dumb question that I hope won't offend you."

"Nothing you ask could offend me," Amerin assured her.

Kai hesitated. No matter how she tried to word her enquiry, it sounded rude. "I...wonder how you became so knowledgeable about high-class living when you're a servant."

"Oh. That's easy. My family was paid *extraordinarily* well for offering me as a tribute to your parents. On top of that, I'm able to dine wherever I please and go anywhere I like on the royal coffers."

She beamed, cheeks dimpling again. "It isn't a bad life. I enjoy it."

Kai pursed her lips and gave it a thought. "I would agree that it isn't a bad way to live, but you've never had experience with any other life."

"I'm happy, my family wants for nothing, I have no needs, and I get to live in the company of a good woman who will in time become an even greater queen. What more could I possibly want?"

"Your every day revolves around my wants. What about your own?"

Amerin tilted her head. "I don't understand."

"Wouldn't you like to take up a hobby? To...I don't know, have a man? Do you have a man? Everyone is so concerned with me having one, but what about you?"

Amerin shrugged. "I have multiple hobbies. I knit. I paint. And I did have a lover for a time."

"What happened?"

Silence lingered between them for a while before Amerin answered. "He is also a servant, but his noble family wasn't so free with his time. It didn't work out, and we decided to end things." She didn't meet Kai's gaze.

"Oh...." Gently, she took Amerin's hand and squeezed. "Hey. You know if you ever need time away from me, I want you to take it. You're not a slave."

Though she'd read it had once existed in the history of Atlantis, the practice was long ago outlawed by her grandmother. Had that queen not ruled it criminal, Kai would have. Slavery had no place in any civilized society, though she wasn't sure if the caste system was any better.

"You have *never* treated me as one, Your Highness, but I thank you just the same for keeping my happiness in your thoughts. Now please, may we speak of lighter things?"

"Sure. Where are we going now?"

"Interested in seeing a little Atlantian history instead of listening to Scholar Proteus?"

"Gods, yes. How much of a walk is it?"

"Not far. About five miles."

They made it three city blocks west toward the historical district when the first shouts reached Kai's ears. She paused and tried to pick out discernible words in the cacophonous din of a few dozen raised voices, but the rumble of four-wheeled coral skippers and the chatter of noisy pedestrians overpowered it. Amerin's hand squeezed Kai's tightly.

"What's happening?"

"Nothing," Amerin said, pulling her faster.

"It isn't nothing if you're trying to rush me down the damned street." Kai pulled her hand free from Amerin's grip and twisted around to see blocked traffic. At least a hundred mers marched down the road wielding signs.

The six Myrmidons trailing behind them moved in closer and tightened ranks, wielding their weapons.

Kai dragged her feet and refused to budge

another foot. "What the hell is happening?" she asked the squad leader.

"A safety concern, Your Highness, but nothing requiring your attention." Then he turned his head and spoke to one of his fellow mer in the Atlantian tongue, "We'll take the most direct route to the palace. Reinforcements will arrive shortly to quash this should it turn dangerous."

"I understood that!" she shouted.

Startled eyes turned to her. Someone had told them she didn't understand the mer tongue, but she'd never heard it clearer. "Someone tell me what the fuck is happening, or I won't budge."

Five seconds later, it didn't matter whether Amerin or her personal guard told her. Kai read a few signs for herself.

Down with the royal family. Down with the
monarchy. Freedom for all.
End the royal line
Royal blood will be our freedom
Death to the leech class
We don't need a queen, we want a VOTE

EACH SECOND OF gazing into the angry crowd revealed a new horror. Her stomach churned with nausea when she picked out a crude drawing of people she presumed were her, Aegaeon, and

Nammu hanging from their necks as sharks fed on their entrails.

Kai's stomach clenched harder than stone, and bile flooded her mouth. The sour taste stayed with her no matter how many times she swallowed. "They hate me." She'd never done anything to them, but the people loathed her so much they drew her death.

The Myrmidon who had addressed her first sighed. His name swam out of her hazy memory. Sergeant Heracles. "They're only a few people, Your Highness. Ignore them."

"Who *are* they?"

"The Atlantian Loyalist Party. They have...some unusual beliefs and desires for the kingdom. But enough of that. We must get you to safety."

"Are they going to attack me?" Her voice cracked when it rose. The parade of mers would reach them soon, and every hateful, glowering face was fixed on *her*.

"Not if we can help it," Heracles said. When he nodded to his fellow Myrmidons, they fanned out in a protective circle around her and Amerin. Her hand-maiden guided her down the road toward the inter-section, steps hastening as Kai's pulse drummed an urgent rhythm between her ears.

"This way," Amerin said. "The glider is—"

An explosion burned the air behind them. Before Kai could take another step, one of her guards threw her to the ground.

Then the shooting began.

17

NEVER A BREAK

Elpis was due to arrive on his doorstep at half past the hour, completing a duty shift overseeing the instructors at the infirmary. Manu did not look forward to the conversation ahead of him. It would either end in bruises or tears. As he knew Elpis well, from over two decades of friendship, both were likely to be his.

Damn.

In the past, Manu had always fucked all of his problems away, but common sense told him his cock would only worsen the problem. He and Elpis did not belong together. Being phenomenal together in bed didn't mean there was enough between them to dive into an actual relationship. He hadn't taken joy in turning her down, but he didn't *do* relationships. And he didn't do them because he lacked the time as much as he lacked the motivation to have one.

Now that she was no longer furious with him, she wanted to talk, and he wondered if it would salvage their friendship. Months ago, when they'd tumbled into bed together after one night at the pub, he'd awakened the next morning without a care in the world, positive it had been just sex. Hot and wild and sweaty sex, but nothing of consequence.

When she invited him to dinner at her place, he thought nothing of it. It wasn't until a month later when she presented him with new bracers that he realized something was amiss. They never gifted one another anything. He and Elpis were comrades who trained together and ran combat drills with each other, instructing her medics alongside his artillery units and Loto's infantry. They were the friends who dragged each other home from the pub and slung the other into bed to sleep it off.

And then they'd somehow fallen into bed together.

Ruining a good friendship with his cock had been, in hindsight, an awful idea.

He dragged on a shirt and fastened it, appreciating a day when he could wear pants and leave the armor behind. Giving Kailani the next morning off from her training meant he was free to sleep in to recover from the night of drinking ahead of him, Loto, and about three other officers among their crew.

It would be nice to have a social life again.

The bell notified him of her arrival. When he opened the door, Elpis stood there in her Friday night best: sapphire blue leggings, scaled boots, and a fitted emerald bodice with a plunging neckline. He raised a brow. "You're dressed for a night out."

Cosmas stepped into view. "Because we're all going out tonight. Loto and I have decided to stage an intervention. Sorry, but this has gone on long enough, the two of you avoiding one another like children. It was only a little sex."

Thank you, Manu thought, though Elpis shot Cosmas such a dark, withering look, he rapidly backpedaled. He set his hand on the small of her back. "Worsened by Manu's tendency to be an unfeeling blowhole, of course. But you were both good friends once. Good friends of *mine.* And I want to see my friends happily socializing with one another again."

"It wasn't my idea," she muttered.

"If you and Loto are staging this so-called intervention, where is he?"

"Completing the usual load of chum at the barracks. He'll be joining us in an hour, which means the both of you have less than an hour to make peace with past events."

"And if we don't?" Elpis challenged, hands on her hips, a brow raised.

"Then we drag the both of you out anyway, and the night becomes an immense load of awkward. I'm prepared. So is Loto. Test us if you dare. It behooves the both of you to remember we were all good pals once. Frankly, I feel like a human child caught in a custody battle. We want to enjoy the company of both of you at once again. Please."

Manu rolled his eyes.

Cosmas shooed her inside and shut the front

door, leaving them to stand just inside the entrance hall of Manu's bachelor residence. He'd liked it for being less than five minutes from the palace and barracks, though it was only a single bedroom and bath, a cramped kitchen, and quarters too small to entertain more than three or four guests at a time.

"I suppose we don't have a choice."

"We don't," he agreed.

Elpis pushed out her lower lip and eyed him, apparently wanting to be anywhere but his living room.

"I'm sorry," he started, swallowing his pride. "I'm sorry for hurting you. I wasn't thinking that night, and it never occurred to me that you might feel more for me than I do for you."

She didn't speak, only studied him.

"But I'm not in a good place for a relationship. It was a rebound for both of us, El. You know that."

When she remained silent, the gnawing in his gut intensified, twisting his intestines into knots. How the hell was he expected to knock back shots with her all night when she glowered at him like that?

"Militiades was a fool to let you go."

"If he was a fool, what does that make you?"

Without missing a beat, he replied, "An asshole way too fucked up to be in a relationship right now." So fucked up he was having fantasies about his future queen, and inappropriate dreams where he stripped the leggings off of her and—

Whoa. Wrong and grossly inappropriate time for his imagination to travel.

El cracked a grin. "I'll agree with you on both counts. Is it Calanthe?"

The question took him by surprise. "What? No. Calanthe and I have been over for a long time."

Her arms crossed against her chest again. "It was certainly Calanthe you were trying to drink out of your head that night. Are you *sure* you're over her now? I mean, the woman *did* pack up and move to the other side of the world three days after you proposed marriage."

"For a once-in-a-lifetime opportunity to serve on the king and queen's personal guard in Pacifica. I encouraged her."

"Mm."

"She would have been miserable if she'd turned it down, El. You know this. There's no honor greater than serving alongside royalty whether it's here, Pacifica, or for the elves. She made the only sensible fucking choice."

"Or maybe she waited for you to do the right thing and fight for her, Manu. Had you truly wanted to marry her, Calanthe would be here alongside you instead of Queen Laka."

He said nothing.

"At first, I thought you were heartbroken over her, but now I can't tell if you're merely grateful it's over."

He clenched his jaw but still didn't honor her shit with a response.

"So, is that why you throw yourself into your duties, Manu? Because you're desperate to fill your father's footsteps? You'll never stand on your own if your only goal is to become the next Lago."

"I'm not trying to become him."

"Then why won't you let anyone in? Calanthe *loved* you."

"She had a funny way of showing it."

"You let her leave."

"I wasn't her owner. If a woman wants to leave, she's going to leave."

"I'm not talking about the offer to immigrate to Pacifica. I'm referring to the fact that you were so goddamned distant the woman was living with a shadow of the man you should be. You'll never be the great General Lago. And maybe if you accept that, he will, too."

It hurt the most that she was right, her words burrowing through his flimsy excuses until he raked his fingers through his hair and groaned. "I know. I know. I've been telling myself for years that I'll never be the son he wants. But still, I have to try."

"You don't *have* to try anything. Nobody could ever be the son he wants. You deserve better, Manu. You deserve to be happy. You deserve to have freedom, and you deserve to have someone in your life."

He jerked back, looking at her. "El..."

"Not me. You're right about being way too fucked up for a relationship right now."

An amicable silence fell between them that didn't feel at all awkward. Manu waited a moment before he offered his hand. "Friends again, then?"

She took it and squeezed. "Friends again."

"Then let's get drunk together like we did in the old days. I need a break from adulthood."

ATLANTIS OPERATED on a combination of hydro-electric power and magic, their society differing in many ways from the world on dry land. But in other ways, they were exactly the same.

Manu sat beneath the spinning colorful lights of the hottest dance club in the city, flanked by a gorgeous lady on both sides. He hadn't paid for a single ale all night, the alcohol plentiful from the moment he arrived. But it wasn't where he wanted to be. He wondered where Amerin had taken Kai, what they were doing, and if the protection detail he and Cosmas assigned to her was up to the task of guarding their princess against any threat.

He shivered, uneasy without knowing why. Loto hadn't arrived yet, and he'd been due to join them a half hour ago. The man was as much a workaholic as Manu, but one defining characteristic divided them— Loto had a family, a wife and a litter of children waiting for him at home each night.

Elpis crossed the dance floor from the bar with a martini. She drank it along the way, set the empty vessel on the table, and took Manu by both hands. She pulled him to his feet. "Dance with me."

"I don't dance."

"You used to."

"I lost the rhythm."

"Liar. Maybe you're getting old."

"Bull. I'm only sixty-two. If anyone's getting old, it's you, El. Don't you have a decade on me? I think the salt water's drying you out." He touched the corners of his eyes. "Looking a little creased here."

"Ha ha." She made a rude gesture with both hands, the equivalent of the surfacer middle finger. He returned it, smiling. This was the El he adored, not the scorned woman dropping hints and alluding to wanting more from him.

The banter continued until the two ladies hoping to keep him company rose from the table, shooting El dark looks for the interruption. When she ignored them, both huffed and strolled away to seek an easier conquest. Manu exhaled in relief.

He glanced to his right and saw Cosmas in the corner with the mortal gaming tables, playing a round of darts. The group of mer waiting for their turn at the board all had hero worship gleaming in their eyes. "Ask him. He's drunk enough to make a fool of himself. And thank you, by the way."

"I don't want to dance with Cosmas." Her eyes lit up with humor. "I want *you* to make a fool of yourself. Besides, you're always the best-looking guy here. You can thank me by joining me on the floor."

"Fine."

The moment he joined her, his communicator beeped with an incoming call, its red light flashing on his belt. He glanced at it and groaned. As unenjoyable as the club scene could be, something told him their night out was about to come to an abrupt and early end.

"Ignore it. That'll be someone at the barracks fishing for an officer. I know it."

"All the more reason to answer if someone's fucked up." It beeped until he raised the receiver, accepted the call, and placed it to his ear. "Manu speaking."

"There's been an attack at the corner of Fifth Avenue and Pearl. Loyalists everywhere," Loto said in a rush. "The princess is caught in the middle of it."

"On my way." He was already in motion before he clipped the device onto his belt again.

Under normal circumstances, riots and other infractions of Atlantian law were the responsibility of keepers, but the princess's presence changed things.

"On your way *where?* What's happening?"

"Attack on Fifth Avenue. Looks like the Loyalists are at it again. Kai—Princess Kailani is there."

One of her ginger brows leapt up toward her hairline. "On a first-name basis with the princess now?"

He grunted and pulled his trident from the stand. "We'll discuss this later."

"You're rushing off to save her."

"She's the fucking princess. What do you expect me to do?"

El crossed both arms and tucked them beneath her breasts. "I dunno. Maybe allow the mers on duty to do their job."

Manu paused. "El, this isn't the time to—"

"Or accept some help from your friends and

fellow Myrmidons. Let me drag Cosmas away from his game, and then the three of us will wallow into the filth together."

She spun on a heel and stalked away, leaving Manu to stare at her retreating form.

It looked like he wasn't heading into battle alone after all.

18

TO LEAD BY EXAMPLE

Blood trickled down Kai's temple. She wiped it with the back of her hand and huddled behind an overturned skipper at the mouth of a narrow alley. They had been pinned for the longest ten minutes of her entire life, unable to leave and risk exposing themselves.

Atlantian civilians didn't have access to gunpowder-based firearms. Such things were banned in the underwater kingdom, weapons of destruction attributed to the predicted fall of the surface kingdoms. But the arms favored by Atlantians also weren't any better than semi-automatic weapons and made hypocrites of the mers. Harpoon blasters charged to shoot energy lances struck her as way more dangerous than the standard 9mm handgun.

In addition to the harpoon guns, they used deadly magical items smuggled into the kingdom from other corners of the surface world. According to Amerin and what she'd learned during her lessons, those were also banned.

Later, when her life wasn't in peril, she'd be able to find amusement in the parallels between the magical underwater kingdom, and the mundane surface world she'd left behind. For weeks she'd thought she'd entered a peaceful paradise. Now she knew better. Not more than two minutes ago, she'd watched a fireball streak down the lane into a building, shattering every window in its frontward-facing wall.

One of the Myrmidons leaned out from cover and scanned down the road. "They don't seem to be after you, Your Highness. I think our presence here was merely a coincidence."

Another explosion sent shards of glass in every direction, tearing metal and crumbling bricks.

"Are you sure about that?"

"They're not trying to reach you. They seem preoccupied with making a point, perhaps. With causing as much damage as they can to this quarter," Heracles said.

"Agreed," said the lone female Myrmidon, Diana. "This isn't an assassination attempt, otherwise we'd be up to our necks in Loyalist scum. This is a riot."

"Why are they rioting?"

"They loathe anything to do with tradition, especially if royals are involved. They're fascinated by the mortal systems of government, which, while flawed, appeal to them over the current state in Atlantis."

Kai couldn't help but think of the many times

she'd watched news coverage of riots in the surface world. There were times when rioting—in her opinion—was absolutely necessary, especially when an oppressed people needed to make a point to the majority. This struck her as more than rioting, however. This was outright assault and terrorism.

"What do we do?" she asked.

"We hunker down until reinforcements arrive to extract us," Heracles said.

"And if they don't come?"

"Then we lead you out of here ourselves."

Poor Amerin was trembling beside her, huddled in a ball with her knees tucked up to her chest. She looked so damned frightened, the situation enraged Kai more than it terrified her. No matter how much these assholes wanted change, they didn't have the right to terrorize harmless innocents like Amerin.

Kai crouched down beside her and slid an arm Amerin's shoulders. "It's going to be all right. We'll make it out of here," she murmured.

"They won't let me live."

"What?"

Though Amerin already shook like a leaf, her sobs intensified until her entire body shuddered.

"Amerin. No one is here to kill you."

"They hate my kind."

Her gaze darted from Amerin to the chaos brewing in the main street. Another plume of fire rocketed into the air, and one of the phosphorescent, tubular skyscrapers near them made an alarming creaking sound. She pleaded for it to remain standing. She'd served in the Navy at the time of 9/11, and while she hadn't been present in Manhattan when the towers fell, she'd watched enough videos to know the devastation it could cause when skyscrapers collapsed in a tightly packed area. The damage was always worse if there were still innocents inside.

Someone screamed in the distance, the voice echoing across the Atlantian dome from above them. As she'd suspected, there were still people in the building above her. Her stomach knotted with tension and fear for the helpless people trapped in the destabilized structure. She had all of the security and protection she needed.

But who protected them?

"We can't just sit here and hide," Kai muttered.

"We can. Until reinforcements arrive to extract you, we don't move, Your Highness. I know it may be difficult to listen to—"

"I'm the future queen. Manu has spent weeks training me to fight against the fucking Gloom, and now you have me hiding from some tantrum-throwing assholes with magical molotovs? This is shit. What the hell good was all of that fighting if I have to cower in a corner now?"

"You don't have a weapon," Heracles pointed out.

Her gaze dropped to his weapons belt. He held a trident, but he had two long, curved blades on his belt, a combat knife in his boot, and a harpoon blaster. The others were all similarly armed. "You have several. Give me something."

"That's—"

Kai straightened her spine. Living up to her future as queen had never seemed more important. If she was going to rule, she had to know how to phrase her expectations. "I'm not asking you. I'm telling you. Give me your harpoon gun."

Heracles unsnapped the weapon from his holster and passed it to her. It had the weight and feel of any long gun from the surface but could have been the bastard child of a shotgun and a revolver, a huge cylinder mounted on top loaded with six translucent harpoon bolts instead of shells or bullets. Electrical magic flickered inside them.

"You two stay with Amerin and keep her safe," she called over her shoulder to two men in the small squad.

Heracles fell into step beside her. "Do you have a plan, Your Highness?"

"Not at all. We need to stop them from detonating another one of those bombs. They're fire bomb potions, right?"

"They are," he confirmed in a clipped voice. "Most likely smuggled into their hands from elven lands."

Another of those magical grenades arced through the air, lobbed by an asshat standing just down the road. It struck the coral front of the building with a boom that almost shook Kai off-balance. Bits of bleached coral flew and rained white dust down upon them. Chaos raged everywhere she looked, from looters bashing in storefronts to criminals terrorizing their fellow mers. At a quick glance, she saw dozens of drivers hadn't been able to escape, and were now trapped in their coral skippers, unable to navigate a road littered with burning rubble.

Most of the people in the street hadn't been the Loyalists' high mer oppressors—the people they were harming the most right now were their own folk of the common classes. And that lit a violent storm of anger in Kai. If being queen meant she hid in safety while others suffered, then she didn't want the fucking title.

"There's not as many as we saw marching," she said as they moved into the street. Some mers abandoned their cars and tried to run away on foot.

"There wouldn't be. The cowards will have spread out to cause as much damage as possible. The ones left behind, however, will be armed."

"Then we need to do something."

"Lead on, Your Highness. We have your back."

A fight broke out behind them, three men from their squad caught in battle with Loyalists.

Kai retraced the grenade to its source and saw a man beneath a street lamp with a duffel bag of glowing apple-red bottles, each one lit bright as an infrared bulb. Her heart started pounded faster than a herd of galloping Thoroughbreds, practically beating its way out of her chest when he shook it. The contents flared brighter, practically white-hot. She aimed the weapon, hoping to hit him in the leg, but fear gripped her index finger and wouldn't let her pull the trigger. She'd never killed a man before, and wasn't sure if she could kill one now, even for another person.

"Someone help us!" a voice cried from above them again on the building's upper level.

Too many things happened at once. Kai froze up. She'd never been combat-trained. She'd been a tech, a brain who worked on wiring and other simple things, though she'd gone through a few drills during her six years and knew her way around a damned obstacle course. One second, a single second of hesitation, cost her the element of surprise that could have saved the people above. Instead of hurling the potion at the building, he tossed it toward Kai and the small Myrmidon squad.

"Myrmidon chum!" he shouted.

At the same time, Heracles yanked the gun from her hands, sighted down the barrel, and pulled the trigger, as did the other mer. One bolt pierced their assailant in his chest, issuing a spray of blood from his mouth and crackling arcs of electricity. The other struck the potion midair, though its liquid contents combusted and became a mist of smoldering embers. Heracles swore and threw himself in front of her to take an attack that would no doubt fry him down to the bone.

At that moment, time slowed down for Kai. Whether it was the adrenaline pounding through her veins, or something magical related to her gifts, every second seemed to stretch before her with startling clarity, frame by frame. As Heracles turned his back on the attack and shielded her with his body, she flung out both hands, one over his left shoulder, the other at waist-level, and a curve of freezing water materialized from thin air. The two forces met in the middle, hot and cold colliding to create a harmless puddle in the middle of the street.

It had been purely instinctual. She still wasn't sure what happened, even seconds later once time returned to its usual speed. Bits of slush clung to the Heracles's glossy left shoulder pauldron and steam filled the air. A bit of ice glossed over his ear.

Before she could ask what had just happened, someone blew a battle horn.

"There's our reinforcements."

He said it like she hadn't just saved him from roasting like a turkey forgotten in the oven.

"Oh. Good," she said, likewise ignoring that she'd pulled off a feat of magic. Because the sooner she acknowledged it, the sooner she would freak the fuck out and wonder what the hell would happen to her next.

THE LAST THING Manu expected when he reached the corner of Fifth and Pearl was for Kai to refuse extrication. He stared at the stubborn princess crouched beside an injured keeper and considered throwing her over his shoulder. Then he remembered weeks of teaching her defensive maneuvers and reconsidered.

He valued his balls too much to risk his little

tadpoles a second time. One day, maybe not this decade or century, he wanted to be a father. It seemed unwise to provoke Kai again.

"Not until everyone is safe." She tore a strip of silk from her own skirts and held it to the man's bleeding shoulder. The keeper shot her an appreciative look akin to hero worship, like the hand of Thalassa herself was on him. The poor bastard. He was probably delirious from blood loss.

"This area will be reclaimed shortly. For your safety, I demand—"

"Fuck whatever you demand."

One of the Myrmidons choked back a laugh, only to become stone-faced again when Manu shot him a cool stare. Heracles wiped the grin off his face.

"Princess Kailani. Consider the—"

"No." She straightened and raised her chin, shoulders back as she stared him down.

Manu set his jaw, wishing he could turn her over his knee like an unruly child. Alas, she was not a child, nor his to discipline, and...her decision was admirable, all things considered. This was the inflexible princess attitude he'd both come to love and hate. But as a member of her guard, it was his duty to discourage endeavors that would risk her life. "There's nothing more you can do here," he told her in a gentler voice. "You need medical care, as does he. Medical aid is en route."

"I'm fine. It's only a bump."

"You're bleeding, Your Highness." Desperate for

help, Manu glanced over the group of assembled mers, silently urging one to side with him.

Heracles gave him a helpless look, shrugging one shoulder. "She wouldn't allow us to keep her in cover, Commander. Our princess is a stubborn one."

"I won't leave until the streets are secure. You wanted to make me a leader, then that's what you're going to get. A leader doesn't leave her people behind to suffer."

Manu gritted his teeth but relented, unable to defeat her logic and all the more irritated that her argument was sound. He'd brought with him three dozen Myrmidons to assist the keepers, and Elpis wasn't far behind, she and her combat medics dispersing to look for wounded mers requiring medical assistance. "Fine. But at least stay close to me or Heracles at all times. You'll wish that you left when you had the chance."

STANDING GROUND

Kai proved him wrong a second time. Shortly after reinforcements came from the keeper depot and Myrmidon barracks, the rioters dispersed into the city and vanished as quickly as they'd come. The whole while they secured the streets, she tended to the wounded with Elpis, helped combat medics apply bandages, and relocated the injured to safety.

Watching her made him damned proud. In only a few weeks, Kai had proven herself to be the princess they needed, but he wasn't entirely convinced they deserved her. This became painfully apparent when he saw a discarded sign on the sidewalk, its hastily scrawled art depicting her gory demise in the jaws of sharks.

What for? While Manu had no true love for the high mer bloodlines of Atlantis, it struck him as igno- rant to wish death on them all for the circumstances of their birth. No one could control who they were born to, otherwise he would have chosen an actual father.

Hours later, long after Heracles guided Amerin and Kailani to safety and the streets were clear of rabble, he retired to the palace and decided to check on their princess.

"Commander, is it true?" a guard asked him when he approached the gate. The two were wide-eyed and alert, youths in their early thirties and barely out of training.

"Is what true?"

"That the princess used the gift," said the other guard. "They say she extinguished a fifty-meter fire raging over the Coral Spire. Saved a dozen families."

"Fifty-meter fire," he repeated.

"That's what they said."

"If such a thing occurred, it was prior to my arrival," he said patiently. Their faces fell in disappointment.

The poor lads were old enough to remember the breathtaking spectacles Queen Ianthe once performed in the coliseum for the entertainment of her subjects. There hadn't been a better magic-user in all of Atlantis compared to the queen; no surprise given that she'd descended from their prime goddess of the sea. He entered the palace and made his way to the royal healer's suite, suspecting Kai hadn't yet been released. His senses led him right, and he heard her protesting further treatment before he even entered the room.

His princess sat on an examination table, eye-level with the old sage who administered curatives and medical care to the palace residents. When Manu strode inside, Kai snapped her attention toward him, away from the attending healer's craggy face. Vitalis was an elderly, no-nonsense sort of mer, hundreds of years old and probably present for the birth of every high mer in the city. Though he seemed moments from crumbling into a pile of dust, his weathered face split into a big grin at the sight of Manu.

"Good day, Commander."

"Manu, tell him that I'm fine!"

"I don't know about that. You may need to be kept overnight," he said slyly, watching her unconcealed exasperation flare into visible fury. A flush kissed her cheeks, though it was so fetching against her golden complexion that he couldn't look away. His gaze remained on her brown eyes—trapped in the depths of them.

"What? Manu—!" Her incredulous screech snapped him out of the moment.

"What do you think, Healer Vitalis? Will it be necessary to amputate? Our princess is quite sassy. I don't know if it can be cured in a single visit." He watched her expression transition from genuine anger to delight as understanding dawned.

The old man chuckled. "She's quite well. I kept her for additional observation, as head injuries can be quite concerning. But I do believe she'll be fine after a little rest."

"Ha!" She set her gaze on Manu. "I told you I'd be fine." She stuck out her tongue afterward.

He rolled his eyes. "Yes, you are indeed fine. A little spoiled, but fine nonetheless."

She swatted his bicep playfully and grinned, wearing a smile on her full lips. He wanted to kiss them but found the strength to keep his desires at bay. Kai was not his to covet, no matter how much she haunted his thoughts.

"What about Amerin? I expected her to be here." He glanced around the small examination room but saw no sign of the servant.

"Healer Vitalis allowed her to leave first. She wasn't injured." As the amusement faded from Kai's face, the corners of her mouth turned down and her brows notched together. "Something happened out there, and I don't know what to make of it. She was petrified and said they'd kill her."

Manu frowned.

"Ah," Vitalis said, clicking his tongue. "The poor child. I sent her off to rest with an anti-anxiety draught. She shook like a leaf, though she wouldn't tell me why. Now I understand."

"Understand what? What's wrong with her?"

"Loyalists hate nobility, but they loathe the servant class most of all," Manu said in a quiet voice. "They see her kind as your enablers and spies. Last year, there was a rash of murders across the city, and they were all servants."

Gasping, Kai raised a hand to her mouth. "No!"

Manu's shoulders dropped when he sighed.

"Unfortunately, it is what it is, Your Highness. The keepers only caught a few of the blowholes responsible. They're cowards and often aim their fury at harmless mers like Amerin who can't defend themselves. They only know how to flee and have no formal weapons training. This is why we don't allow her to travel alone without a protective detail."

"That's awful. I thought...when you assigned so many to me, I thought it was for my safety."

"It's for the both of you to remain safe, Your Highness."

Her lower lip pushed out, and it killed him that there was nothing he could do to return the smile to her face.

A mer rapped his gauntleted hand against the door frame. "Pardon my intrusion, Commander. General Lago requests your presence in Lord Regent Aegaeon's private to discuss this evening's bombing."

"Ah. I'll go at once. Thank you."

When Manu strode for the door, Kai jumped down from the exam table.

"What are you doing?"

"Following you," she said.

Because he knew better than to argue with indisputably the most quarrelsome woman in all of Atlantis, he gestured with a hand toward the door in an unspoken invitation for her to lead. They walked in silence. He didn't need to be a seer to know concern for Amerin weighed heavily on her thoughts.

"She will be safe, Princess."

"I know she will be. I won't let anyone hurt her."

His respect for her continued to rise, skyrocketing in great leaps and bounds. He couldn't wait for her to come fully into her powers and prove the Loyalist scum wrong. Life for their people was difficult enough without Atlantis tearing itself apart from within.

UNDERSTANDING the depth of Amerin's terror only fueled Kai's determination to become the powerful queen of Lago and Aegaeon's expectations. Even if she had to bleed to make it happen, her suffering was worth it as long as another servant like Amerin never had to cower in fear for her life. The longer she dwelled in Atlantis, the more easily she recognized the flaws in their civilization.

The underwater kingdom and surface world weren't so different after all.

Here, she could make a difference.

Here, she could create change.

"It may bring you some amusement to know a strange rumor met me at the palace gate," Manu said as they descended the stairs side by side, almost close enough for their hips to brush.

"Oh? What rumor is it this time? Another tale about the princess swimming stark naked in the gardens?"

He gave one of those husky chuckles that always made her core clench tighter than a drum. "No. They said you channeled a fifty-meter wave of slush into the skies and extinguished a fire in the Coral Spire. Figured I'd share that one since you could use the laugh."

When Kai didn't laugh, Manu glanced at her with slow-dawning wonder on his face, eyes slightly enlarged, lips falling open.

"It's not a tale," he guessed. "You really did it."

"I don't know what happened. I ordered Heracles to give me his rifle, but when I had it in my hands and was facing this Loyalist, I...I couldn't pull the trigger. I couldn't kill another person. I froze." She swallowed the dry tension at the back of her parched throat, relieved when Manu didn't laugh at her. Instead, he paused, and he took her hands in both of his.

"I understand. Taking the life of another mer is never easy, even when that mer is infected by the Gloom. When they're not, it's even harder."

"I could have gotten myself killed. I could have got one of them killed. I mean, I pulled rank and ordered him to pass his weapon over, and then I just stood there like an asshole holding it. Anyway, this Loyalist wound up like he was pitching a fast ball, then suddenly this thing was flying at us. He'd been throwing them at the Coral Spire, hurling them into windows. People inside were screaming for help."

Manu's thumb stroked over the back of her knuckles. "So you found your powers when they were needed most."

"I did. One of the Myrmidons shot the fire bomb, but the liquid ignited in the air. Instinct just took over at that point and I whipped a wall of ice water at it."

"Then you saved the Coral Spire."

"Yes. I still can't believe I did it."

When Manu didn't release her hands, she didn't tug either free, appreciating the strength of his grip and the comforting warmth imparted by his callused fingers. She could have stood there all night soaking it in, but he snapped out of it first and dropped both hands to his sides. "We shouldn't keep the general and regent waiting."

"Oh. Right."

Kai cleared her throat and fell into step beside him, saying nothing else the remainder of the walk to Aegaeon's study. A palpable kind of tension seemed to emanate from the room long before they crossed the threshold, like an inaudible siren screaming for her to turn tail and leave. Her uncle sat behind his desk and Lago stood near one corner of it, big arms crossed against his massive chest. Loto, Elpis, and Cosmas were also there.

The moment she and Manu stepped inside, Aegaeon's brows knit in consternation. "Shouldn't the princess be in her chamber resting?"

"Her Highness wanted—"

"You were given orders to see to the princess's safety, Commander Manu," the general spit out, further irritating the hell out of Kai because the man had been nothing but rude to his son in every encounter she'd witnessed.

"The princess is right here and doesn't appreciate when others discuss her as if she isn't present," Kai said. Cool blue eyes darted her way, narrowing.

She stood her ground with Lago. "I'm not a child. If you're serious about me one day taking the throne, then you need to include me in whatever you six plan to discuss."

"Very well then," Aegaeon muttered. He vacated his chair and gestured for her to take the seat behind the desk, opting to stand beside her. "Still, I don't understand what they thought they could possibly accomplish by rioting in the middle of the street."

"Neither do I," Manu said.

"Isn't it clear?" Lago straightened his back and gazed out the window. In the distance, Kai saw the lingering fog from the fire bombs clouding the air. "This was a test of our defenses and response time. The moment our Myrmidons arrived, all hostilities ceased and the perpetrators scattered to the waves."

Aegaeon's brows knit in consternation. "Why would they test our response times when they've seen the Myrmidon force react to emergency situations in the past?"

"It means they're up to something," Kai suggested. "It means the next time we hear from them, they'll have a plan, and it won't end when our forces arrive."

20

A LIGHT IN THE DARK

MANU GAVE KAI THE NEXT THREE DAYS OFF FROM training. Though he claimed to be occupied with Myrmidon matters, she thought he was showing her pity when she awakened the morning following the Loyalist attack aching from head to toe. A migraine throbbed behind her eyes, and light sensitivity kept her in bed with the lamps dimmed. Aside from rousing once around noon to peek in on Amerin, she listened to her body and slept.

The next day, much of the discomfort had dissipated, leaving only a dull ache.

"It's the magic use," Amerin explained, sitting opposite Kai at the round table in the nook. Cook had already brought them a delicious brunch to enjoy together. "Using magic taxes the body, and since it was your first time using the gift in years, your mind will have to adjust."

"Oh." As her belly rumbled, Kai stared at the smoked fish and sweet strands of seaweed salad, for once doubting it would be enough. She could have eaten a whole tuna. "I guess it's another skill I'll have to practice. Manu mentioned it once, but he said he didn't want to overtax me by introducing so much at once."

"Manu isn't a high mer, so he can't really instruct you. I overheard the regent and general discussing whether to have Cosmas teach you."

Kai thoughtfully forked a bite of salmon into her mouth. "I don't see why they'd change my tutors now. Manu did a fine job teaching me to use my tail."

"True."

They stayed in together and enjoyed a quiet day of reading. Kai had determined the only way to improve her understanding of the underwater language would be to immerse herself in it completely.

On the third day of her break from training, Aegaeon called her to join him on the balcony overlooking Atlantis where he often took his morning tea. If not for his summons, she would have lain in bed insensible for another hour at the least.

"Something wrong, Uncle?"

A big grin slid across his face when he offered her the morning newspaper, the paper thick and green-tinged. The *Atlantic* printed squid ink on paper pressed from kelp pulp. "On the contrary, Kai, something is finally right. Feast your eyes on this, my niece."

Upon unfolding it, she saw a photograph of herself knelt beside a fallen keeper, feeding him small amounts of healing tonic from a vial. Above it, a bold headline stretched across the top.

PRINCESS KAILANI, OUR LIGHT IN DARK TIMES

"Someone photographed me."

"Indeed. Someone captured this, and it took a few days for news to reach the *Atlantic*. I had no idea about it, but I'm thrilled nonetheless. This is an enormous step toward proving yourself to the citizens."

"The Loyalists will still hate me."

"They hate everyone. You and I are no exception. They are foul people with no love for anyone or anything."

"Is what they want that bad, though? Votes, a government, a hand in the decision-making process—why is this all so awful?"

"It isn't awful, but it isn't up to me to change Atlantian law. Our kingdom has been this way for centuries, my dear, and we thrive. If they wish to be like the surface, then the surface awaits them. We have contacts within many of the human governments, and the ability to plant them into surface society." He shrugged one shoulder. "Regardless, these laws have guided us for nearly two millennia. Have no worries about the Loyalists. They will be squashed soon."

"How do you know?"

His shark-like smile sent ice trickling down her spine. "A belief that our keepers will triumph. But please, I'm sure you have better things to do with your morning than to listen to the ramblings of your old uncle." Then he paused, appearing to reconsider dismissing her. "Actually, how are you recuperating from your magical use?"

"Well, I think."

"Good. The first large expenditure can be quite taxing. But you are your mother's daughter. You'll rebound in no time. Next week perhaps, we'll assign a tutor...."

And there went the rest of their brief conversation, their discussion surrounding her studies and a planned visit to the healing house to see the keepers overwhelmed during the riot. Aegaeon appeared delighted by the idea of future photo opportunities to prove her worth to the Atlantian people.

So she agreed.

By the time Kai returned from her impromptu breakfast with her uncle, Amerin had become her usual bubbly self.

"How was it? Is everything all right?"

"He wanted to show me the morning paper. Someone photographed me working alongside Commander Elpis and her medics." Kai sighed as she thought back to that night and the hours spent seeking the wounded. She'd worked until exhaustion overcame her, not that the experienced medics had needed her mediocre help.

"That's a good thing, isn't it? Then everyone who doubts you can see what the rest of us do?"

An involuntary smile crept onto Kai's face. "And what do the rest of you see?"

"An amazing mer who cares about others more than she cares about herself. I..." Amerin dipped her chin and toyed with the hem of her fitted blouse. "Thank you, Your Highness. For looking out for me. I'm sorry that I fell apart."

"You don't need to thank me or apologize. You were afraid. You can't control that."

"You did. When I saw the Loyalists, I thought..." A small shudder overcame the other woman, and a single tear squeezed from the corner of her eye, trickling down her pale cheek. "I can't do anything valuable. Nothing but style your hair and help you with clothing, things you'd learn to do on your own in time without me. Maybe they're right. Maybe servants are useless. We do nothing more than things the high mers can learn to do on their own. We are absolutely disposable."

"Hey. Hey." As Amerin's mood deflated, Kai stepped forward and took her by the shoulders. "You are not disposable. And you're not worthless, either. You're a good person, and there will always be a need for good people." She paused a moment. "I learned that from Mr. Rogers. You'd like him, I think."

"Mr. Who?"

"One day, we'll go to the surface together, and I'll show you old re-runs." The shows in Atlantis weren't as entertaining, most of them action flicks, detective noir-style mystery, period pieces, and Greek historical drama. The one hidden blessing was that reality television didn't exist, as she couldn't imagine the underwater version of *Survivor*. In her head, she dubbed it *Shark Bait*. Though something told her it would be rather similar to the surface show's actual premise, a group of mers trapped on a tropical island in the middle of the Atlantic, given only the bare necessities to survive.

Kai snapped her thoughts back to the present, cursing her wandering mind. "I want to do something today. Are you up for heading out of the palace? I think I'm fed up with lying in bed."

"Of course, Your Highness. What would you like to do?"

"Tell me what would you would like to do."

"Me?" the handmaiden squeaked.

"Yes, you. We've done all the things I like. If I weren't here in Atlantis, what would you do with your free time?"

Amerin hesitated for a moment, lips pressed firmly together. Within a few moments, her sad eyes brightened and elation spread over her face. "I can show you one of my favorite places, but you'll want to wear sharkskin or scales. Going by coral glider isn't the same. To really appreciate it, you have to swim there."

"Sure. Let me change."

After Kai squeezed into her favorite set of Gigas fish scales, they set out from the palace and passed beyond the Atlantian gate with a few Myrmidons as their escort. Two men led by Heracles hung back a respectful distance while Amerin and Kai swam ahead down a road paved by white stones.

"Where are we going?"

"The Fields of Gold. It's one of my favorite places to go to when I want to think."

"I've never been there." Manu preferred to remain close to the dome, often taking her no more than a few miles beyond the city gates. "What are they?"

An impish smile livened Amerin's round face. "You'll see."

No matter how many times Kai ventured beyond the city limits, the sight still took her breath away. Miles and miles of underwater terrain beyond the city dome had been aquascaped into carpets of algae, seagrass, and flowering corals covered in phosphorescent anemone. All of this was hidden beneath the murky cloud protecting Atlantis from human discovery, lit by solar lanterns providing the necessary light for growth.

They passed fields of kelp grazed by hippocampus livestock and sea cows resembling oversized manatees, traveling farther than Kai ever ventured with Manu.

"We're almost there. It's just over the ridge," Amerin said.

"Race you."

When they crested the ridge, Kai understood how the place came by its name. Hundreds, if not thousands, of gilded starfish glowed amidst clouds of fuzzy carpet algae, no doubt sifting through the soft fibers for food particles. Flicking her tail, she swam down the low hill to the golden field.

Amerin touched down onto a green patch first. "Watch your step if you use your legs. There are sink holes here from the sandworms. It's safe to walk on the bubble algae. The barren places are where they've been digging."

"Thank you for bringing me to your special place."

"Our special place," Amerin corrected her. "We used to visit the gardens as children. King Neptune would bring us here sometimes, and we'd play for hours among the starfish and collect a basket of them."

"What did we do with them afterward?"

"Eat them, of course."

Kai's belly twisted inside out. Sheer willpower kept the horrified expression from her face. At least, she imagined it did until Amerin burst out laughing.

"You'll get used to dining on Atlantian food again soon."

"We...ate them?"

No matter how much she wanted Amerin to be teasing, a sinking feeling in her gut told her that was not the case.

"Have I steered you wrong yet when it comes to the food in the underwater realm?"

"No," Kai said reluctantly, deciding to be adventurous. "I've eaten a lot of things without asking what the hell you're feeding me. I regret asking about the whale milk cheese though." Despite her disgust, it had been creamy and absolutely delicious melted over the baked oysters.

"Then trust me now." Amerin plucked one of the golden stars from the seaweed and snapped the poor creature in half.

And Kai, having no other option, took the unfortunate animal without grimacing.

"Well...to memories."

They tapped their starfish halves together and bit in.

TRUSTING Amerin turned out to be a good thing.

Between Kai and her new friend, they ate about a dozen of the tender, sweet and savory critters, scooping out the edible parts of the spongy insides and leaving what remained for ocean scavengers. Kai sprawled on her back in the seaweed and gazed at the illusory ceiling over the underwater realm. The magic glittered sometimes, resembling stars scattered in a midnight sky. Amerin sat cross-legged beside her while watching a colorful hermit crab hauling away a piece of star fish exoskeleton.

"Thank you for bringing me here."

"You're welcome. I was happy to."

As she lay there contemplating her life, Kai wondered what made Amerin less valuable than the high mer in their fancy shell manors and glass homes. It seemed silly, treating a portion of their society as less, simply for being born to the wrong mothers, into the wrong families.

"Amerin?"

"Yes, Your Highness?"

"I truly enjoy being with you. Between you, Cosmas, and Manu, you've done the most to make me feel welcome here. I know it's your job but...I do sincerely appreciate all you've done." A few heart-beats passed before she added. "Being with you reminds me of my sister from the surface."

"I do?"

"I know you're not her, but when I'm with you... being away from them hurts a little less." Kai blinked rapidly a few times, thankful for the water to disguise her tears. "I miss my family and I worry about them. I don't know if it's silly to worry about them when they're safe on land, but I worry. I worry about what they're doing now that I'm gone. What they must think about my disappearance. I just..." She sighed and dropped her head, hating that she'd ruined a special moment and feeling quite ridiculous. "Ignore me."

"I don't think you're silly for worrying about the people who raised you. I only wish I could meet them. Your surface mother must be a wonderful person."

Kai pushed up into a sitting position. "She is. She's the only mother I can remember. Being here and enjoying life feels like a betrayal. Does it make me an awful daughter that I'm here moving on while they probably mourn me?"

Amerin's lips pressed together in a taut line. "No, it doesn't. You're only in this predicament because of what happened to you as a child, and that isn't your fault, Your Highness."

"Kai." When the handmaiden blinked and canted her head, Kailani took both of her hands. "Call me Kai. Not Princess Kai—just Kai. Please. I don't want a servant. I want a friend. This evening with you was the most at home I've felt since reaching this city."

"It helps that there are no explosions," Amerin said, features solemn until a tiny grin snuck onto her face.

A tiny bubble of laughter escaped Kai despite the serious topic. "It certainly does. Come on. Want to help me collect some of these for later?"

"Yes!" Amerin clapped as she crawled to her hands and knees, gathering stars in the apron of her dress. "And some for Commander Manu as well."

Kai flicked her tail and drifted off the ocean floor. "Why Manu?"

"No particular reason. I just figure he'd like a star." The devilish glint in Amerin's eyes set an uneasy knot in Kai's belly. Something told her there was more to it, but the only way to discover why was to go along with her friend's mischief.

21

JUMPING THE SHARK

Shark riding wasn't too unlike horse riding, though the ocean was more forgiving when a disobedient animal threw its rider. Instead of flopping from the saddle onto unyielding Texan ground, the shark's wild ride sent her rolling off his back into the water with an inelegant splash.

Cosmas cracked up, deep belly laughs echoing across the open blue. It was fall now in the northern hemisphere, and he'd brought her up to the surface to practice beneath the clouds. She had no idea of their location in the Atlantic, but the sun shone warm and the water was pleasant. While she appreciated the sentiment, she did *not* care for his amusement.

"That's not funny!"

"It was damned hilarious is what it was. You should be hoarse from that scream at the end."

"You're not much of a teacher if you're going to laugh at me."

The corner of his mouth ticked up. "You're not

much of a student when you disregard my instructions. You brought it on yourself."

Despite how much she wanted to call him a slew of names, he was right. And now she had to leap back into the figurative and literal saddle somehow, so she could make a fool of herself *again*.

"Perseus! Get back over here."

Obedient for his rider, the enormous shark cruised back to them and waited, huge maw gaping open.

"No treats for you until you're good for the princess. Go easy on her, my friend. She knows no better."

"I really don't," she said, sighing. "I don't think I have the same intrinsic magical talent as the rest of you high mer."

"You do. And it'll be strongest in you, remember? You're our queen, the only true direct descendant of Thalassa and Pontus."

"Maybe I was lost for a reason, to save you all the trouble of making me into something I can't be." It meant to leave her in a teasing voice, but the catharsis of voicing her unspoken worries left her feeling raw and exposed.

Cosmas frowned as he bobbed on the surface, treading water easily by only kicking his feet in lazy movements. "Hey. None of that, Your Highness. That's no way to look at it. No one excels their first try. I've been on sharks and hippocampi since I was able to crawl on dry land. It takes practice. What you see here"—he jumped into the leather saddle on

Perseus's back—"is the result of seven decades of work."

"Seven decades? Gods. I'm so hopelessly behind I'll never catch up." Until then, she'd never considered Cosmas's age.

"Your High—"

"Kai." His brows rose. "Just call me Kai. No 'Your Highness.'"

He nodded, but the disturbed expression on his face didn't ease. "Kai it is. Still, whether it takes you seven decades or seven days to grasp the basics of maintaining your seat, you have time. Our people are long-lived. There's no rush here."

That wasn't what Aegaeon had said. Kai pushed her sopping hair away from her face. "How can I rule as a proper queen or stop the Gloom when I can't convince a shark to obey me?"

"Perseus is a bit of a blowhole. It would have been kinder of me to bring Malleus or even Hecate. Both are headstrong and stubborn fish, but gentler on new riders. Come on." He offered her a hand then helped her into the saddle in front of him. His arm fit around her waist with ease, a band of steel encased in tiger sharkskin.

Kai leaned against his chest and tipped her head back, peering over one shoulder. "Thank you."

"Don't mention it. And don't allow my uncle to worry you about becoming an overnight warrior queen. All things take time, Kai."

"I can't stop thinking about it."

"You must. The animal can sense your trepidation and your worries, and you pass this anxiety on to him. When you're on a sea creature, your thoughts must be on the task ahead of you and nowhere else. He *wants* to listen and obey, but how can he when you're distracted by other matters?"

"I guess."

"There's nothing to guess, Kai. Queen Ianthe didn't become a legend in a day, and neither will you. What Aegaeon and Lago haven't told you is that centuries of training created our beloved queen. Like you, she learned through trial and error, through practice, and through mistakes."

"Did you know her?"

"I did. I swear you remind me so much of her. She was as beautiful inside as she was outside. No one could meet her without becoming enchanted by her wit or her humor. Or her courage. She'd put herself between a Gloombeast and one of her citizens without a second thought. *Any* citizen," he added, when she raised a skeptical brow.

"Even a servant?"

"Especially a servant. I heard her once tell my father the way we treat our most helpless is a reflection of our entire kingdom. So be kinder to yourself."

She nodded.

"Breathe." He splayed his palm against her stomach. If he was Manu, it would have incited little flutters. Cosmas's touch did nothing. "Breathe deep and close your eyes."

Despite the rising doubt, she closed her eyes and

became aware of Cosmas edging back, away, and finally off the shark's back.

"You aren't one rider and one shark. You're one mind. One being. Feel the smooth glide through the water, the waves cresting over your fins."

"I don't have fins right now," she muttered.

"*His* fins are your fins," Cosmas corrected her.

Perseus slid through the water, gradually descending until the white-capped ocean waves rose from her hips to her chest. She opened her eyes and stole a glance to her left to see Cosmas dutifully swimming alongside the shark with powerful strokes. Whether the beast sensed her determination or her frustration, he didn't rear and throw her again.

Hours later when they returned to Atlantis on the majestic beast, Kai's aching thighs barely allowed her to walk into the city. Cosmas laughed at her again, though it was a good-natured chuckle as he slipped one arm around her waist. She couldn't help but laugh along.

"That was fun. Despite all of my bitching and moaning, I loved it. Thank you."

"You're welcome." A snap of his fingers leeched the water from their garments and hair. Every droplet merely pulled away and dropped to the floor. She marveled over it, fascinated by the simplest spells. "I have another great talent if you're interested, one far superior to my teaching skills."

"Yeah?"

"Not bragging, but I was once told I could have had a lucrative career as a masseur."

He spoke the magic words. Kai's core clenched, not in anticipation of having *his* hands on her, but because her body remembered too well how much she'd wanted Manu to explore its every inch. She stumbled for a step, but Cosmas's strong arm tightened around her.

Stupid, traitorous body, finding attraction towards the wrong man. She cursed it inwardly but put on a smile. "Not this evening, I don't think. I'd like to get to bed early. Read a little perhaps, now that the language isn't gibberish to me anymore."

"Oh." He masked his fleeting disappointment behind a kind smile. She adored him all the more when he didn't pressure her. If there was one thing Atlantian men had in their favor, it was their ability to take "no" for an answer. "Let me walk you to the palace then."

The moment she reached her private suite, she shut the door behind her and leaned her back against it, eyes closed. Amerin popped up from where she sprawled across the divan with a book.

"Is everything okay, Kai?"

"Just peachy."

Far from it. Given Cosmas's perfect qualities, she'd resigned herself to accepting him as her mate. How sad. She was soon to be engaged to one man, and absolutely smitten with another. To make matters worse, they were the best of friends.

Amerin's skeptical gaze followed her across the room. "You don't look peachy. Did Commander Cosmas upset you?"

"No. *I* upset me. I—ugh, never mind. It's stupid."

"What's stupid?"

"Nothing. I'm tired from riding in the sun all day," she lied. One afternoon beneath the sky hadn't been enough, but she hesitated to ask for more favors from Cosmas. He didn't seem to be the sort, but her experience with men on the surface told her he'd eventually want something in return, and she wasn't quite ready for that.

Or maybe she was. Maybe a romp with him was exactly what she needed to fuck Manu out of her mind. The sooner she stopped dreaming about the hunky warrior, the sooner she could embrace a future as Queen of Atlantis with Cosmas at her side.

Manu had been gone for three days and was scheduled to be absent for many more, leaving behind Cosmas as an adequate substitute for her training. Still, a jolt of guilt shot through her every time he reached for her hand or twined their fingers.

Because aside from the occasional moment of appreciating his good looks, she felt nothing for him. Cosmas wasn't the man she dreamed about kissing at night, and he wasn't the man who had dominated her thoughts since the moment she saw him at a beach-side bar in Galveston.

22

———

CLOSURE

HUMANS MAY HAVE FUCKED UP A LOT OF OTHER shit throughout the centuries, but they did one thing right when they invented coffee. Irritable from his lack of sleep, Manu sipped the sweet black brew and observed the tidy lines of new recruits in the training yard before him, thanking the gods he wasn't instructing today—merely an observer.

Some of the lads were just shy of adulthood, youngsters desperate to make a difference in their enormous kingdom or to earn a living to help their families. A few came from as far as hundreds of leagues away for training, some from distant colonies, others from farmland on the Atlantian outskirts, the eldest sons of share-croppers who worked the land for nobles too good to get their hands in algae.

It was a shame more of the noble-born didn't take after their princess.

And there he was thinking of her again. All trains

of thought led back to Kailani for some reason, no matter how much he tried to focus on his day.

Kai shouldn't have occupied Manu's mind as often as she did, but the woman was inescapable. He thought about her at all hours of the day, whether he was training, teaching, or attempting to sleep in his bed each night. There, she was a persistent thorn in his sleeping schedule, a barb burrowing into his subconscious, because then he dreamed about her.

In short, he was in hell. A hell where the woman of your dreams floated beyond your reach, absolutely unattainable. Not only was she royalty, but she belonged to a good friend he respected too much to make a move on her. Cosmas didn't appear to be too excited about potentially courting the princess, but the man could be strange, accustomed to rich and spoiled mer heiresses throwing themselves at him. They found it sexy that he was both highborn and a Myrmidon, a risk taken by too few of their haughty counterparts.

In the old days, even a few centuries past, it wasn't uncommon for high mer to enter the military. He wondered what led to the change—*when* it changed. As long as he'd been alive, mers like Cosmas were an anomaly, a rare breed envied by their peers for their bravery and honored by the commoners for their sacrifice. As if being wealthy and more magical than others made them greater.

Pondering these things took his mind off of what was becoming a very troublesome and concerning addiction to the princess, which was why he'd needed a few days off for his sanity. He'd given her some crab-and-eel story about wanting her to rest, but the truth was that when focused and motivated, she'd turned into a damn machine.

A mer stepped up to his side and saluted. "Commander. You have a visitor."

"Who is it?"

"Princess Kailani's handmaiden."

"Amerin?"

"Yes, sir."

"I'll meet her in my office. Have her wait for me there."

When he reached the room, Amerin had taken a seat opposite his desk with her hands folded in her lap. She'd dressed in a sleeveless silk dress and wore her braids decorated with polished coral beads. In a word, he'd call her pretty—delightfully cute, but too impish for his tastes.

"Greetings, Commander. I hope I didn't pull you away from important matters."

"Likewise, I hope I didn't keep you waiting too long. What can I do for you, Amerin?"

"I come on behalf of Princess Kailani."

His heart gave a violent thump against his ribs before common sense told him to calm. There were a dozen reasons a woman could send her handmaiden to a mer on her behalf. "Why is that?"

"She doesn't know that I'm here, but..." Thank the gods. He relaxed. "She misses her family. I thought perhaps..." Amerin bit her lower lip, looking shy. "I could be wrong, but you like her, don't you?"

"Everyone likes the princess."

"Yes, they do, but with you I sense it's more than the loyalty a mer feels for his queen, more than a liking in the fraternal sense, and definitely more than any amicable sort of friendship. I see how you look at her when no one else is present, when it's only the three of us. You forget that I'm there. It's all right. Most people forget that I'm present, but I like it that way. It allows me to see the things most would conceal from others." When he didn't respond, she carried on. "What I see when I watch the two of you is mutual interest."

Manu said nothing. He didn't dare confirm such a foolish notion with the woman's personal servant, knowing she was bound by loyalty to repeat anything Kai asked about.

"You do want her. Oh, don't worry. I don't plan to share my suspicions. They are, after all, only suspicions." Amerin giggled. "But you should have seen your face when I suggested you could possibly feel romantically for her." Then she tilted her head. "Or at least, something lustful."

"I don't."

"You're a liar."

"I—"

"But that's not why I came. We're off the topic now. I came because my princess worries about her family and how they've fared since *you* took her away. You may have been under orders, but you snatched her, giving her no chance to say goodbye to her loved ones."

"I didn't realize she had loved ones then," he growled.

"Now you do. And now you can fix it. So...what do you say, Commander? Do you have it in you to visit the surface world for a chat with our princess's mortal kin?"

"They're not even her kin. They're humans who took her in and raised her, but they're not related. They're not *blood*."

Amerin tilted her head. "No, they're not. But given how you feel about *your* blood, one would think you'd realize that relation isn't everything."

He didn't respond. Did everyone across Atlantis know that he had an asshole for a father?

"I'll leave you to think about it," Amerin said, rising gracefully from the seat. She then set a wrapped bundle on his desk.

"What's that?" He eyed it with as much trust as he'd give a lump of fire coral.

Her cheeks dimpled when she smiled. "Something from the princess."

Something told him to decline the gift, but his curiosity got the better of him and he tugged the sparkling twine binding it. The packaging fell apart to reveal a pair of golden starfish tucked in an open coral box.

Manu stared at them. He really stared, because part of him thought if he continued to look at them, they would morph into something that made sense.

"Well," Amerin said, still grinning cutely,

mischief in her eyes. "I'll leave you to it. Good day, Commander."

The gift couldn't be correct. Though they weren't in Pacifica, he knew the traditions well, branded into him by his mother as a child. A starfish given there symbolized one thing, and one thing only, when gifted to another mer: love.

WERE IT ANY OTHER MATTER, Manu would have approached his father. But since his father was a world class dick, he bypassed the general and requested a private meeting with Regent Aegaeon in the man's personal office instead.

He rehearsed his request in his head on the way. Worst-case scenario, Aegaeon declined, and when his father found out, he spent weeks in shitty assignments until the man got over it.

Manu reached the door and paused instead of rapping his knuckles against the thick panel. The usual pair of guards weren't at their post. Something struck him as amiss, though he couldn't place it, and the fine hairs on his nape rose, his arms breaking out in goosebumps.

"You shouldn't be here," Aegaeon was saying. Someone replied, their voice an indiscernible hiss in the otherwise quiet room. Manu knew he shouldn't eavesdrop, but he strained to hear the other speaker. "I told you, the risk is too—"

"Lies." The voice sounded female.

The room fell silent again. A chair scraped against stone.

Manu tensed, again poised to knock. He thumped his fist twice against the door despite the eerie sensation crawling over his skin.

"Enter," Aegaeon called. Then the door swung inward to reveal the high mer lord sitting behind his desk, a warm smile on his face.

Manu stepped inside and shut the door behind him. "Good day, my lord. Thank you for agreeing to see me today." Somehow, he resisted the urge to check out the room, though nothing stood out of place. Had anyone left the office, they would have had to pass him, he was sure.

"Any time, Commander. You're a little earlier than I expected, but my office is always open to you. Now, what brings you here to see me?"

He had to steel his nerves and prepare for pitching the ludicrous idea to their interim ruler. After a deep breath, still feeling quite ridiculous, Manu said, "I'd like permission to return to the surface. For Princess Kailani."

Aegaeon's brows rose. "To what purpose?"

"She worries about her mortal family. I fear the distraction prevents her from attaining her full potential."

"And what do you hope to accomplish during this visit?"

Ignoring the perspiration slicking his palms, and the niggling self-doubt arising—borne from years of listening to his father's negativity—Manu raised his chin. "Provide them assurance of her safety. Explain what she wasn't given the chance to say."

Unconvinced, Aegaeon leaned back in his seat and crossed his legs. "They're mortal. What good does it do to tell them the truth?"

"They wouldn't be the first surfacelanders who know about Atlantis. Thousands work with our kingdom each year, Your Grace. They import and export our goods."

"And you believe they'd keep their silence?"

"I do. Princess Kailani thinks highly of them both. Notifying them of her survival would provide her with much-needed closure to focus on the tasks ahead. She's already seen tremendous improvement since the events at Fare, and I believe she'll only continue to grow once her past life related to the surface is behind her." The traumatizing events at the Pharae colony had been a decisive chip in her stubborn psyche, chiseling a facet in the otherwise unpolished jewel known as Kai.

It hadn't broken her, after all. It made her *shine*.

Aegaeon didn't speak for some time. He rubbed his face and cradled his cheek against one palm, elbow supported by his armrest. Manu held his breath.

"All right. Request granted."

Fuck, yes. He didn't pump a fist in victory before their interim ruler, however.

"If this is what you feel is necessary for Zephyr—Kailani's happiness and emotional well-being, who am I to stand in the way? Will you leave at once?"

"If permitted."

"Then please, by all means, leave as soon as possible. The earlier she is able to move forward from her past life, the better. Perhaps we can make arrangements for her to meet her mortal friends in time, once she's settled into Atlantian life." His fair brows slid inward. "Or invite them to visit her. They would not be the first humans."

"Perhaps," Manu agreed, still celebrating the victory. He'd visited the man with every expectation of failure.

A worry line creased Aegaeon's brow. "But what of her training in your absence?"

"I plan to visit Commander Cosmas. During my absence, he can provide her a week of instruction with the sharks. We can't expect her to be a well-rounded Queen of Atlantis if she's never ridden a battle shark. Who better to teach her to ride than our cavalry commander?"

"Excellent point. Go with my blessing, then. Cosmas will make an adequate substitute in the meantime. There's no better time to begin training her water magic than now."

LESS THAN THREE days after leaving Atlantis behind, Manu stood on Galveston's golden-brown shoreline and wondered what the hell he was doing. Traveling to the Texas city had seemed like a good idea at the time, but now he sorely regretted allowing Amerin to talk him into her little scheme.

When he'd set off from Atlantis, he'd had every confidence in the simple plan of giving Kai's mortal family the closure they deserved.

Too late to turn back. He'd stood up to his father for it, even accepted that somewhere across the ocean, Cosmas Stormshark was probably teaching the most perfect woman in all of Atlantis how to straddle a beast capable of swimming one hundred miles an hour. The fastest sharks in all the world lived in their kingdom, a crossbreed between a mako shark and a skiafin. The latter was an endangered magical species found cruising only at the bottom of the Mediterranean.

As much as he wanted to envy Cosmas his fortune, his fellow commander deserved a good woman, though he didn't understand the mer's reluctance to marry her. In his eyes, Kai was more than the best. What she lacked in training and strength, she made up for with intentions. Heart. Love.

He'd already decided that the pair of starfish had to be a joke or Amerin meddling in their business. Kai barely knew Atlantian culture, so it seemed foolish in hindsight to believe for a moment she'd learned about rituals in Pacifica. There, a young merwoman who decided to accept a potential mate's courtship gifted him with a pair of starfish.

Fuck. He had to get her out of his head. And a good way to start would be by addressing the task that brought him to mortal shores. Putting all thoughts of

Kai from his mind but those that mattered for his mission, he ventured from the beach and approached the front of her family's house. The white two-story building stood on wooden stilts overlooking the beach, though the front of it straddled a stretch of green grass. One flight of steps took him to the front door. He knocked.

"Just a minute!" Then the door opened, and the blonde woman on the other side peered out, kind blue eyes studying him. "May I help you?"

"I am looking for Sunshine Queen."

"That's me. Do I know you?"

He sucked in a deep breath and thought back to what he'd rehearsed during the days of travel. "Not personally. I'm a friend of your daughter."

"Sadie?"

"Kailani."

Her grip on the doorframe tightened, turning her knuckles white. "I...I'm sorry to be the one to share this news with you, but my daughter is gone. She..." Her shoulders trembled, and she blinked away the moisture swimming in her eyes. "She's gone."

"Yes. She is," he agreed in a gentle voice. "May I come inside to speak with you? I won't take more of your time than what's needed, but I have something I must show you. Something your daughter would want you to see."

"Yes, yes, of course. Forgive my manners."

"Forgive mine. I'm Manu, and it's my honor to meet you."

Sunshine gestured for him to follow her. After

shutting the door, she led the way to the kitchen and moved a kettle to the stove. It was then that she raked her gaze over his sharkskin suit, noticing it for the first time. "You say you were a friend of my daughter?"

He didn't sit. "I *am* a friend of your daughter. You are right that she is gone from this place, but I came here to pass along a message. She wanted you to know she's returned to her people."

She dropped a mug. Bits of ceramic skittered across the floor.

"And she also wanted you to know she is well, that she is not dead. She is home again where she belongs, but she will never forget you. She hopes you'll one day forgive her for leaving as she did. And that in time, she may even be able to visit."

Time stood still. He waited for her to order him out, to scream, to deny his words or claim he was insane. She did none of those things. Instead, she broke into tears and clutched a hand to her chest.

"Thank you," Sunshine breathed, shoulders shaking, a sob shuddering through her body. "*Thank you.*"

"Thank you?" He'd expected an argument about it, given how infrequently mortals accepted the existence of magic when it wasn't in front of their eyes. When she didn't scream and demand he leave, he crouched and picked up the broken pieces.

"I always knew Kai was special. Always knew there was something different about her. I thought..." Her shoulders shook. "Thank the goddess. No...thank *you.*"

"You believe me?" Manu asked, straightening to set the pieces of shattered cup on the counter.

"Why wouldn't I believe you? Kai was..." Sucking in a few breaths seemed to calm her shudders. "I knew from the moment they brought Kailani to my doorstep that she was different from other children. But I loved her. I loved her for so many reasons. There was never a moment she didn't make me proud."

Funny how he felt the same way. Despite her struggles and the moments when she drove him mad, he couldn't ask for a better student. Though it would have been nice if she wasn't the sexiest warrior goddess to ever pull on fish scales. "She is amazing, and I consider myself fortunate to be her friend." Though it was a strange and unusual kind of friendship.

"She doesn't know I'm here." He couldn't help the smile curving his lips. "But she will soon. Take this."

When Sunshine held her hand out, he placed a palm-sized clam shell upon it. "What is it?"

"A way used to communicate within Atlantis."

The older woman's eyes grew wide, but she slipped her thumbnail between the two shell halves and popped it open. "Atlantis?"

The inside glowed with a mirror shine, the mother of pearl interior enchanted to connect to another paired device. The lower half reflected the viewer's face in dazzling definition, or whatever they were transmitting to the other participant of the conversation. The top half displayed the ceiling of Kailani's personal chambers.

"Honestly, Amerin," Kai's voice echoed from the open thing. "I don't have time to play with toys. I have history lessons in fif—"

"Kai?" Sunshine blurted into the shell.

All noise on the other end of the line went silent. He stood close enough to see Kai's face when she appeared in the reflection. She screamed. "*Mom?* How are you—how did—?"

"Baby, I'm so happy to see you," her mother managed to choke out before pressing a hand to her mouth. "So happy to know you're alive and safe. I thought you were gone forever. Thought we'd lost you."

"How am I seeing you right now? I don't get it."

Amerin said something, her voice too low for Manu to pick up her words.

"Mom, is there a really large guy there with you?"

"Manu? He's right here." Sunshine tilted the shell enough to capture Manu in the frame. She wiped her face with her other wrist. "I wish I could hug you right now. Are you safe? Are you happy?"

"I'm safe," Kai replied, still appearing dumbfounded. "I just don't understand why Manu is there or how this is happening."

Manu leaned forward into frame again. "Your uncle permitted me to bring this communicator to your mother. As long as you both hold one, you'll be able to make contact with each other."

"What am I allowed to say?"

"Whatever you desire as long as your mother is able to keep the nature of our world a secret. Our safety depends on few humans knowing the truth."

"I'll guard it with my life," Sunshine promised. Her shoulders stilled, the last of her shudders subsiding and sobs quieting. She wiped her cheek again and sat on a chair in the kitchen nook. "Words can't express how much we've missed you."

Granting them privacy, Manu wandered to the adjacent living room, where framed photographs decorated the shelves and walls. The pictures of Kailani followed her all the way from her childhood to her adulthood, one of them an image of her in a sailor's whites. He grinned.

Nearly an hour passed before the mortal woman emerged from the kitchen and found him. Instead of the clam shell, she held a glossy red bracelet. "When Kai was brought to me, she was holding this. She wore it sometimes as a child, but when she turned older, she lost interest in it. I don't know if she'll want this back now that she knows her origins, but I feel like I should send this with you."

Manu froze, not because he recognized the bracelet—though he did on sight—but because he thought he'd never see it again. He'd seen it a thousand times before on his mother's wrist: a bangle made from polished coral engraved with the names of her son and husband.

It seemed like only yesterday when his father had taken him along for a visit to the artisans' quarter and they'd picked out the wrist bangle and had it inscribed with their names for her birthday.

After her death, General Lago became a stranger. Changed.

Blinking away the stinging behind his eyelids, he took the bracelet and smoothed his thumb over the faded lines. A single scratch marred the otherwise perfect surface.

"Thank you. I..." He paused, wet his lips, and glanced toward the window at the setting sun. Lingering longer than necessary hadn't been his intentions. "This came from the woman who brought her to your shores."

Sunshine nodded. "I thought so. No one ever knew where she came from. She couldn't be identified, and her clothes were so strange. No one reported a missing young woman, so investigators shrugged it off and closed the case."

"She was my mother."

Sunshine's eyes softened. "Would you like to see where she's buried?"

Manu wasn't prepared for the way heartache clenched around his throat. "You'd take me there?"

"Yes. Come on. The cemetery isn't far."

23

FAMILY MATTERS

Kai and her human little sister had a lot in common. The two weren't blood relatives, but Sunshine must have instilled certain qualities in her adopted daughters...like the refusal to accept eelshit from men.

Sadie recognized him on sight when she arrived from school. Whether it was clever deduction, or the connection was that damned obvious, she promptly jumped to the conclusion that he had something to do with Kai's disappearance. Which he had. To her credit, she listened to her mother's explanation and didn't blink when Manu told her about Atlantis and that her sister was a mermaid queen descended from a goddess. Appearing more level-headed than Kai, she listened from start to finish in silence, asking at the end about their realm and how he'd found Kai.

So he told her the details about that night, as well.

Then she hit him. Hard. With enough power in the punch that he felt it. It didn't rock his head back, but he heard her knuckles crunch and the bones come perilously close to breaking, the girl putting all her weight and power into the blow, driving the right cross from the hip like someone had taught her how to fuck someone up from an early age.

That had probably been Kai.

Sadie ducked away and clutched her hand to her chest, swearing. His instinct was to go to her, because human beings could be so very fragile. One had never broken a hand on his face before, though.

"Sadie," Sunshine began in a warning tone. "Baby, are you okay?"

"No, I'm not okay! He took my sister." She didn't cry over her injured hand, but her accusation came with a ragged sob. "He took her away from us."

"Sadie—"

"Fuck him. All this time we thought Kai was dead—that she—that she—" Her voice broke, wavering, and then an awful, raw sob tore from her throat. "But it was just this dickhead had abducted her."

And he felt lower than low in the face of Sadie's righteous anger, not because she was crying, but because she was right. He'd taken Kai from people who loved her. He may not have realized the depth of their affection for her at the time, but hindsight was a powerful bitch.

"I never meant to hurt either of you," Manu said in a quiet voice, stepping closer. "I didn't realize her importance to your home. I was blinded by the urgency to get her away from the surface and it never occurred to me that she might be loved, that she belonged with you as much as she belonged with us."

Sadie didn't look at him. Her mother tried to take her hand to examine it, but she snatched it away. "Leave me alone. Maybe you won Mom over, but you're shit."

She stormed from the living room, heading upstairs with her injured hand.

Brow creased with stress, Sunshine watched her leave. "I should have warned you. Sadie has a bit of a temper."

"So does her sister."

"She's taken Kai's loss particularly hard. They've always been close, with Kai looking after Sadie."

"I should leave."

"No." Sunshine sucked in a breath. "You're some kind of Marine, right?"

"I am."

"Then you've faced dangers greater than a heart-broken twenty-one-year-old, I'm assuming. If you could just talk to her, help her understand, I'd appreciate it."

"You can just show Kai's comm to her and—"

"I could, but I want you to do this." The woman locked gazes with him. "Because this is your mistake. If you're genuinely sorry for what you did to my family, you'll do this and right the wrong you made. You owe that much to Kai, but you owe it more to the girl who has spent these past weeks thinking she drove her sister to suicide."

Put like that, Manu didn't have much of a choice. "All right."

Sunshine told him where to find Sadie, then he trudged upstairs to meet his fate, passing several portraits of Kai along the way. She'd always been beautiful, even as a pre-teen, dredging up faint memories of young Princess Zephyrine in the palace, though he'd been much older, a young Myrmidon occasionally assigned to duty guarding the entrance doors or palace gates.

He reached the second door on the left and knocked.

"Go the fuck away!"

"Not until we've spoken," Manu replied. Sighing, he leaned his forehead against the cool wooden door. "You have every right to be furious with me. I wasn't thinking. Your sister had just been attacked, and I removed her from the situation as my training dictated. That was my error. It was heartless."

She didn't respond.

"I'll stand here all night talking to this door if I must."

The pounding spray of a shower began from the attached bathroom. Manu groaned into a hand and waited it out. A good half hour or so passed before it quieted and steps returned to the bedroom.

"Will you at least allow me to look at your hand?"

"Are you a merman doctor or something?"

Finally! She speaks. "No, but I've seen enough injuries of the type to know when serious medical care is needed."

The silence resumed. Just when Manu considered retreating, the door opened to frame Sadie in leggings and a blue U.S. Navy sweatshirt he suspected belonged to Kai, as it swallowed the girl like a tent. "Are you seriously going to stand here until I talk to you?"

"Yes," he lied, like he hadn't been three seconds from leaving. But Sunshine had a point. Myrmidons didn't give up, and surrender wasn't in his nature. They didn't make excuses; they accepted responsibility for their wrongs. He'd have no doubt been back within a few minutes after devising a new strategy. "Look, I know I fucked up—"

"You speak English well, for a guy from the sea. Swears and everything."

"Magic."

From that moment, he had her hooked. Both brows jumped up and Sadie fell back a step, gesturing for him to step inside a feminine, frilly room decorated by a combination of butterfly-themed art and what he presumed to be popular human movie posters. He recognized a couple imported to Atlantis. "Magic? Like, Merlin and *Harry Potter* magic spell casting?"

Not so honorable that he wouldn't use her curiosity to his advantage, Manu grinned. "While I am familiar with *Harry Potter*," he said, noting the way her eyes grew large when he nodded toward the untitled *Deathly Hallows* poster of Harry and Voldemort facing off, "and the tales of Merlin, it's a different kind of magic. I don't actually speak

English. Mastery of language is a gift we're all born with in Atlantis. When I speak to a human, my tongue is automatically translated to something you can understand. Slang gets a little tricky, though, especially if I haven't visited a land in a long while. It's always changing, and words gain new meanings."

A computer desk and chair occupied one corner of the bedroom, a television set and futon close by. Sadie gestured him toward the latter and rolled the desk chair up. "Keep talking." Good. He still had her hooked.

"Kai just learned the language. Relearned it, rather. She was away from us so long she'd lost many of her gifts."

Sadie flexed her hand quietly, listening to him. He could tell from the way she moved it, and the lack of swelling, that she probably hadn't damaged it enough to require further care. "Is she happy?"

"I think so. She...your sister is an amazing person, and I consider myself fortunate to be in her service, Sadie. There are no words to express the regret that I have for how I took her from you both. But time wasn't on our side that evening. As I said, she was in tremendous danger."

"These things that want to hurt her. They're real? All of this is real?"

He nodded. "Every word."

"Then I guess...thank you for rescuing her that night. I don't have to like that she's gone, but it's better than her being dead."

Gaze dropping to her hand again, he nodded and held his out palm up. "May I?"

"Fine."

Once he had her smaller hand in his, he palpated the knuckles and felt for breaks. At most, he suspected a hairline fracture. "I expect it'll be fine, but you should ice it," he murmured, letting go. "You know, you throw an impressive right."

"Kai taught me."

"I'm not surprised. She hit me with one of those, too."

Sadie appeared delighted, her peal of laughter no doubt inspired by the grimace he exaggerated. "Did she almost break her hand, too?"

"On the contrary, she almost broke my face."

Her grin only widened. "Too bad I couldn't do the same."

THE AROMA of frying meat and garlic wafted to Manu before he made it downstairs, a delicious and savory smell permeating the entire lower floor of the two-story home. His stomach rumbled loud enough for Sadie to glance at him.

"What the hell do you people even eat? Tuna?"

"Among other things."

Giving him no chance to sneak out the door, Sunshine emerged from the kitchen with a towel in her hands. "Where do you think you're going?"

"Uh. Home?"

"No, you're not. Go sit down somewhere. Sadie, show Manu a movie while I finish dinner." As if sensing the protest on the tip of his tongue, she held out a hand. "Non-negotiable. Sit down, put your feet up, and watch a movie."

A devilish glint shone in Sadie's eyes.

Less than an hour later, Manu was sucked into the perils of Middle-earth with a plate balanced on his lap, Sunshine's daisy-themed dinnerware loaded with an assortment of what had to be the most delicious cuisine to ever touch his lips. Why were humans so angry and violent when they had access to the culinary delight of fried chicken and beer?

He'd never seen *The Lord of the Rings*, on account of disinterest, rather than inaccessibility. Frodo's tale had long ago made the cut, one of a small number of imported movies brought from the surface realm. Their government didn't like to bring too many, afraid of introducing too much human culture.

"This is one of Kai's favorite movies," Sadie told him. "Both sets are hers. We only saw *The Hobbit* trilogy in the theater, but we'd watch all six at least once a month together, sitting here on the couch with popcorn and pizza. Mom sat with us, too, most of the time, because she's a big fantasy lover and crazy about anything to do with magic. If there are witches involved, she's down for it."

"That's a nice tradition to have. I can understand why she favors them. Which is her favorite part?"

"We're not there yet. Her favorite from *this* one is coming up though."

"Brownies are in the oven," Sunshine called from the kitchen.

He ate those as well, wondering what the hell had just happened and if the two humans had cast some sort of addiction spell over him, because nothing, not even his sense of order and responsibility, could move him from the couch. He needed to know the fate of the two hobbits as much as he needed air. Or water. Or another drumstick from that endless pile of delicious, mouthwatering sin. Surface cuisine would be the end of him.

Kai called on the communicator during some point near the middle of the second film, having concluded her evening responsibilities in Atlantis. While the three women talked in another room, he stuffed his face with *more* fudge brownies.

No wonder Kai didn't want to leave the surface world behind. If he'd grown up with the *Lord of the Rings* and fudge, he would have held a grudge against whoever took him away from it too.

24

THE ACCORD

In the ruins of a sunken ship rotting two hundred leagues southwest of Atlantis, Calypso awaited intel vital to the success of her newest scheme. While it had been decades in the making, it may never have been possible to crush her enemies so thoroughly if not for the return of her nemesis's little brat. And what a brat she was; the inferior progeny of a nigh-unstoppable goddess, a weakling spawn unable to hold her own in battle and distrusted by the mers in authority.

Those imbeciles didn't understand the latent power Zephyrine commanded. Otherwise, they would have put the young princess in play at their first opportunity. Every second they hesitated to place her on the throne was to Calypso's benefit. But they were afraid, far too willing to ignore her existence and pray for a miracle from their goddess. And then there were some, like her Atlantian benefactor, who chose to offer the Gloom

Queen a fragile alliance. Even worse than the traitor who crawled to her, licking her figurative feet, were the idiot Loyalists hoping to depose the monarchy altogether.

Fucking marvelous. Those spineless worms would hand the kingdom to her on a coral platter.

Every delicious tidbit of news from Atlantis turned her ever more gleeful. Twenty-five years she'd waited to end the line of Thalassa, forced to take her victories in nibbles and bites, never able to satiate her appetite for vengeance. Now it was finally possible, Zephyrine's return presenting her with a golden opportunity to crush her enemies.

Calypso had sent her favorite daughter to the rendezvous with their confidante. Meeting them beyond the city would be a risky maneuver for their conspirator, but it was the safest method to avoid detection by inquisitive Myrmidons. After all, they'd come close too many times before.

A low voice stretched across the water, the caress of magic and spirit touching her consciousness. *He has arrived, Mother.*

Bring him to me.

Calypso swam down the dim ship's passage, propelled by the many dull gray tentacles replacing the lower half of her body. Her dark hair, once a magnificent mane of golden curls trailing down her naked spine, rested in brittle strands of dark green kelp against the tough barnacles covering her back. Strength and power beyond measure hadn't come without a cost; Phorkys and Keto's blessing had corroded her natural nymphly beauty, transforming and mutating her into something different.

Would she have made the same choice again if given the chance today? The question boggled her mind. Until now, the sacrifices had never felt worth it. Until now, she'd doubted she would ever take vengeance for the wrong committed against her.

Narkissa and their guest waited in a private cabin in the belly of the ship, hidden from eyes of Myrmidon patrols. Every so often since her arrival, she'd noticed the headlamps from their gliders in passing, or she felt the disturbances of their craft. If they knew she'd dared to come within the usual boundary, they'd have called in their forces at once. Not that they stood a chance of defeating her.

The Myrmidon in the cabin was a handsome creature with high cheek bones and full lips, silver and blue hair bound in shoulder-length braids floating around his gorgeous face. She coveted him at once, desiring him for a lover though the likelihood of ever having him was as great as her chances of walking on dry land. Impossible. Narkissa watched him too, pursing her dark lips and spiraling a dark strand of hair around her finger. The Gloom hadn't defiled the beauty of her daughters as greedily as it had taken Calypso's—after all, the price had been hers to pay.

He jerked his attention from Narkissa and bowed stiffly, placing one fist across his chest. "Greetings, Lady Calypso. I am Erasmus. As a show of good faith, I came in person as requested to deliver my master's message and to negotiate the terms of our continued alliance."

Calypso grinned, pleased when the mer didn't flinch from the sight of her teeth. Her cohort had sent her a strong one. A brave one. "And what does your master say?"

"We are willing to uphold our part of the bargain for the continued safety of Atlantis. You need only lay the trap that will lure your prey into the open, and we will do the rest."

She drifted around to his side and behind him, trailing her fingers over the shell cuirass covering his chiseled torso. He didn't flinch when she touched his face. "I find those terms acceptable, but perhaps we should seal the deal with a more...intimate arrangement."

His dark brows rose. "That was not part of our deal."

"It wasn't." Playing it safe, she disguised her disappointment and straightened, pushing her shoulders back as another scheme took root, of equal merit to her original plans. A better idea. If it could not be her, then it would be one of her dear daughters. "But long has it been since Atlantis has given me an offering."

His expression told her everything, the mask of polite indifference giving way to a grimace. And there died any hope she'd had of him seeing her as normal, as a woman once more. If this young and magnificent specimen of the Atlantian Royal Army chose to see her as a monster, what did it harm her to become one?

"I should like more children to do my bidding," Calypso pressed, "now that my dearest Desma is gone by the hands of your people. Pass my message along, or we have no deal." Of her three daughters, Desma had been the cleverest, the fiercest lieutenant of the Gloombeast legions and also the one most like her parents, a true force to be reckoned with.

Queen Ianthe had killed her.

"Lady Calypso, the arrangement has already been made—"

"Unfortunate," she hissed, drifting away. "Pass my demand to your master, or I may be forced to forget certain accords between us. It need not be you. Any strong mer of your Royal Army will suffice to conceive the child I desire." She stole a glimpse over her shoulder at him and watched, holding his gaze.

"A child," he repeated after a time, one of his gauntleted fists clenched at his side.

"Yes. Gifted as I may be by Keto and Phorkys, I am unable to conceive alone. The seed must be planted."

"There are few in my confidence I would trust with such an endeavor, my lady. Our numbers are too few, otherwise we risk discovery."

"Then it must be you, or dare your master come to me to do the deed himself?"

Erasmus said nothing, sullen reticence at odds with the proud mer who had met her gaze moments earlier.

"I thought so." Her path to the door continued, and she paused, feigning deep contemplation. "Or...perhaps one of my daughters would do."

"Which?" he asked in a quiet voice.

Hooked him. "Maybe Narkissa or—"

"Astraia will do," Narkissa cut in, smiling devilishly.

That, too, had been expected, for Narkissa was her favorite remaining daughter, but also too cunning and conniving to miss an opportunity to pass a burden to her sibling. "Very well. Find your sister. Tell her there's work to be done."

25

A TASTE OF THE FORBIDDEN

Of all the presents Kai had received since assuming her role as Princess of Atlantis, nothing surpassed the gift of seeing her family again. She spent the night talking to them, deferring her evening magic lessons with Cosmas until the next day because a couple of hours wasn't enough time to recount all of the unbelievable things that'd happened since her disappearance. Cosmas didn't mind. At least, he claimed he didn't mind, responding with a smile and kissing her forehead before he promised to return the next morning instead.

Surprising her none, Sunshine fed Manu and took him in overnight, refusing to let him embark on the journey back to Atlantis without rest. Kai expected nothing less. Anyone who entered the Queen residence was promptly treated like one of Sunshine's children.

That additional night Manu spent away from the

kingdom gave Kai time to plan and determine how to appropriately express her gratitude. Thankfully, Amerin had no shortage of ideas. Kai told a Myrmidon at the sea traffic control center to call her when Manu returned, then she bribed the master of keys to let her into his cottage. Not that bribery was necessary. As it was on royal property, just within the boundary of the palace grounds, no team of guards trailed behind her, and she had complete privacy.

Kai seriously missed her independence. She missed walking on the sidewalk alone without looking over her shoulder or needing someone to babysit her. She missed swimming in the ocean and sprawling across the sand unobserved. She missed a lot of things, but what she missed most of all had been returned to her. In a way.

Manu lived in a humble home, his living space barely large enough to entertain more than a handful of people, a pair of worn divans positioned opposite each other and a thin-paned televiewing screen mounted on the wall nearby. Nothing separated the room from the nearby dining nook and its round table.

Just after she wheeled the cart of ingredients and tools into the kitchen, something wet slapped against the floor, startling her. Kai jumped and whirled to see nothing.

Then a tentacle slid around her ankle, and if she'd had a spear in her hands, the poor critter crawling up her leg would have died an abrupt death.

"What the—? He has an octopus?" The creature

resembled a blue-ringed octopus, only much larger. From what she understood of their unique Atlantian physiology, most venoms and poisons didn't actually hurt them.

So Kai risked leaning down and accepting it onto her arm. It slid around her wrist and eyed her. "Hello there, pretty one. Do you belong to Manu?"

Something resonated in her thoughts that sounded like a 'yes'. It missed its daddy, which only endeared Manu to her even more, knowing that he could have an adorable little creature at home who *loved* him the way this animal did. The fondness for its owner just ebbed out from it like the tide.

"Aw, you're so cute. Well, he's going to be home today. Let's go make him a dinner together, okay?"

She cooed over the nameless octopus, who clung fearlessly to her shoulder the entire time she made dinner preparations. It never left her side.

Thanking whichever god was listening that ovens in Atlantis operated similarly to their surface counterparts, she followed Amerin's instructions and did as she'd practiced in the castle, whipping a chocolate batter by hand while awaiting Manu's arrival. He'd be storing his glider, checking into the barracks to report his return, and slowly wending his way back home. One of the watchmen at the barracks called and tipped her off as she removed the pan of oven-fried chicken. She set it in a warmer she'd borrowed from the palace kitchen.

Kai wondered what the chefs thought of her unusual desire to cook.

"Awesome. Tell Commander Loto it's time to initiate Operation Chum Bucket. Delay him as long as you can. I need another thirty minutes."

The Myrmidon chuckled. Kai had yet to ask how, but she'd discovered weeks ago that even Atlantians knew about *SpongeBob SquarePants*. It must have aired on one of their channels. She'd had no time to really enjoy their handful of networks. TV just wasn't a huge thing in their realm. "As you wish, Your Highness."

The guy's best happened to be another thirty-five minutes, just enough time to mash the potatoes and make a delicious chicken gravy. When Manu stepped into his home, looking ragged and exhausted, one hand on the shaft of his collapsible trident, she met him with a big smile.

"Hey, stranger. Long time, no see."

He met her greeting with a bewildered, "What are you doing in my house?" Seconds passed until common sense broke through the confusion, and he corrected himself. "Good evening, Your Highness." His gaze darted to the octopus on her shoulder. If he disapproved, he said nothing.

"Good evening. I hope you're hungry."

"You're cooking for me?"

"Uh huh. Figured I'd recreate the meal my mother made for you. She mentioned feeding you that first night." She grinned at him and wiped her hands on a kitchen towel. "And she also revealed you're a fan of chocolate fudge brownies. It took more work than you'd want to believe to gather the ingredients here, but I managed it." She'd had three days of advance notice of his fondness for it, put in the proper requests with their importers, and paid a considerable sum for a rush order. As flour, chicken, and other ingredients weren't items native to Atlantis, they'd come from Spain.

"Go and sit down, or do whatever you need to do to unwind."

Manu lingered in the middle of the floor, studying her. As often as he took care of her, protected others, and guarded the kingdom, she wondered if anyone had ever returned the favor for him, or if his entire life had been sacrifice and service. "A shower would be nice," he muttered.

"Go ahead. I'll pull dessert out of the oven soon."

WHEN MANU STEPPED INSIDE, he'd planned to order supper, stuff his face, and collapse across the bed until morning, when he'd no doubt report for duty as usual. Instead, the most beautiful sight in the world greeted him—dinner served by a sexy woman.

Princess Kailani wore a fancy apron over a high-necked dress that tied behind her neck and exposed her back, fitted until the skirt flared out over her hips and glided behind her across the floor. The red looked good against her skin, contrasting the gold-scale thigh-high boots beneath. Fuck, he had been salivating before his mind even processed the savory aroma of poultry filling his quaint cottage.

And she'd somehow bewitched his fucking octopus. Launa never liked anyone, and had especially loathed Calanthe, trying to strangle his ex in her sleep once.

Not a sign. This doesn't mean anything.

As Kai needed more time to complete her preparations, he let her be and entered the bathroom where he stood beneath the water until he felt alive again, and less like a compressed ball of tension. Nothing felt better than fifteen minutes of steaming hot water after a two-day drive in a cramped coral glider. Of course, stopping only for fuel had shaved a full day off his travel time, returning him to Atlantis ahead of schedule.

He should have been home over an hour ago, but the moment he stepped onto the docks, a deluge of eelshit began. First, Loto called him to his office to discuss eelshit any other commander could have handled. Then, Cosmas caught him in the hall, wondering when they'd go out again to make up for the ruined night out. After that, a grunt at the coral glider depot claimed he hadn't logged out of the system, recalling him back to the machine.

Returning to the living room treated Manu to the sight of Kai setting two plates on the small table. She beamed at him while pouring white wine into his cheap glasses. Her pours were definitely on the generous side. "Your friend abandoned me."

"Yeah, she's in her tank again."

"Oh. Well. She's really pretty. What's her name?"

"Launa." He'd had Launa since he was a boy, one of the last gifts he'd ever received from his mother. At the time, his father had been fiercely against him having any kind of pet, but Malie had ignored his wishes and caved to Manu's pleas, buying him the creature during a visit to see relatives in Pacifica.

"She kept me company while I cooked." Kai gestured to the dinner spread. "All finished."

"That looks amazing," he said, not sure if he meant her or the dinner. She'd prepared crispy drumsticks, garlic asparagus, and creamy mashed potatoes, things that must have been staples growing up in Sunshine's home. His belly growled aggressively with hunger. Fuck. That looked outstanding. And expensive. None of those things grew in Atlantis, and chickens were a pricy delicacy only the wealthy could afford.

"Do you not have a shirt?"

He blinked at her, jerked out of his appreciation for the food. "Uh, not when I'm at home. You told me to get comfortable."

"Oh." Kai skated her teeth over her lower lip. "Well. Have a seat."

Not yet accustomed to the paradox of a princess serving his dinner, Manu sat opposite her and ate his weight in chicken legs while she regaled him with chatter about her riding lessons with Cosmas. As he demolished a second serving of asparagus and mashed potatoes, Kai popped over to the counter to fetch another bottle of wine.

"I think I prefer sharks over dolphins. Dunno

why yet. Of course, Perseus was a real blowhole and tossed me off him *three* times before I caught on that he was trying to intimidate me. He's so smart, Manu. I've always thought sharks were beautiful, but I love his pattern. He looks like a tiger."

He watched her work the cork out, lean and toned arms flexing as she pulled it free. The wine looked pricier than the chicken dinner, a dark bottle of red she'd likely nicked from the palace cellar.

"Since I'm free from lessons tomorrow, I figured it wouldn't hurt to cut loose a little."

"Princess Kailani?"

"Hm?"

"What is all of this about?"

"The wine is going to be amazing with the brownies, I think," she said, pouring two big glasses.

"Your Highness?"

She nibbled one and sipped her wine. "Yup. I was totally right—"

"Princess Kailani," he growled out, rising from the seat and dropping both palms on the table. "I'm not one to complain about a gorgeous woman making me a meal, but what in the name of Styx is going on here?"

She froze, and her smile wavered. "I didn't know any other way to thank you for what you did. You gave my family back to me. You didn't have to drive to Texas to hand-deliver a magical fucking videophone to my mom, but you did it without me asking. Without wanting anything in return."

His mind drifted back to the gold starfish. Unable

to bear eating both of them, he'd placed them in a tank in his bedroom and kept the delicate critters as pets.

When he didn't respond, she collected the dirty plates and hurried them into the kitchen, placing both in the sink. "Anyway, I should leave you to rest. You've been on the...sea-road, or whatever you call it, for a long time. Enjoy the brownies, Manu."

Kai got as far as the door before he found the nerve to dig deeper. "Your Highness?"

She glanced over a bare shoulder at him, hand on the door handle. "Yes?"

"I never thanked you for the gold starfish sent to my office, but something needs to be addressed. Do you understand the significance of them?"

A shy smile touched her lips. "You're welcome. And yes, I think so. Amerin called them a gift of friendship among the Pacificans. I mean, I do consider you a friend. A *good* friend."

A good friend. If he read between the lines, he could take it a few different ways. Though his dick wanted to take it down a dark and dirty road that ended with both of them in bed, sheets twisted around their naked legs. "It's more than that." He hesitated, reluctant to embarrass her, but positive her handmaiden had stuck her nose where it didn't belong.

"Oh?" A slight furrow creased her brow. "Then what is it?"

He stepped closer, crossing the living room floor, aware of how much the mere memory of her gift aroused him. "Golden starfish are what my people gift to lovers or mers they plan to take as lovers, Your Highness. It's an offer of sex. And depending on the relationship between those mers, it's an admission of *love*."

"Oh." She didn't break eye contact as she stepped toward him, cheeks rosy and flushed with mutual arousal he'd somehow missed. Fuck, he could smell her need, and she wasn't freaking out about the message.

Something very wrong was happening, and hell if he knew what to do about it.

"What...is happening here?" he asked slowly.

"I don't know." She placed one palm against his chest. She didn't have to tilt her head far to make eye contact, standing only three inches shorter, taller than most other female mers. "I..." Her breath quickened, pupils blown, with a narrow ring of chocolate brown color surrounding them. "Manu..."

He thought they both moved at once, but he couldn't be sure. One moment, he was studying her face and wondering how soon before he surrendered to his baser urges. In the next, one arm was around her waist, and she moved in against him of her own volition, silky skin scented like lilies and plum blossoms.

His self-control disintegrated.

Chocolate and wine flavored her tongue, lips soft and pliable beneath his mouth. Even as he came to his senses and tried to draw back, Kai laced her fingers through his hair to anchor him in place.

He never wanted to stop kissing her, wanted to hold her in his arms forever. He crushed her closer, swallowing her low moan when he squeezed a handful of her ass. Her hips nudged forward, grinding against him. The moment she gasped in surprise, he knew that she felt his hardening cock. Every inch was throbbing for her—his princess, his future queen.

Manu surrendered to the taste of her, the heat of her tongue, the way her nipples tightened pebble-hard through the thin silk, their stiffened tips brushing against his chest. Weeks of urgent need flooded to the surface as his mouth traced an invisible path from her lips to her bare shoulder. He nipped, found her throat, and relished the way she tipped her head back. Then he almost lost his mind the moment her hand slid between them and fumbled for the laces on his trousers, eager to free his cock.

Nothing in all of the underwater world could have prepared him for the moment her bare fingers touched his naked shaft. Sensation sizzled down his nerve endings and tightened in his balls. He could have come right then if not for the mantra he chanted to his inner self not to shoot like a school-age boy.

Holding him in her fist, her fingers slid up and down until he involuntarily thrust in her grasp, fucking her fingers the way he wanted to claim her body. His princess stroked him expertly, squeezing and sizing him up with her fingers. His cock was an iron bar, throbbing so hard it hurt.

He wanted to be inside her, *needed* to be inside

her. He pulled at her skirts, hiking them up until they bunched around her waist and those lovely, naked thighs were against the trousers sliding down his legs. Just one thrust, one moment, and she could be his.

It was wrong, so painfully, deliciously wrong. Painful because he knew he needed to stop, delicious whenever her thumb flicked over the tip of his cock and swirled over the satiny skin. He shuddered against her, claiming her mouth again with raw hunger.

As much as he wanted her, as much as he wanted to carry forward, one night with Kailani wasn't worth potential imprisonment in the Royal Jail for defiling a princess.

Kai wasn't wearing undergarments. The fight against his conscience and self-preservation raged again, flaring up like gasoline-fed flames. He held her warm cheeks in his hands, knowing if he moved his palm a few inches, his fingers would be delving between her strong thighs. Nothing less than Herculean effort provided the willpower to drag his lips away from her hungry mouth. "We can't do this."

Her husky chuckle tickled against his cheek. "Do we need the mer equivalent of a condom or something?" She paused before asking, "*Are* there condoms here?"

"No. I mean that this can't happen." Though it ripped his heart in two, he dropped her dress and hauled up his trousers, concealing himself from her. He stepped away. "I didn't mean to do that. For it to go so far."

Her gaze darkened with confusion, a crease deepening between her brows. "I thought...you seemed to be into me."

Into her? He was all about her, he wanted nothing more than her, just to hold her in his arms for a night and kiss away the frown dragging down the corners of her mouth. He wanted to pledge his life to her as more than a soldier in the Royal Guard.

But she was not meant for him, a mere warrior.

"You're the princess. This can't happen between us. You belong to—"

"Don't you dare start that again. I know how Atlantian law works. I'm not bound to anyone, I don't belong to anyone! It's so stupid. I never asked for this."

"It is stupid," he agreed in a quiet voice. "But it's tradition, and this can never happen again, Your Highness. I'm sorry. The law forbids it."

"Don't worry about it."

"The law—"

"I understand." Then Kai opened the door and marched outside, shutting the door behind her.

KAI LEFT EVERYTHING BEHIND, including the equipment she'd promised to return to Cook. Between the humiliation of Manu's rejection and the creeping realization that she'd abandoned her best-ever batch of brownies, the night was inarguably a failure.

The taste of him was still on her lips, and she couldn't stop thinking about holding his shaft in her hand. Just a few seconds longer, and the hottest merman in all of Atlantis would have been hers for at least a night, if not for their antiquated traditions. Instead of scratching an itch, she'd only amped her curiosity higher.

Damn him. Like she would have ever uttered a word to anyone. Didn't he trust her?

She walked the Royal Plaza for a time, lingering at the park, where passers-by glanced at her but didn't intrude on her privacy, then eventually wound her way back to the palace.

Amerin greeted her at the door of her suite, bubbling over with anticipation. "Well? How did he like the dinner?"

"He liked it."

"That tells me absolutely nothing, Kai. Did—" Then she cut herself short, gazing at Kai with compassionate eyes. "It didn't go well."

"It went well until the end. I feel like a dumbass. I made a pass at him like you suggested, and everything went to shit."

"Why?"

"As far as Commander Manu is concerned, I am firmly the property of Cosmas and too far above his station."

"I was positive he..." Amerin sighed. "He took the gold starfish."

"Yeah, about that." Kai said in a quiet voice.

"Next time you want to help me with my sex life, Amerin? Don't. It sucks enough on its own."

Then she crossed to her room, stripped out of her pretty dress, and crawled into bed to wonder what the hell would happen next.

26

PERSEVERANCE

A HIGH-VELOCITY ARC OF WATER RACED THROUGH the air with the force of a firefighter's hose, striking Kai in the chest and thrusting her back. She stumbled two steps until she reached down deep and found the font of divine strength supposedly imbued in all children of Thalassa. It still hurt. Still stung her skin, feeling like it was peeling it away layer by layer. She gritted her teeth against the force and put up both arms to shield herself, but it battered her, forcing her back, damned near turning her end over end onto her ass.

Kai tumbled onto the shore and received a mouthful of sand. "Fish sticks!"

The onslaught stopped abruptly. Spitting sand, chest still heaving, she pushed up onto her hands and knees to stare at the mer standing opposite her on the sandy shore. Cosmas had brought her to one of many nameless, uncharted islands. A week of the sweltering sun had turned her skin dark brown.

"Kai?" Cosmas finally said.

"I know, I know. That was eelshit."

"I wouldn't call it eelshit," he muttered, though she thought he was far too polite for his own good, considering her poor performance. "Seriously though, Kai. You're not that awful, but you are distracted. Why are you using your hands when you have a shield? I never said you're not permitted to use it. The object of this lesson is for you to deflect it, no matter the tool you use."

"Uh."

"As I said, you're distracted. What's wrong?"

He'd pummeled her into the sand twice already using a funnel of water channeled from the shoreline itself. Kai was supposed to deflect it, but Cosmas did not take pity upon her. That was a point in his favor, reminding her of Manu. Manu, who hadn't been alone with her since that train wreck of a dinner.

A bundle of Kai's belongings from Galveston—packed lovingly by Sadie, to include many of her favorite books, outfits, and even a scrapbook—had arrived the following morning, delivered by a young Myrmidon. Apparently, Manu couldn't bear to see her alone, or in person. After that, lessons with him took on a painfully professional tone. He didn't appear unless Cosmas was present, and had she not seen the two of them joking one afternoon while awaiting her arrival, she would have thought Manu spilled the beans and his pal held it against him. He didn't. As far as she could tell, Cosmas didn't have a clue about what took place, and maybe it was for the best, despite Amerin swearing up and down no such thing as cheating occurred until there was a bond or marriage in place.

In their society, tradition expected young mers to explore their options. It made her wonder how they could be so progressive in some areas, while horribly behind in others.

The dates with Cosmas went on, as did their magic lessons; her combat training with Manu tapering off until she saw him twice a week. Other commanders filled the gap. She'd trained using martial weapons with Loto and learned emergency medicine from Elpis.

"Nothing is wrong."

He cocked a brow then crossed his muscular arms over his chest. He wore metal-reinforced shell armor and the usual leggings, a dazzling blue-green from some mystical beast imported from the Pacific deep. "You're an awful liar. I want you to know that. You have this thing you do where you cut your eyes away for a few seconds. Makes it very obvious."

"I don't." Except Sunshine had always known when she was fibbing as a child because...dammit. He'd caught on quickly.

"All right. I can't make you speak with me, but I am here if you need me. Are you ready to resume?"

"Ready."

Their training picked up again, though this time she whirled to the side and ducked beneath the immense spray, rolling her shield from her back onto her arm. Water crashed against the glossy construct of metal and tortoiseshell, creating a high-pressure jet.

Cosmas put more magic into it. Harder, forcing her to lean her body against it and change her center of balance, booted feet sliding on sand and barely able to find purchase.

"Don't give up!" he called.

She envied him for even being able to speak while channeling so much magic.

Her hamstrings and calves cried out for respite before she made it halfway to him, crossing the most arduous twenty meters of her life. Her arm shook.

In Atlantis, when she'd put out the fire in the Coral Spire, she'd pulled the moisture from the air, condensing it into a single hard stream. The water channeled by Cosmas resisted her efforts to take control of it, too slippery for her thoughts to command.

"You're almost here, Kai. Come on! There are merchildren able to withstand this! Or maybe we should give up and let Aegaeon keep the thro—"

Like Manu, he knew how to make it sting. Determination pressed her forward and she threw her weight into it, leading with the shield to deflect the oncoming stream of water to the ocean. In the split-second that followed, she bashed the curved face of the shield into her tutor's chest, driving him back onto his ass. Light exploded from the point of contact, flashing over the island and sending energy rippling over the waves, blowing her hair back from her face.

Kai became aware of two things at that moment.

One, the water assault ended, a stream of waves landing with a splash into the greater body of the Atlantic again. Two, Cosmas was sprawled out on the wet sand with an enormous fissure down the center of his armor. He groaned, then went still.

Gods. She'd killed him. She'd killed her teacher.

Kai tossed the shield aside and fell to her knees beside him, touching the deep split in the hard armor. "I'm sorry! Are you all right? Cosmas? Cosmas?" Helplessly, she glanced around for aid. A small squad of cavalrymen had accompanied them as part of her official escort, but they weren't watching her training, ordered to remain underwater until it was time to leave.

"I'm sorry. I don't know what happened, I thought—"

"I'm fine," he wheezed. "Moment."

A few of the Myrmidons emerged from the waves, no doubt wondering what the hell happened.

"Commander?"

Cosmas made a weak gesture with one hand. One man raised a dubious eyebrow but sank into the water again. The second hesitated, then followed suit. The third lingered, no doubt prepared to carry gossip back to his companions.

"I'm sorry."

"It's fine. That was...godsdamn, that was spectacular."

"But I hurt you."

"Yeah, well, I put you up to it." He crawled to his feet, glanced at his chest, and then flashed her a weak grin. "For my own safety, I'm going to call it for today."

"What the hell just happened?"

"Your divine gifts are awakening, as Hipponax anticipated. The longer you remain in Atlantis and the more you work with your talents, the more powerful they will become. You're only five generations removed from Thalassa and Pontus, Kai. The rest of us were made in their image, but we'll never have the same gift you've inherited by blood."

"Doesn't it get diluted with each generation? I mean, technically that means I'll never be as strong as my mother."

"That isn't how it works. It's strange, I know, but supposedly godly powers are indivisible as long as the predecessor passes on their gift. Part of her, and your mother's power, lives on in you and will always be with you. At least, that's how the old man says it. That old fart has been around since the time of your grandmother. You may be overdue for a meeting with him."

Kai blinked. "That makes him hundreds of years old, doesn't it?"

"Yes." Cosmas touched his chest, wincing. "Let's return to the city. Dinner?"

"My treat at the palace?"

"Sure."

Cosmas arrived late to their dinner, smiling

sheepishly at her when he approached the small table for two. "Apologies, Kai."

"No need to apologize. Are you okay?"

"You cracked a rib."

Guilt sank her good mood like the Titanic. "Gods. I'm so sorry. I didn't mean—"

"It's okay." He held up a hand. "We've spent three months coaxing these gifts out of you. I'm not going to accept apologies from you when we finally succeeded at getting what we want. Rage seems to be your thing. You don't like being told what you can't do."

"Never have."

His crooked grin lifted some of the weight from her heart. "You need to take that feeling and channel it. Put it to good use."

When the first course of their dinner arrived, the conversation fell away. Kai applied herself to her soup and salad, wondering what other powers lay untapped and undiscovered inside her. It was difficult to believe that three months ago, she'd been a normal woman, unsuccessfully seeking employment in a busy city. She'd had one job prospect, working at Moody Gardens Aquarium. Right now, she should be testing the pH of marine aquarium water or tending to sea horses in a hatchery.

Now she swam with sea horses through pristine ocean water far below the muck polluted by man.

"Did I lose you?"

Kai snapped out of it, blinking at her dinner partner. "No. Sorry. Was thinking of how things had changed."

"Ah." He tilted his head, dark hair spilling over one shoulder. He'd exchanged his broken armor for a gold-trimmed red tunic of some sort in the old-fashioned Greek style with a contrasting, royal blue cape thrown over his shoulders. Clothing in Atlantis tended to be modernized versions of the ancient styles, though she'd also seen garments inspired by topside fashion. "Are you feeling better about what troubled you earlier?"

"No."

He didn't press her. Another course came out, urchin sashimi and bubbly sea grass. She picked at her food and sighed.

"I think Manu is upset with me. You're a great trainer, but..."

The consternation on his face softened. "You miss his company. Ah, Kai, why didn't you say so?"

"I thought..." She glanced down at her plate, feeling childish and silly. Men on the surface—at least the ones in her romantic acquaintance—didn't compare to the males in Atlantis. "I didn't want to upset you by pining for another guy."

He barked out a laugh, then winced and held his chest. "No, love. Manu is your friend. Hell, he's my friend, too. I noticed he's been distant lately, but I imagined it had something to do with personal matters."

"Personal matters?"

"Not my business to discuss," he said quickly. "If he wants to mention it to you, he will."

"How can he, when he avoids me?"

"He isn't avoiding you."

"He was supposed to be topside with us today but he never showed."

Dark brows jumped up. "Far from it. He's occupied with some other matters. General Lago tasked him with investigating a recent Gloombeast sighting to the southwest. He's leading a fireteam that way. We tend to send the artillery units in their coral skippers and whale thumpers to investigate those matters. They're faster, and they're protected from the corruption when they're in gliders. Don't need filtration masks to avoid breathing in poisonous octopus ink."

"Oh. I have another question. You're both commanders, but you're always out leading squads instead of delegating the task to your captains or lieutenants. Why?"

"Manu likes to take a hands-on approach to our duties." Cosmas shrugged. "I suppose I picked up the habit from him. Most of us do. Besides, one must lead by example. We command numerous patrol squads in this ocean at any given time, and also oversee additional training to the dozens of ports across the Atlantic."

"It sounds like you overwork yourselves."

"What else are we to do with our free time?"

Feeling silly, she stuffed a piece of tender urchin into her mouth. "Never mind me, then."

Before she could finish her bite, Cosmas reached

over the table and took her hand, gazing at her with compassion-filled eyes. "Back to the original topic at hand: I'm not the sort to become jealous over a friendship, Kai. Nor are most men of Atlantis. You're a free woman until you're bound by an engagement. Remember that."

"I know. Amerin reminded me."

"However..." He reached into the pouch hanging from his belt, and she knew without a doubt before he came up with the clam shell that she wouldn't like what happened next.

Cosmas left his seat, and he knelt beside the table.

There wasn't a servant left in the room. She didn't notice when they all slipped out, but the spacious chamber suddenly felt tiny, suffocating.

"I don't need to court you longer than I already have to know I couldn't be happier as your husband and king, Kai. Will you do me the honor?"

What else could she do but say yes when the entire kingdom counted on her?

27

TO THE END

*T*HE FIELDS...

Kai jerked awake for the fifth time that night. Despite the comfort of her bed, she'd spent most of the night staring at the ceiling with a dozen thoughts fighting for dominance in her brain.

Could she become the queen they needed?

What would it be like to marry Cosmas, a man she didn't love or feel even a hint of attraction for? They hadn't so much as kissed, and she felt no pressing urgency to try it.

It felt wrong and untrue, like she was cheating on the spirit of the relationship she could have with Manu if the rigid traditions of their society didn't dictate he run like an asshole from her to protect his neck from the guillotine. She didn't think Aegaeon would jail him or pursue execution, but he had a legitimate fear of losing everything he'd worked his entire career to achieve.

And she couldn't take that from him. Fate had

been against them from the start, but what bothered her the most was that they hadn't even had a chance to see where it would go—if they could mesh and whether they belonged together.

More importantly, Kai wondered if she'd become powerful enough to overcome the Gloom. Each day she dwelled upon the matter made her wonder how she could ever hope to defeat a goddess twisted by hate and envy, a goddess with centuries of time to plot the demise of their city.

Those and so many other concerns flooded her mind until she surrendered to her subconscious and crawled from bed.

The fields...

The whisper crept into her thoughts again, though it could have been a figment of her imagination, or the rustle of the breeze blowing through her curtains. She didn't understand how it worked on a magical level, but Aegaeon had explained it once. Oxygen exchange occurred somehow, the ocean current passing through the barrier—which wasn't actual glass at all—and sending wind currents over Atlantis.

Kai heated water for tea with a kettle enchanted to boil water when placed on its matching slate tile. Cosmas had brought her samples of his favorite loose leaf blends, so she brewed a kettle of seaweed-infused green tea and settled on the balcony off her solarium overlooking the city. Even at the early hour of three in the morning Atlantian time, the world continued to move down below in the city that never slept.

It made her miss New York, for the one time she'd visited Manhattan with friends years ago. They'd been stationed in Norfolk and had a weekend to themselves, so they drove northeast over the terrifying Delaware Memorial Bridge and spent six hours in a crowded sedan because one of the ladies had been invited to a party.

Had Kai been recalled for any reason to their base, she'd have been up shit's creek, but they'd just returned from a long deployment and had been desperate to dance the night away on dry land. They'd also shopped far too much. Kai remembered splurging and spending two grand during that weekend, then wondering what the hell happened when she looked at her bank account later.

Still, she wouldn't take it back. The only regret she did have was never keeping in touch with those girls after her discharge. Most of them chose to stay in. She hadn't. She'd missed home, missed her family, and wanted to get a college education.

Kai sipped her tea, musing over her past and how much of it had been worthless, wondering if any of it impacted her now. Yes, she decided. Everything she'd done, every class she took, every day she served, all added up to the woman she'd become, and she wouldn't take any of it back. None of it. All of those experiences made her.

The kettle yielded three cups of tea, all of which she sipped while watching distant coral gliders and tiny pedestrian dots. She couldn't get the damned Fields of Gold out of her mind and contemplated visiting them. It was a twenty-minute swim at the most.

Refusing to wake Amerin over something as simple as squeezing into her suit, she dragged shark-skin over her lower body. The first time she'd dressed on her own, it took almost twenty minutes to stretch out all the wrinkles and force the form-fitting material to obey.

It came on easier this time, broken in to her shape.

Kai made it as far as the guard post at the city gates before she encountered resistance.

"I don't know...we should contact Commander Cosmas. We were told you're not to leave the city without an escort, Your Highness," a stoic-faced guardsman told her. His gaze drifted to the armband above her elbow.

Mers did not trade rings, as they slipped from wet fingers and were easily lost in the water. Instead, they gave their betrothed elaborate bands, chokers, or even belts carved from shells, jewels, and precious metals charmed to resist oxidation. Hers was pretty and pink, decorated with flowers carved from shells.

"Right, but they were all asleep. Can't one of you come with me? I'm not going far."

"Definitely not. As great an honor as it would be to swim by your side, only the designated mers can serve as your personal guard. They were all hand-chosen by Commanders Manu and Cosmas."

"You're not serious."

"Quite serious, Princess Kailani."

One of them got on a communicator just out of her earshot, and she remained there, feeling like a naughty child under their watch, until Cosmas arrived about fifteen minutes later. He looked smug and altogether too satisfied for a man dragged out of bed in the middle of the night.

"I'm told you made an escape attempt."

Kai rolled her eyes. "It's not that dramatic. I didn't try to creep past them or anything. I presented myself at the gate and said where I'd like to go. Even asked for one of them to come with me because I knew you and Manu would lose your shit if I left the city alone."

"I have better bowel control than that."

Kai stared at him, unamused.

He merely grinned, reminding her too much of Manu. No wonder the two were goddamn friends, because they both delighted far too much in making fun of her. "If you're going to make that face at me, I may change my mind about accompanying you."

"Am I a child, to be babysat now at all hours of the day and night?"

"No, but you're our princess, and you mean something to me. I won't force my company on you, but as a fellow insomniac, I'd like to join you."

Kai sighed. "Well, when you put it that way...maybe."

"I'll introduce you to Leilei."

"Who's Leilei?"

"You'll only find out if you become my companion."

"Fine."

"Excellent, so where are we going?"

"The Fields of Gold. I picked starfish with Amerin there two days ago, and I can't get the place off my mind. It's like—ugh." She pursed her lips, unable to describe why she awakened with a desire to see the starfish. "I don't know."

Cosmas canted his head. "A stop at the armory then."

"Seriously? We're only going for a walk."

"A swim, technically. No Myrmidon leaves the city limits unarmed."

"Manu does."

"Trust me, Manu is always armed. You simply haven't seen the weapon."

LEILEI TURNED out to be a gorgeous Atlantic dusk-tip, a navy-skinned shark bred for agility, with bright purple and pink spots on her caudal and her long pectoral fins. They reminded Kai of a sky at twilight, and she had to be the most beautiful creature Kai had seen since her arrival. Her turquoise eyes and her markings glowed like starlight.

She was also quite the attention whore and swam back and forth, letting Kai stroke her sides and rub her nose, behaving more like a water puppy than one thousand pounds of ferocious underwater beast.

"Cosmas, she's *beautiful*." The man's talent for riding sharks reminded her of an aquatic Cesar

Milan, somehow owning over a dozen animals of five different breeds. She'd visited his farm outside of the city where he owned a few hundred acres of fenced, magically compartmentalized water, granting each animal territory and freedom to be sharks. Prey could enter and exit, but the sharks couldn't, and she suspected even if they could, none would leave because they loved their daddy, and when he was present, they didn't fight amongst themselves. "She's definitely the most gorgeous you've shown me."

"I'm glad you think so, considering she's yours."

Kai stared. "What?"

"She's yours. Manu chose her from the rider program for you, but I wasn't sure until now whether the two of you would mesh." A big grin stretched across his face from ear to ear. "Seems she likes you."

"Manu chose her?"

"Yes. He asked me yesterday if I'd introduce both of you. I planned to fetch you in the morning to bring you to the stables, but we're both awake, so." He shrugged.

"I thought..." Thought he hated her. She hadn't thought it possible three months ago, but she missed his company and had decided that, even though Atlantians didn't celebrate Christmas, the only gift she wished for herself, was for her friend to talk to her again.

"We'll speak later about this issue with Manu. For now, come on." He nodded toward Leilei. "Remember how to saddle up?"

"I think so."

On a shark of Leilei's size and build, saddle design required the rider to sit before the dorsal fin, leaning forward. Cosmas only had to correct her once when she incorrectly looped the excess girth. That went behind the pectoral fins. She found shark riding oddly similar to horseback riding. The motions differed, more natural underwater. Sharks had no gait, instead cruising smooth as glass through the currents.

Since he wanted Kai to begin bonding with her new friend, Cosmas swam alongside them, pulling off an Olympic-worthy dolphin kick Lochte or Phelps would have envied. Leilei had a lot of energy, and she wondered if her smaller size was relative to her age. Some of the other battle sharks were massive monsters almost twice her length. Every mile or so, she had to cue the shark to slow down before they left Cosmas behind in their wake. Not that her concern was necessary. The third time Leilei bolted, Kai glanced to her right and found Cosmas keeping pace beside her, cruising through the water with a sleek shark tail.

"About time!"

"About time what?"

"You've never brought out a tail before."

He chuckled. "Not often a reason to show off, but I figured we should give the little lady what she wants. Care for a race?"

"A race? Dude, I'm on a fucking shark. You won't keep up."

"Precisely. She's your shark, and she's faster than

me. Your job, and your only job right now, is to tail me. Consider this our next lesson. You'll have to control her and her speed. Think you can do that?"

Giving her no chance to decline his challenge, Cosmas darted into the lead, leaving her in his wake. Not about to accept defeat, she and Leilei gave chase, racing alongside him and pulling into the lead.

"You're failing, Kai!" Cosmas shouted. "Remember the terms of the race!"

Curbing Leilei was easier said than done, her mind young, enthusiastic, and playful. She wanted to impress her rider. Kai coaxed her to slow down, pitting her consciousness against the filly's until she obeyed.

The first time Cosmas stopped and Kai had to put the brakes on her mount, Leilei resisted her, an echo of thought reverberating through her mind.

Her shark wanted to speed against Cosmas in a true race.

No, Kai thought at her, deciding to be stunned later, much, much later, about actually hearing the little voice inside her own thoughts. *It isn't yet time to go fast.*

Go fast!

Despite urging Leilei to decelerate, the creature twisted into a tight circle, pulling off a maneuver that almost wrenched Kai from the saddle. She held on and dropped her heels, tightening with her thighs, refusing to be thrown.

"Shit!" Cosmas swore, knocked aside by the powerful tail. "Are you all right?"

"I'm fine!" she shouted despite Leilei taking her on a ride, like an aquatic bronco with something to prove at the rodeo.

"Back out of her thoughts, I'll take con—"

"No! I have her."

"You most certainly do not. Kai, she can hurt you."

"I have her!" she insisted, queasy from the motion of whipping left and right, turning tight figure-eights.

Gripping the reins so tightly her nails buried in her palms, Kai gritted her teeth and hurled her next thought with all of the mental energy she possessed. *Leilei, you will obey me now! There will be a time for fun, but this isn't it. Listen to me now, or we won't go out again. I'll take another shark next time. Do you want that?*

Silence. The underwater acrobatics slowed.

You don't want that do you? I want us to have so much fun together, but to do that, you have to listen to me. Do you want to hurt me?

No.

Then listen. Be a good girl, Leilei, then we'll be able to have all the fun later.

Drifting back from them and watching the entire exchange, Cosmas rubbed his face where the tail had struck him, his cheek already showing signs of a bruise.

"Are *you* all right?" she asked him.

"Nothing but my pride is damaged." Slanting a skeptical look at Leilei, he moved into the lead again. The algae mound bordering the field was already in view. "That was very well done, by the way. I didn't think you'd be able to control her, but you did."

"She's like a child. Most children don't want you to be disappointed in them. How old is she?" Kai asked, cresting the hill overlooking the Fields of Gold.

"Two years old. A young one compared to most others at the breeder's. Why?"

"Curious. She's a little..."

"Playful? Yes." He chuckled. "Manu thought her persona complemented yours."

Kai glanced at him, feeling skeptical. Manu had thought about her quite a bit for a man who had practically fired her from their friendship. "He did, did he?"

"He did. Goddess's honest truth."

"Hm. Why aren't you on Perseus?"

"He'd only distract Leilei. A first swim between a rider and their shark should be with minimal interference," he explained. "And my presence here is enough. I thought it would be better for her to give you one hundred percent of her focus, and it seems I was right."

"Ah."

The stretch of starfish-speckled ocean floor was prettier than ever. A synchronized smack of fuchsia bioluminescent jellies passed above it, their number no less than five dozen. The many undiscovered ocean creatures never failed to amaze her.

After admiring the departing group for a time, Kai slipped from Leilei's back and touched down on the sandy bottom, cautious due to the sinkholes Amerin had mentioned.

"They're certainly hauling ass," Cosmas muttered, regaining his legs. "Must be a predator nearby."

"What are their main predators in this area? Other jellies? Turtles?"

"Doomlantern jellies can suck in about a dozen of them at once, if not more. Quite a sight to see."

"Doomlantern?"

"Yep. Not something you'd be familiar with on the surface, as they're native to these waters and only spawn near Atlantis. Roughly the size of a bed sheet." Kai stared, but he only grinned wider and continued. "They were almost hunted to extinction a few decades back until your mother forbade their slaughter. Said it was better for our people to merely avoid them. Live and let live, because there's enough sand under these waves for all of us to thrive."

"She said that?"

He nodded. "She did. Like most members on the Council of Lords, my father returned from court outraged about it. But it only endeared her to me. I thought she had to be one special queen to stand up for the defenseless."

"Technically, they're not defenseless if they're as large as a bed sheet."

"Compared to us, they were. Mers would go out armed with harpoon blasters while riding greater shark breeds to hunt them for sport and food, though we had ample other creatures to eat. They're not even particularly tasty, but from a distance, Kai... they're gorgeous, fascinating creatures. They'll test even us if they encounter a mer in passing, and we lack the willpower to persuade them away."

"They sound beautiful, and a little scary." She pursed her lips. "We should go on a hike one day. Or whatever the mer equivalent of a hike is. Riding on our sharks. I want to see all of the local fauna. I've only seen a little while out training with Manu, but there has to be more."

"There's plenty more, especially once you get to the outskirts of the Atlantian safe zone. We'll make it a picnic." He squinted at the starfish spawning field, a wrinkle creasing his brow. "I've never known it to be this serene. It's almost unsettling."

A stillness settled in the golden expanse, the atmosphere different from what Kai remembered during the visit with Amerin. They'd chatted among the stars for hours that day while watching sea creatures Kai thought long extinct. Every hour of exploration in the Atlantian kingdom was a dream come true for her, especially when Cosmas took her to view the laomedon riders in action, a special cavalry regiment under him trained to ride the fierce, bottom-dwelling crocodilians that reminded her of a cross between a mosasaurus and a dolphin. They could hold their breath for hours.

"Amerin told me the golden stars spawn year-round."

"They do, making this a popular feeding ground."

Now there wasn't a single scuttling hermit crab

or any inquisitive fish scavenging through the sand, making the area too quiet, almost unsettling, once the jellyfish departed. Without them, the area dimmed further. If the starfish were absent, the only light would have been the single lamp installation at the northern corner of the field. Serving underwater street lamps, the Atlantian techs planted bioluminescent, thirty-meter poles of hard coral every quarter mile throughout the hundred-league radius surrounding Atlantis. Beyond that, they relied on subtler markers on the long stretches of sea-road connecting the various colonies and townships of their kingdom. They didn't want mortals to find those.

Hoping to feel something romantic for Cosmas, she took his hand and ignored his startled eyebrow. "I have it on good experience that these little guys are delicious. Wanna share one?"

He laughed. "I've had them before. If you're able to stop at one, your willpower is greater than mine, Kai. Let's not tease ourselves."

"Fine. We'll gather as many as we can carry back to Atlantis."

"Better." He glanced at the watch strapped to his left wrist, the glowing ink below the glass highlighting the time. "Let's place a little wager on it," he said, withdrawing his hand.

Kai crossed both arms. "Uh huh. What kind?"

"Winner finds largest starfish in five minutes. Beat me, and I'll convince Heracles to let you ride the kraken he imported from Crete. She's a real—"

"Deal."

"You didn't even wait to see what I get if I win."

"You won't. I want on that kraken."

"For the sake of full disclosure, when I win, you're taking on an additional hour of weight training each day—"

"Ew."

"—underwater with Loto's junior Myrmidon infantry recruits—"

"The *kids*?"

"—as their mentor," he concluded while she stared at him.

"You're serious? Ugh, all right. It's not like I intend to lose." They shook on it, and at the start of the minute, rushed to their knees on the algae-covered ocean floor to sift through stars, gathering their best finds and comparing each tasty, gilded creature with another.

A flicker of luminescent gold caught Kai's attention in passing, shining brighter than the others. She brushed a few stars aside and plucked up a few tufts of hairlike algae, unearthing a glossy, polished gem.

"Hey, Cosmas. I found a really pretty rock over here."

"Are you trying to distract me so you can win?"

"No, for real."

Clutching her largest star in one hand and the gem in the other, she rose and picked her way over to him across the green patches, watching each step. A sandworm had been poking the tip of its tail—or was it the head?—from one of the soft burrows littering the area, and she also didn't fancy an enormous hermit crab testing the limits of her bladder control by dragging her inside.

Cosmas already had an impressive star in his hand. He rose to meet her as she held up her discovery. A subtle glow surrounded it when Kai raised it on her palm. "It's so pretty."

The moment his eyes went big, anxiety roiled through her. "Kai. That's not a rock."

"Please tell me this isn't some small monster or creature's shit."

"No." A quiet moment passed, during which her heart tried to break free from her chest. "I think you found the King's Treasure, the pearl missing from the king's trident."

"Really? But...I thought my parents died hundreds of miles away from here, closer to—" Kai caught a hint of something rancid, strong enough to cut her off with a gag. "Do you smell that?"

"Huh. I thought I smelled something rank, but there's always some detritus on the ocean floor. Could be a hermit crab eating a snack nearby." He gestured to the golden sea to emphasize his point, only to go rigid, tension filling his spine. His nostrils flared, then he said in a quiet whisper, "Kai, head to Leilei. Now."

"What's wrong?"

"There's a Gloombeast in the area. Possibly many. Mount up and get out of here." He tapped the comm pinned to his shoulder. "Commander Cosmas to Central Command. We have a breach within the

Atlantian perimeter. Possible scylla in the Fields of Gold."

Central Command did not answer.

"Central Command! We have a breach in the perimeter approximately ten leagues west of the city. I need a coral glider fireteam in the Fields of Gold. Do you copy?"

Silence continued. He tapped the device a few times, then the green light blipped red and went dark.

"What the fuck? It has a fresh charge."

The smell intensified from a subtle odor to an overpowering stench that flew up her nose and choked her with its foulness.

"Cosmas, we need to go." She tugged his hand. "They don't hear you."

The sand floor swelled and rolled with movement beneath it. Cosmas shoved her toward Leilei, urging her to mount up, but when she grasped the saddle pommel, a gray tentacle shot from one of the many sandworm burrows. Panicked, Leilei shot away into the darkness, damned near taking Kai's fingers with her.

Then the rest of the creature emerged from the ground with an enormous conical shell on its back, though it had the sucker-covered arms of an octopus. Cosmas lunged between her and the monster with his trident, features grim. His tail returned, muscular thighs merging together.

"Go after her. Push yourself and you won't be far behind her. She knows the way home to Atlantis."

Cosmas squeezed his trident in a white-knuckled grip and eyed the ocean floor. It shifted, rolling with hidden Gloombeasts beneath the sand.

A cold wave broke out over her body, beginning in her chest and spreading until it reached her toes. "You're not coming with me?"

"They'll follow us if I do. They're fast as we are, sometimes faster."

Fuck. That. "I'm not leaving you behind." To die for her as her parents had likely died for her. In recent days, they never strayed far from her mind.

Kai wondered if it was a memory surfacing.

"You have to. Where there's one, there's always many. Now follow my damn order and get out of here."

Hoping to disguise the trembling in her voice with rage, Kai extended her spear and moved into battle stance. "I don't have to do a damned thing you tell me, because you're not the boss of me."

"Kai," he said, a warning in his tone. The thing advanced, feinting with a tentacle to break through Cosmas's defenses. Testing them. It whipped forward and tried to sneak past the commander, but he slapped it aside with his tail.

"Myrmidons don't abandon each other. Myrmidons battle together until the end."

"You aren't one of us."

A ripple cut through the water to Kai's left. Whirling, she followed blind intuition and thrust, impaling it on the first stroke. Sparing only a glance at the slaughtered squid on its end, she kicked it off with her boot and shot Cosmas a look.

"You're not getting rid of me."

Cosmas grunted. "Fine. Then listen to everything I tell you to do, and maybe we can survive this until my communicator comes online again."

28

BLOOD AND GOLD

IF MANU HAD BLINKED, HE WOULD HAVE MISSED it. He hadn't slept the previous night and had been drowsing during a portion of the patrol, searching to no avail for a plague of Gloombeasts sighted west of one of their rural settlements. He'd led a strike team with five other coral gliders into the wilderness, and none of their scouts turned up a single monster.

But to his left, his headlamps reflected off the glossy surface of a glowing shark eye. He saw it for only an instant, the telltale turquoise shade of a dusk-tip. As the color was a special morph designed by a topnotch breeder, it wasn't possible to find their kind in the wild.

Manu tapped the comms. "Hold up, mers. Veering out of formation to investigate an unusual sighting at eleven o'clock. Cover me."

He banked left and accelerated to catch up to her. Nearing her allowed him to see the fine details, making her a distinct figure with colorful patterns instead of a svelte silhouette against the blue tones of the ocean bottom.

His blood rank cold. He knew those patterns, because he'd babied that shark for three long months. He knew that pattern; he'd thought Leilei's fins resembled a dazzling nebula and wondered if the princess would appreciate a piece of the sky even while underwater in their realm.

The shark was swimming in a panic, slicing through the water fast as a knife and without her rider. Kai was nowhere in sight.

"It's a domesticated dusktip belonging to Princess Kailani. She's saddled and riderless. Spread out and begin a search. I'm going to follow her into the stables." One of the earliest things they trained their young sharks to do was return home, differing from a battle shark trained to fight alongside a Myrmidon. Some were better suited for combat than others. Leilei had been bred for speed, but she was a frisky thing, young and still skittish. But he'd seen a fire in her he thought would match Kai perfectly. What he didn't expect was for Cosmas to agree with his observation.

Why the fuck was Leilei loose in the wilderness?

He tapped the comms again. "Commander Manu to Central Command. Has Princess Kailani left the city?"

"She checked out about a half hour ago from South Gate with Commander Cosmas as her escort, sir. They went for a ride."

Manu checked in with Cosmas next, praying the

young shark had merely gotten away from Kai and been too spooked by an ocean predator to heed either of their commands. "Cosmas, this is Manu. Where are you?"

No answer. He tried again, stomach twisting into knots.

"Cosmas, report!" he finally barked.

His ribs hurt and the heart behind them thrummed erratically, desperately, sending tendrils of pain through his chest. This wasn't normal.

Leilei fled back to the stables. After parking, he met her there and a young merwoman with a bucket of chum strode up to meet him, grinning. "Commander Manu, hi! Did Her Highness enjoy her first ride on Leilei?"

"I wouldn't know, as I found Leilei alone and followed her here."

The girl blinked. "Alone?" Her gaze darted to Leilei, thrashing in the corral and looking increasingly agitated. "She's afraid."

No shit, genius. "At any time did they mention where they're going?"

"Something about gold fish...or...was it gold starfish?"

Manu stepped away and spoke into his communicator again. He needed a full patrol of gliders to the Fields of Gold, and he needed it yesterday.

LOTO DISAGREED with Manu's assessment. "No

Gloombeast would come within one hundred leagues of Atlantis. That's the clearance zone. Everything within the borders is clear. You know this. I understand that you're concerned about our princess, but she's capable of holding her own now. You've said as much yourself after Fare, remember? Besides, Cosmas is with her."

A gnawing in Manu's gut wouldn't allow him to let it go, however. If it was so safe, why did they take so many precautions with Kailani's life within the city? Anything could have occurred once they were beyond the wall, including an attack from the Loyalists. He leaned over the console in the communication bridge and called Cosmas three more times, waiting for an answer. "Commander Cosmas, report. What is your status?"

"I'm telling you. There's no reason to be alarmed. The shark is young; she got away from them or was spooked while they were indisposed and too distracted by other acts to control her. It happens."

"I don't believe that, Loto. Assemble a squad."

Loto raised one hand to his brow and groaned, scrubbing the same hand down his face. "Manu, if you do this and it turns out nothing is wrong, that they're only having a bit of private time, your father is going to assign you to whale shit detail for a year. By Styx, he'll take it out on me, too."

"It isn't a bit of private time. They're not answering comms."

"I turn mine off when I'm having a romp with the missus."

"It's against protocol. Anything could happen during your...five minutes."

Loto barked out a sharp laugh. "Five is generous these days, man. When you have five children, you're not given a lick of time or privacy. You need to get in, do your business with the wife, and be out again. We snuck a quickie in the closet three days ago with our hands over each other's mouth so the little blighters wouldn't find us."

Manu blinked. "Really? I thought—anyway, back to the matter at hand. Something is amiss. It isn't like Cosmas to do this."

"We've never known Cosmas to be engaged either."

Manu's heart sank. Fuck, he wanted to be happy for Kai and Cosmas. He could understand the man wanting a few private moments with his new beloved, disabling his comm, and setting the device aside for a private moment. Kai deserved that.

But he also couldn't leave it to chance. If they died because he didn't trust his gut, he'd never forgive himself. "Then it's all on me, brother. If I'm overreacting, feel free to tell General Lago you tried your best to talk sense into me. I'll take responsibility for it all."

Manu grabbed the speaker, pressed the broadcast button, and called their people into duty.

And he prayed that they interrupted a romantic early morning tryst between two newly engaged mers, because the alternative—that they were already dead—hurt too much to consider.

A SQUAD of coral gliders cut through the algae-choked countryside west of Atlantis, zipping along the sea-road leading to the Fields of Gold. Manu piloted the craft at the lead of the formation, with a dozen more behind him. That was all he could round together and call into action on short notice, unwilling to wait longer.

Prior to their departure, he'd set Captain Leander to the task of organizing additional squads to follow in their wake, demanding no less than a platoon, overkill for a small incursion, but appropriate for the swarm that had felled Helike and Fare.

"Commander Cosmas, we are currently en route to your last known location," Lieutenant Philemon barked into the communication channel. "If this has changed and you are no longer at the Fields of Gold, please respond. I repeat, we are en route to the Fields of Gold. Please respond if your location has changed."

Manu's pulse thudded louder with each league they crossed. If he was wrong, there'd be blood to shed when General Lagos returned from his tour of the other Atlantian outposts. If he was right—and gods, he prayed he wasn't—Kai and Cosmas were already in danger.

The odor of Gloombeast was already in Manu's nose, death and rot, the offensive stink of it searing into his nasal passages, though it wasn't possible for it to permeate the sealed craft. It had to be his imagination. Yet the smell assaulted him, and it only grew stronger the closer they came to the Fields of Gold.

His heart only raced faster, hurting his chest and making him fight for every breath.

A blip darted across Manu's console screen, followed by additional specks of orange against the sonar's black field. "I'm picking up activity due west, Commander," Philemon said.

"As am I."

A few became a dozen, and a dozen became a hundred colorful pinpricks of light indicating mass movement over the starfish spawning ground.

"A lot of activity. Arose out of nowhere, though we've been scanning since we left the city. Do you think it's a swarm?"

There hadn't been a Gloombeast swarm within three hundred leagues of Atlantis in years, and even then, it had been a passing danger headed north.

Manu rolled the accelerator forward, pushing the coral glider to maximum speed until it shot over the top of the hill and came within view of the fields.

A warzone awaited them below the mound. As Manu decelerated and initiated the targeting system, fingers a blur of motion over the console, battle reflexes came into play and he saw every inch of the field before them in astonishing clarity, burned into his mind and frozen in time. He saw his princess and his best friend fending off an onslaught with their backs together, the former armed with her spear, Cosmas with his trident. Clouds of blue Gloombeast blood dyed the water around them, turning the fields murky with their filth and disturbed sand. Corpses littered the ocean floor and floated around them in a nimbus of slain creatures.

He also saw the scylla looming above them, an ocean chimera with a dozen venomous sea serpent heads connecting a squid's tentacles to the bloated torso of a merwoman resurrected to serve the Gloom. Such was the fate of all mers taken by Calypso.

Manu fired a salvo of bolts from his harpoon guns. Each shot forced the monstrosity backwards, ripping into her tentacles and tearing through flesh. Cosmas snapped his head toward them and palpable relief shone in his eyes.

Thank the gods they'd held out. Thank the gods he'd followed his instincts and listened to his gut.

In a few more shots, he reduced her lower half to harmless pieces in the current. For fear of striking Cosmas or Kai, Manu redirected his assault to the encroaching hoard. The once-golden field was reduced to a land of craters and sinkholes.

"Fan out, men. Alleviate the pressure from Commander Cosmas and Princess Kailani. Philemon, cut off the swarm."

"Understood, Commander."

The moment Kai and Cosmas dispatched what remained of the scylla, a Doomlantern glided toward the pair, emitting a sinister dark violet glow. It shone brighter than a living black light with a long stinger trailing behind it across the sandy bottom. Manu caught the diseased beast in his sights and squeezed the trigger, but he only clipped the edge of its gelatinous mass, wounding it. It shot away into the dark, and his remaining energy rounds hurtled harmlessly into the Gloom where they crashed against an upraised swell on the far side of the field.

Manu's gaze darted back to Kai. His chest could have burst from pride when she launched her spear into the chest of a hippocampus taken by the sickness, the once beautiful creature twisted by Calypso's curse. The spear flew back into her hand again, and she whirled, turning a somersault in the water, powerful tail propelling her from the path of a monstrous hermit crab with ridges of spines on its shell.

Together, she and Cosmas made a deadly pair, his future king and queen. She was quicker than her battle companion, moving with the preternatural speed he'd expect of a mer with divine blood rushing through her veins.

"Commander," Captain Leander spoke over the channel. "We are fast approaching the Fields of Gold. What is your status?"

Meters ahead of him, a tangle of octopuses converged on a glider, crushing it in their inescapable arms. The glass cracked and water flooded the craft. Their tentacles had prevented the escape hatch from opening and ejecting the pilot.

They crushed him inside it, even as Manu and another glider fired upon them.

"Overwhelmed," Manu replied. "They're surging from the old sandworm tunnels beneath the fields. We need to cut them off at the source and secure an escape route for Commander Cosmas and the princess."

"Acknowledged."

The fight wore on, a never-ending tide of aberrations rushing from deep within the Earth itself, coming from gods only knew where. Another glider fell, and they were down to Manu and three others.

At last, there was a break in the storm of monsters, enough that Cosmas urged Kai to flee. Manu saw her eyes, watched her gaze dart to the gliders, the shape of her mouth asking why. Whatever response Cosmas gave, it was lost when the mer turned his back. Kai's spine turned rigid.

Another disturbance moved the sand bed.

Each second Manu waited for her to leave was a second anxiety compressed his lungs in a vice, barely allowing him any air. Just as they bolted, the ground erupted again, sand and ocean detritus stirred by another of Calypso's sea monsters. He lit into it, precise and careful shots chipping at a conical shell on the monster's back.

They started moving, the two mers just flickers of color in cloudy water, coral glider headlamps reflecting off their scaled lower bodies. Taking up a position as their escort, Manu followed without removing his fingers from the triggers.

Before they reached the edge of the hill overlooking the fields, a single limb burst from the ocean floor. No monster, no gelatinous body, only a wicked cross between a manta ray's barb and a scorpion tail protruding from the swaying kelp bed. Just as it swung forward toward Cosmas's chest, Kai pulled off an impressive stunt with her tail, throwing herself in between them. It pierced her armor and shattered the golden cuirass. Manu saw the moment it entered her chest, the moment her eyes flew wide with pain.

He couldn't hear Cosmas's scream, but he saw it, fury and anger boiling across his features. A trident thrust into the sand bed, presumably even hitting the mark. But it was too late.

Against everything he'd been taught while piloting an underwater craft, Manu flooded the chamber and ejected from the coral glider, abandoning it and subjecting himself to the sudden pressure of the ocean pounding in on him from every direction. Mers had an adaptation that allowed their survival, but it still hurt. The brief moment of discomfort was meaningless as his future queen floated lifeless in the water, trailing rich, red blood against a sea of golden stars.

29

DOUBT AND FURY

THREE HOURS AFTER SURVIVING A SUCCESSFUL surgery to repair her heart, Kai lay beneath a healing lamp while the enchanted light of Apollo glowed golden on her skin. Vitalis claimed to have pulled every magical trick from of his repertoire of spells and tearfully professed the princess's survival to be in the gods' hands.

Manu had little confidence in their neglectful Atlantian deities, as they were the very gods who had allowed the Gloom to overtake the Atlantic Ocean in the first place. The same gods who allowed Calypso to cause rampant destruction across the kingdom for two millennia after driving her mad with envy to begin with. No matter the faith of his fellow mers, Manu was sick of gods.

While seven of Atlantis's key decision makers squabbled, Manu waited by the healing suite's door beside Cosmas. The other mer should have been recuperating, pale from blood loss but too stubborn to lie in his own sick bed.

The room was stifling, overcrowded for a place of healing, and still yet more people were bound to storm inside and blather their unwanted opinions. Chief among the expected visitors was General Lago, though he'd no doubt blame Manu for what happened.

And that was fine. Manu blamed himself. If he'd been faster and had his eyes been sharper, he would have seen the fucking thing lying in wait and filled it with holes.

"I've done all that is possible with medicine. All that remains is prayer," Vitalis said. "We must now wait."

"Wait until she becomes a monster, you mean. You know as well as the rest of us what happens when any Atlantian falls to the Gloom," Lady Nammu retorted.

"Agreed," said Lord Euripides. "What happened is a grave misfortune, but should she arise infected by the Gloom, I can only imagine the creature she would become. For the safety of all, we must lay Princess Zephyrine to rest."

"Kailani," Aegaeon said in a quiet voice.

"Excuse me?"

"Her name is Kailani."

"What matter does it make?" asked Sophocles, another high mer of the Council of Lords. "What does her name matter now that she is dying before us, and with her, any hope we may have had of defeating the Gloom?"

They cared nothing for whether Kai died. To them, she was a symbol of their continued importance in Atlantian society. She represented safety and an end to the Gloom. She represented a continued life of privilege in their pink shell manors. Without her, nothing guaranteed the Loyalists wouldn't reenact the French Revolution and introduce a few high mer necks to an executioner's axe. Manu suspected it wouldn't be long until the royal-hating traitors constructed a few guillotines.

Another lord sighed, dropping his heavy shoulders. Epicurus was a well-built mer, a retired Myrmidon and rarity among the nobility, like Cosmas. "Death will come for us all in time, Sophocles. What does it matter if it is now or tomorrow? I say let her live. Let her live, and then put down whatever the Gloom makes of her, should it make anything of her at all. Hours have passed, and yet look at her. There is still life in her face. Perhaps there is a chance, a hope of her recovery after all."

"Thank you, Epicurus," Aegaeon murmured.

Epicurus inclined his head.

"Am I the only one here besides Nammu with a brain to see the foolishness of this? I will not stand by as you endanger all of Atlantis," Lord Aeschylus said, a scowling mer with a perpetually curled upper lip, as if his surroundings always carried a foul odor. "It's an unnecessary risk. One we cannot abide. Princess or not, we must put the girl down. Were it any of us, we'd be long dead."

Manu told himself it wasn't worth the jail time. Introducing Aeschylus's nose to his fist would only cause unnecessary drama. He clenched his left hand, knuckles cracking.

Sophocles sighed. "Look at us, arguing over the fate of our future queen."

Lady Nammu jolted back a step, a hand raised to her heart. "Future queen? Whether this had happened or not, she never had any future as our queen. She is a *child*."

"I beg to differ, Lady Nammu. All queens must begin somewhere. The blood is in her veins, and more importantly, she has the gift of Thalassa."

"We don't need the gift of Thalassa." Lady Nammu clenched her jaw. "Has Aegaeon not kept our world safe from harm for all these years? No less safe than his brother and wife did."

"My love—"

"Don't you 'my love' me," she snapped. "If you won't speak for yourself, I will. This supposed queen has already proven herself unsuitable for the throne. She endangered my nephew by rushing into danger, and just look at what her childish antics have wrought."

Perhaps it was for the best, angry as Manu was, trembling with indignation, that Cosmas strode forward first to challenge her. "That is *not* what happened. I love you, Aunt Nammu, but you won't tarnish her name while I stand here. Kai wanted an evening swim, and I voluntarily took her, as was my right. As was the plan arranged between all of us should her personal protection detail be unavailable. What happened out there wasn't normal. I've never seen anything like it!"

"You are blinded by your affection for her. You can't be trusted to think rationally, Cosmas. Why aren't you in bed? You have internal injuries, my dear."

"I'll return to bed when this matter is resolved."

"You'll return now. You may think this misfit *un*mer is the only eligible maid to wed you, but there will be many others, Cosmas. She—"

Regent Aegaeon glanced at his wife, blue eyes lit by fury. "That is *enough*, Nammu!" His wife shrank away, blinking at him but still trembling with rage. "This is no decision to make overnight. It cannot be rushed. My niece is the last direct descendent of the royal bloodline, and I will not take her life until all other options have been exhausted."

He turned on a heel and strode from the room. Nammu followed, but she cast a murderous glance over her shoulder toward Manu before gliding into the hall.

The others filed out one by one until only Cosmas and Manu remained, standing on opposite sides of the bed.

Cosmas swallowed, throat bobbing. "I'm sorry."

"You owe no apologies to me. And it wasn't your fault."

"It *is* my fault. She protected *me*."

"She did what was in her nature to do. I...I want to blame you. I want to be furious with you. But it isn't your fault."

"Manu—"

"Get some rest."

Cosmas lingered, one arm against his ribs. "Will you sit with her?"

"Someone has to. I don't trust what might happen if one of us isn't here to protect her."

"Thank you."

Once the door shut behind Cosmas, Manu dragged a chair to the bedside and gazed at her pale face, the sweat gleaming on her brow. She looked bloodless, a still doll with algae bandages wrapped around her torso.

Manu leaned closer, daring to take her clammy hand. "I know you're still in there, Kai." Her hand was so boneless and lax in his grip, slick with sweat. "They want to murder you in your sleep. To kill you now before you succumb to the poison in your veins and arise as part of the Gloom."

With his other hand, he stroked a damp lock of hair from her perspiring temple. "I won't let them harm you. Not if I can help it. Not until we know you're not our Kai anymore."

Impulsively, he leaned down and kissed her, hoping he'd have the courage to do it again while her eyes were open and filled with life.

And to tell her how he felt, whether it was wrong or not.

THE COOL AIR in the royal healer's suite smelled like herbs and the sharp medicinal tang of alchemy. Manu rubbed his tired face, finding comfort in the astringent scent filling the room, preferable to the smell of Gloombeast still clinging to his skin. He didn't dare leave Kai's side, afraid the moment he did, the moment he let down his guard, they'd come to kill her.

Forty-three years of Myrmidon training told him Kai should have been laid to rest. His heart wanted her alive. Wanted her in his arms, her pulse pounding strong and eyes glittering with laughter. The clash of training and desire alerted him to his own hypocrisy —affection for her versus common sense and centuries of tradition steeped in experience. He'd yet to see a mer recover from the Gloom once Calypso took them in her vile clutches.

A tiny, niggling voice of self-doubt told him she was gone, and that despite all her effort, he'd only brought her to Atlantis to die. For that, he couldn't forgive himself. Lord Aegaeon, General Lago, and Hipponax had dared to believe a load of idealistic eelshit, and now a brave and witty beautiful young woman was dying, the world soon to be much poorer for having lost her. Why couldn't they have let her be?

Manu knew the answer. Even if the underwater realm had allowed Kai to remain on the surface,

Calypso's vile abominations would have torn her to shreds. It was unfortunate, the future carved for her all because she'd had the misfortune of inheriting a few drops of divine blood, condemning her to a life of battle and warfare cut far too short.

His eyes burned, red from lack of sleep. Not tears. Myrmidons did not cry. But they did grow exhausted, his shoulders sinking and chin dipping toward his armored chest.

"Commander Manu?" Amerin's gentle voice came from the door, a whisper in the quiet room with the power to snap him out of the brief drowse.

Manu jerked upright, heart pounding. "Any news?"

"No." Amerin crossed the room with an enormous fuzzy blanket in her arms and unfolded it over Kai's legs. It looked like it belonged to a child, cheerful yellow seahorses over pastel anemone print. "I thought you'd be resting by now." She paused beside Kai's bed and ran her fingers through the princess's dark hair. "I thought Kai would like the blanket her mother made for her. Have you slept?"

"No."

Amerin slipped into the chair beside him. "You should, you know. A little rest will do you some good."

Rest could come when Kai was awake. Or when she'd found peace. Until one event or the other happened, he couldn't imagine leaving her alone in the room at the figurative crossroads between life and death.

"I'll be fine, Amerin. Thank you for the concern."

"At least shower and get out of your armor, Commander. Please. For her sake. Kai wouldn't want you to suffer at her bedside." Cosmas had come and gone again, sitting alongside Manu for two hours while Kai fought for her life. Eventually, Aegaeon and Vitalis dragged him back to his own recovery room, citing his need for rest was just as great.

"I don't—"

"I will remain here. I won't let them take her."

"You won't have any choice. When they come for her, they won't ask your permission."

"Commander Cosmas sent me to keep an eye." Her gaze snapped to the door, lingering. "He's behaving now for them, biding his time. If...if they try—"

"There's no if," Manu said, voice quiet and hollow, as empty as his soul felt since the moment he saw the barb piercing Kai's chest. "They will. No one's ever come back from the Gloom."

"We don't know that. A queen has never been infected before. Never in the history of Atlantis, in the line of our queens, has one of Calypso's monsters infected a mer from Thalassa's blood. We just have to fight for her." Amerin bit her bottom lip. "You have to fight for her."

"I will fight for her if I must, because I'll be damned if they take her life before we...before we do know. Before it's fucking certain."

Kai deserved that much, to have the chance to speak her goodbyes.

Manu had promised to protect her. He would with his final breath, whether his princess was in sickness or health.

30

ELYSIAN WAVES

Kᴀɪ ᴏᴘᴇɴᴇᴅ ʜᴇʀ ᴇʏᴇs ᴛᴏ ᴀɴ ᴜɴᴅᴇʀᴡᴀᴛᴇʀ wonderland more spectacular than any Atlantian park or city. A thousand corals glowed all around her, their colors too numerous to count. A pink jellyfish swam past her to the left, and a school of neon fish swirled by to the right. There were enormous plant beds of crimson and pink aquatic flora, though these grew wild and untamed without a caretaker's pruning. No matter which direction she turned, the endless twilight of the ocean displayed unfettered beauty.

This was how the ocean ought to have been from one pole to the other. Filled with life and beauty instead of pollution and death.

A Technicolor squid shot past her, and a tiger shark cruised in the distance. She floated there, lost in time and space, wondering where the murky sand bed of the battlefield had gone. As memories of her final moments returned, Kai turned again and came face to face with her own image, standing tall in sculpted sharkskin armor.

It took about five seconds to realize it wasn't her mirror image, and that there were laugh lines framing the woman's full mouth and crinkles around her gray eyes. Her hair was violet from root to tip and flowed behind her on the underwater current, pinned from her face by a tiara shaped from coral.

Neither paintings nor statues had done Queen Ianthe justice. And seeing her now, standing there at the bottom of the ocean with her serene smile and quiet nobility, told Kai she hadn't survived the stingray's barbed tail piercing her chest. Her brain had put together a final dream before death took her.

"Mom?"

Ianthe stepped closer and embraced her, imparting so many sensations of love and affection at once. Her mother's hug was pure heaven, better than a warm blanket on a cold winter night. "I have loved you from the moment I knew I carried you, my dear sweet Kai."

Her heart hurt. Her mother knew her name.

"You seem surprised."

"You called me Kai."

"Is Kai not the name you have adopted since our loss? I could call you Zephyrine, but you are no longer she. You are a new woman. You are better and stronger than I ever imagined or dreamed you could be. Why would I not recognize that?"

Hallucination or reality? The rapid pulse behind

her breast seemed ready to burst free. "I don't understand. How are you here? *Where* are we?"

"We are in the threshold between the world of the living and the land of the dead. Just as Elysium has lands and valleys for heroes, so too does it have shores and oceans."

"I'm dead?"

"No, my love. But you are close to it."

"You're not upset that I took another mother? That I forgot you?"

"What?" Ianthe's gaze softened. "No. Never, my love. What took place was what needed to happen to ensure your survival and happiness. More than anything, I feel gratitude to the woman who raised you, the woman who allowed you to live as a child should: in happiness and joy."

For years, Kai had fantasized about what it would be like to meet her biological mother. She'd grown up loving Sunshine and appreciating everything given by her adopted mother, but she'd always wondered about the woman who birthed her and how she'd wound up on the shores of Galveston with a dead woman.

The reality of her mother lived up to every expectation and dream.

"I...never stopped wondering about you."

"I know." Her mother's serene smile wavered. "But I sense there are doubts within you. The goddess *never* abandoned us, my dear sweet Kai."

"Then why wasn't she there to help you? Why hasn't she saved Atlantis?"

"Even a goddess tires, my sweet. The battle against Calypso weakened her, and for years, she has hidden, regaining her strength and recovering from the ordeal. She could fight our battles no more than you could fight an entire army. Do you understand?"

"But there's been no sign of her. Everyone in Atlantis believes she's abandoned the city and our people."

"Oh, my sweet love, no. Never. There are signs of her in this world, if you know where to look. She awakened your gifts the day of the *Sea Angel's* wreck, waiting years until the ideal moment for your return to Atlantis. She could not send you earlier, Kai. Not until you were strong in mind and body. Not until you could withstand the forces of Calypso and her daughters." Her mother smoothed the hair from her face, tucking it behind Kai's ear.

"Tell Daddy I miss him."

"Tell him yourself."

"What?" Kai glanced past her mother's shoulder into the bearded face of her father, standing tall and proud a few feet to Ianthe's rear with a trident in hand. He looked more regal in person than he did in his statues, ruddy skin weathered from the sun and green eyes bright.

"I'm proud of you, Kailani. We've been there with you every step of the way and always shall be. Through each struggle and every accomplishment, we are always at your side. How I wish we had a few moments longer. But our time is nearly up here. We must go."

"No! I can...I can go with you. I want to go where you are going."

"No." A sad smile flitted across his lips. "You cannot. Where we go is a plane for heroes. For the warriors slain in battle and dreamers who gave their lives for better days. One day you will join us. But not now. It isn't yet your time. Until then, we count on you to defend Atlantis as we once did for centuries."

"But...I've only just gotten to know you."

"Our time is past and now the future is yours. Claim it, my dear daughter, and continue to make us proud. But I've come to bear a warning to you." His shoulders moved with a deep breath. "What they do with you now is not your true purpose. They fail to see your value; they smother you. You must claim what is yours. For the good of Atlantis, you must retake the kingdom and become the queen you were meant to be."

"But I don't know how. I don't even—I don't know where to begin."

The two mers exchanged a brief glance before her mother spoke. "Begin with what your heart tells you. You sense the changes we left incomplete, the changes that are needed across the kingdom. We were not guaranteed tomorrow, and now you have learned, neither are you."

"Learn from our mistakes. Do not take tomorrow or even today for granted. Not one hour, nor a minute. Each second is precious and valuable, whether it is a moment to learn or a chance to act.

Trust in yourself, as we trust in you, to do what is right."

Why did it hurt so much?

She drew in a ragged breath and her shoulders shook, but then his strong arm curved around her waist and drew her near, cradling her between both of them the way she remembered them holding her as a child.

The way they'd hugged her before Commander Malie spirited her away from the battle and they hung back to cover their rear. Memories slammed into her mind with the force of a tempest, and she recalled the last time she saw her parents, her mother and father holding back the forces of hundreds of Gloombeasts to ensure *her* escape. They'd given their lives to guarantee she'd live, fighting an impossible battle.

And she could not let them down.

31

HOPE FLOWS ETERNAL

In the end, Manu did leave the palace to shower and freshen. Amerin wanted to bathe the princess and change her clothes, so in the interest of maintaining Kai's dignity, he left. He returned to find both women where he'd left them, with the addition of Aegaeon in Manu's seat, leaning forward with his chin propped on both thumbs, fingers steepled over his nose. He looked older. Worn. Faint creases had become canyons, and deep purple crescents smudged under his eyes. He clearly hadn't slept either.

"Any change?"

"None," Aegaeon replied, leaning back in his seat. "The poison is neither advancing nor receding. Vitalis believes that to be a favorable sign."

Manu swallowed the hard knot in his throat and stepped closer. "What's the verdict out there, my lord?"

"They're biding their time. Lago's on his way to

the palace now to weigh in. It's split at the moment, but his vote is critical to—"

"What in the name of Styx is happening here?" Lago bellowed, voice thundering across the suite's walls as he stormed into the room. "What is this farce?"

And so died any hope Manu had of a peaceful evening at Kai's side.

Aegaeon rose from his chair. "We're standing vigil over the princess, Lago."

"Why has she not been put out of her misery? These are our rules—our laws. You put the safety of all Atlantis at jeopardy by allowing her to live. You don't know what she could become, the power that could be created from her divine blood and Calypso's curse." He strode forward, extending the haft of his shortened trident to its full length. "This isn't a matter for a fucking vote and you know it," the mer growled.

Then shit became real, because Aegaeon drew his trident, too. Aegaeon, who had only three decades, if even that, of combat experience against his father's centuries. Lago, their brilliant strategist— their strongest mer and most powerful combatant to ever lead all the forces of Atlantis—only cocked a brow before his features went harder and colder than an arctic glacier.

"You have no chance of stopping me, Aegaeon. Out of respect for you and the office you hold, I won't take this as a challenge, but I have come here for one thing, and one thing alone."

Aegaeon stood taller. "Unless I'm mistaken, I'm the regent and you follow my commands."

Lago's cheeks flushed fuchsia. "Your power is granted to you by the Council of Lords as an interim ruler. You're no king. Don't pretend to be. Your days in the throne room may be coming to an end, considering the number of lords I encountered in the palace halls begging me to put an end to your madness."

Tension rippled down Aegaeon's spine. "Lago, please. If you ever considered me a friend, hear us out."

"It isn't about friendship," the older mer murmured in a quieter voice, losing some of his steam. "This dream of ours, it was merely that—a dream. She was never prepared and could never be what this kingdom needed." He cut a hard look at Manu, blame broiling in his eyes. "As those under my leadership have failed so thoroughly, I'll be the one to—"

Manu maneuvered between his father and the foot of Kai's bed. Aegaeon made a micro-adjustment in position, and Amerin fled the room just as she'd promised she would, footfalls echoing down the corridor. "I can't let you do this. I won't allow you to hurt her."

"That's insubordination." A low scoff barked from his father's throat.

"It's doing my duty. I swore to protect Princess Kailani, heir to the Atlantian throne. And I will protect her, even if it's from you."

Lago's fingers tightened, knuckles a bloodless white. "Stand aside."

"No."

Cosmas burst into the room, still grimacing in pain, the size and number of his bruises creating a watercolor splash of indigo from his right pec to his waist. He clutched his ribs with one arm while Amerin squeezed into the doorway to support him from the other side. "What's happening here?"

"I am correcting Commander Manu and Regent Aegaeon's oversight," Lago said. "Return to your bed, Commander. There's nothing here I want you to see."

"In that case," Cosmas murmured, peeling away from Amerin to stand beside Manu, "it is also my oversight."

Rage distorted Lago's expression, twisting his features into a mask of anger. "Both of you dare to defy me on a matter of Atlantian law? You forget your places in our society."

"I've forgotten nothing," Manu said. "My place is between you and Kailani, General. I can't allow you to hurt her."

"As is mine," Cosmas agreed.

"And mine," Aegaeon said, revealing more steel in his spine than Manu thought possible from the high mer.

When Lago took a menacing step, trident poised for the attack, Manu slid before him. Their tridents clashed and prongs locked together, enchantment-enhanced steel against steel. Sparks flew up and electricity arced between the tips of Lago's weapon. "Move aside, son."

Son. How many years had passed since his father had last shown him an ounce of affection or love, or anything that wasn't mountain-high expectation, a demand for physical perfection and absolute obedience; to be as flawless as a mer of the warrior class could be?

Not since the week before his mother's disappearance and presumed death.

"No. I can't. If you want to kill her, you'll have to take my life as well."

Manu locked gazes with his father and endured a silence heavier than a blue whale. After what felt like a lifetime, Lago growled and spun before storming from the room. His retreating footsteps echoed down the hall.

And then there was only peace. Blessed peace and four souls who had been ready to die for a woman who might never recover.

MANU WATCHED her decline from that point forward. It had been a foolish, childish wish to believe a mer born from divine blood could resist the effect of the Gloom. Part of him had hoped her relationship to the primordial goddess of the sea would provide a greater resistance and save her.

Reality wasn't so kind.

Their vigil continued into the night. Though he

and Aegaeon stepped outside to allow the healers and Amerin time to perform their duties, one of them always stayed at her side, never leaving Kai unattended, distrusting anyone—even the palace healers—with the princess's safety.

The toxin spread. At first, it had been only a blue puckered wound located on her upper chest, padded by poultices. Later, it spread tendrils of violet toward her throat. He watched her breaths grow erratic while sweat glistened on her brow.

He and Amerin took turns bathing her forehead. While Aegaeon met with the Council of Lords to hold the final vote that would determine whether he died this evening in her defense or lived to fight another day, Manu wrung a cool cloth out over a bowl of water infused with a few drops of the golden liquid kept at Thalassa's altar.

He didn't know if it helped. He didn't believe in gods anymore.

But Kai certainly had. And that was enough for him to follow Hipponax's guidance.

"I know some part of you is there, Kai," he murmured, leaning close. "I know you're not gone yet. As long as your heart is beating, I'll do whatever I can to protect you."

Because at some point during their journey together through weeks of training, through an unusual friendship, against the odds, he'd fallen for her.

And he didn't know if he could crawl out of the deep, bleak hole she'd leave behind if she died.

"I need you to return to us. Not only for this kingdom. But for me. You're my biggest regret. Not because I failed you in providing instruction, in making you a warrior—I didn't fail at that. You *did* become a warrior. You're just and compassionate and everything Atlantis needs, the only mer to hold a candle to the legacy your mother and father left behind."

All he had were hopes and prayers, and even those seemed flimsy. Sighing, he fell back into the seat and dropped his head, wondering.

Even if he had taken her to bed, they would have only had the one night. And one night with Kai could never be enough.

He remained that way for a while, fighting sleep and ignoring his body, occasionally drowsing, only to stir at the sound of her clear and even breaths.

Clear and even breaths.

Manu jerked up in his seat and blinked at her, at the time, noticing two hours more had passed. The blue veins crawling over her chest had retreated, and only the raw, angry puncture remained beneath the crust left behind by the most recent application of ointment.

He bolted to the door, Vitalis's name on his lips. His fingers had just grazed the knob when sheets rustled behind him.

"Manu?"

With his heart in his throat, Manu turned to find his princess sitting upright in bed, watching him with wide eyes. The pallor previously clinging to her cheeks had turned rosy and she was flush with health. Warm and alive again.

"You're awake," he breathed, desperately wanting to kiss her until his soul no longer burned.

"I am. And everything has never seemed clearer." Kai touched her chest where the ray's barb pierced her. "Manu?"

"Yes, Your Highness?" he asked, moving to her bedside again.

"We need to speak soon. Not now. But *soon*. Right this minute, though, I need you to tell me everything I've missed."

So he told her. Every word, from Aegaeon's loyalty to his own father's decree that she die.

Afterward, Kai swung her legs over the side of the bed and shakily rose. "Do one last thing for me?"

"Anything, Your Highness."

"Tell Amerin I need clothes. Find my uncle and tell him I have one request: gather *everyone* of importance to Atlantis for a meeting in the Chamber of Heroes. Let him know I said to tell them, not ask. I have an announcement to make."

CURRENTS OF CHANGE

Iᴛ ᴡᴀs ʙᴇᴛᴛᴇʀ ᴛᴏ ʙᴇɢ ꜰᴏʀɢɪᴠᴇɴᴇss ᴛʜᴀɴ ᴀsᴋ permission.

For all the time Kai had spent in Atlantis, she'd learned they were a rigid people with a culture steeped in tradition, but their traditions had done little to protect them over the years. Instead, it hindered their growth.

They'd retrieved her from the human world to be their queen then inflicted an outdated system upon her.

They claimed to be better than humankind but treated their weakest citizens like dirt.

They asked for a ruler but saw her as a child.

To Kai, the answer to all of their troubles seemed simple.

"Your Highness, are you certain of this?" Hipponax asked, licking his lips nervously. "Perhaps you should still be in bed recovering."

"She should definitely be in bed recovering,"

Vitalis said in his high, nasal voice. "Though I understand her reasoning and intentions, I disapprove of her making this step so soon after escaping certain death. Your Highness, I beg you to reconsider. For your health." Everything about his pleading voice struck her as genuine. Vitalis was a good man. The same could be said of Hipponax, who radiated fear and worry, not condescension.

"No. I need to do this. It's mine. This is the reason I was brought back to Atlantis."

For months, she'd listened to her elders and obeyed their commands, following their instructions and assuming they knew what was best for Atlantis, but if they'd known, Helike and Fare wouldn't be watery burial grounds. Had they known what was best for the kingdom, the Gloom wouldn't have reached their kingdom's doorstep.

Kai reached out and grasped the scepter. The moment she touched it, radiant light exploded from the gemstone, warmth washing over the Chamber of Heroes until every statue came alive with golden light. It slid neatly from the statue's grip and pulsed with what she could only describe as acceptance. Glowing approval.

"This is mine. It belonged to my mother before me, and hers before her."

Waiting for the men who had tried to control her, Kai traced her thumb over the glossy jewel. It reacted to her touch, gleaming brighter—more eagerly—as if it had waited for her all along and bided its time, if an inanimate object could do such a thing.

As the great doors opened, her heart pounded into hyperdrive, drumming faster than a mako shark pursuing its prey. A commotion broke out as expected, bickering between Royal Guardsmen and irritable high mer. Her uncle moved at the forefront of the group alongside Lago, Loto, Manu, and other familiar faces of the Myrmidon forces—save for Cosmas, who she'd been adamant would have to stay in bed. He'd taken a beating out there in the fields.

Worse than she did. To protect her.

"What is this about? Last we were told, the princess was dying," one of the council lords declared, wearing a sour look on his weathered face. The rest of his peers appeared equally resentful. All save two kind faces in the crowd.

"Our princess stands right before us," Manu said sternly. "I advise you ask her yourself, Lord Fridericus."

Ah. Lord Fridericus senior. His son had been an asshole with an asshole name, and now she knew from where he'd inherited it. Blowhole was too kind a term for mers like them.

A second mer stepped forward, dispassionate and scowling features telling Kai he would have cheerfully lopped off her head. "I will happily ask. How are you standing here now when I saw you on your deathbed?"

"Deception!" Lady Nammu cried. "I saw her as well and stand in complete agreement with Aeschylus. I don't know what game you're playing, but this child was covered by the Gloom's taint only hours ago. Perhaps it is a scheme, and they seek to deceive us, to conceal that she has turned."

Aegaeon whirled to face his wife, but the healer beat him to the response.

"It grew worse before we saw improvement, Lady Nammu," Vitalis said in his even-tempered voice. "But I can assure you, all signs of her infection are gone. As a healer, it is against my code to allow such vile artifice in my name. In my healing house. What you see is our Princess Kailani, alive, thriving, and deserving our respect."

"What respect has she earned?" asked a man with sapphire hair and a regal bearing.

Aegaeon shot the man a dirty look, his expression speaking volumes. "All of it. Especially since she nearly died saving your son's life."

The mer blinked. "What do you mean?"

"I meant what I said, but that is a discussion to delay until another time. Kai, what is the meaning of this? Gods know I'm thrilled to see you're alive. I don't even know where to begin but..." His gaze drifted to the glowing scepter in her hands. "I haven't seen it shine this way in years."

"Twenty-five years to be exact, Uncle."

He nodded.

"I asked Manu to gather Atlantis's decision-makers for a reason. Is this everyone?"

"Every single mer," he replied, stepping aside and sweeping his hand in a broad gesture toward the committee of twenty-five nobles, in addition to their military and religious leaders, the group of them talking amongst themselves, bickering like children instead of the kingdom's great advisers.

"Thank you for that. I'll begin now." Kai cleared her throat. "Manu tells me a small number of you stood at my bedside while I lay dying, and that you asked for my death. I'm here now to say that I live. To show you that I live. I...still haven't decided if what I saw during my sleep was a hallucination or the truth, but I spoke with my mother and father."

"Ridiculous. They've been dead for years," Fridericus cut in. "And the dead do not speak."

"Hallucination," said another mer.

"Is this why you've called us? To discuss dreams?" Lago demanded, glowering down the bridge of his nose at her. "I have matters of great importance to plan, yet we stand here tolerating the mouth of a child who—"

"We're standing here to discuss my recovery. Manu and Cosmas both told me, in no uncertain terms, that a mer who is pierced in the heart is a mer who succumbs to the Gloom. But I'm here. I survived. When I was asleep, I saw them, and they told me Thalassa herself protected me. I've had time to think about that while waiting for you to show up." Kai's heart did a nervous skip behind her ribs, making it difficult to breathe. She hadn't expected them to believe her, but she also didn't predict they'd all but call her a liar.

"No one's heard the voice of Thalassa in decades," Hipponax murmured. "But it could be possible."

"My mother and father didn't rise from the Gloom. You were all so worried it would happen to me, that you neglected to remember my parents never rose. All you found were their remains. Don't you see? This means I can't be infected. If Calypso could have had my mother and father as part of her army, she would have taken them then."

A low murmur spread over the crowd of lords, no one voice more comprehensible than the next. Aegaeon held up a hand, gesturing for silence.

"That is a sound theory, Kai. What else did they say?"

"Aegaeon, you don't seriously believe—"

Her uncle shot Fridericus another dirty look. "Let her speak."

"That it's time for me to take the throne. Regardless of whether I have a king or not. You've all told me a hundred times that Atlantis is a matrilineal throne. It shouldn't matter if I have a husband or not, because this here," she said, thrusting with her scepter, "belongs to the queen and you don't have the King's Treasure."

"Your Highness—" one of the lords began.

"I am still speaking," Kai cut him off, enunciating each word with force. He blinked at her. Out of the corner of her eye, she saw Manu, Loto, and Elpis hiding grins. "But I saw it. Just before the attack began, I found a golden pearl just like this one.

"We already knew about the pearl." At her eyebrow raise, Loto continued. "Cosmas mentioned this to us. We were in the war room planning a retrieval, hoping it's still there. You dropped it, right?"

Kai nodded. "I did. I had it, but then monsters came out in force. It's somewhere out there among all the sandworm holes. I think I can take you to it."

"I don't need a child to swim in my formation," Lago growled. "We will retrieve this thing on our own. Someone put her back in bed where she belongs."

Once again, just as she'd expected, the old men walked all over her and did as they liked.

But she wouldn't allow it for much longer. Change was coming whether they approved or not.

⚔

It wasn't often that Manu felt the dire need to punch his father in the mouth, but his disrespect for their princess was one of those moments. He clenched one fist and bit his tongue, conflicted when it came to loyalty for his princess versus his sire and his superior officer.

"She isn't a child," he said at last, deciding to go for broke. He'd stood up to the old man once and hadn't landed in jail for insubordination. What was one more time? "She's our future queen and should be treated as such, with the deepest respect."

"*Future* queen," Lago snarled.

"As I said before, it's time for me to take the throne. I understand our realm and culture. I know the laws of society." She raised her chin and stared at them, the defiant and powerful queen Manu had expected her to become one day, there before them *now*. "And my memories have returned. I know who I am. I know each of you; yes, *even you* Lord Leonidas. I know my mother couldn't stand you and called you a greasy little guppy who can't be trusted. And I know she planned to remove most of you from the Council of Lords. That she planned to organize a system of voting, allowing our citizens to choose new representatives from among the other classes. *All* the classes."

As disagreement rolled through the room, shocked voices raising in volume, Manu searched the faces there. Their expressions ranged from horror and disbelief to outright fury, rage turning Leonidas's face purple.

"It was a foolish notion," he gritted. "Atlantis has been this way for centuries."

"Then change is even longer overdue. I *will* take the throne." Kai glanced at Aegaeon. "I'm sorry, Uncle, but it's time."

He inclined his head to her then shrugged one shoulder. "It is. I'll do whatever I can to support the transition."

At that moment, Nammu spun to face him and jabbed a finger in his chest. "You can't be serious. She knows nothing. She isn't prepared to take over the rule of an entire kingdom."

"Neither was I when my brother and Queen Ianthe fell. Yet I made do."

"We won't approve it," Aeschylus said.

"Nor will I," Lago growled. "I've had enough of listening to this girl's naïveté." He whirled, cape billowing behind his broad shoulders. With one gesture he ordered the commanders to follow him. Obedience wasn't an option. They did, after all, have a mission to plan and a magical relic to recover from the ruin of the battlefield once their scouting vessels returned with news.

"Give it time," Manu heard Aegaeon saying to the princess. "They'll come around, dearest niece. Give it time. They have no choice in the matter. The transfer of power will occur whether they desire it or not. It's out of their hands."

Manu hoped so. Their city had been divided enough by the conflict between Loyalists and the monarchy's royal supporters. Anything else would rip their kingdom apart and further weaken them against Calypso's dark machinations.

And as Kai had said, they were long overdue for change.

33

OUT OF THOUGHT, OUT OF MIND

AFTER A LONG SOAK IN THE BATH TO FEEL human again, Kai emerged from her royal suite to visit the healing house and see Cosmas. According to Aegaeon, it'd be days longer before he recovered and Vitalis released him to return to duty.

Meanwhile, Lago and the others planned to initiate war without him.

"Up for a visitor?" she asked, peeking inside the room to find Cosmas propped up with several bed pillows behind his back. His open shirt revealed a deep patch of color across his ribs. He'd have been cut to pieces by the shattered breastplate if not for the sharkskin padding he'd worn beneath.

"I'll never turn away a beautiful visitor. But shouldn't you be resting?"

"Nope. All healed."

"Ah, then in that case, have a seat." Cosmas patted the bedside, inviting her to join him. Then his bruised face screwed up into a frown. "Manu already told me about the outcome of the meeting. I'm sorry."

"Why are you apologizing when it isn't your doing?"

"Because my father and aunt were there, and they *are* complicit. I plan to speak with both of them about it."

Kai gingerly sat on the bedside, afraid of disturbing him too much. "You don't have to do that."

"Don't have to, but I want to." He glanced at the scepter in her hand. "It looks good with you, by the way."

"Does it?"

He grinned. "Damned right it does. Look at how it gleams when it's in your hand. It may have ignited anew when you returned to the water, but it's never been this bright. Not since your mother's reign."

"About that...did Manu tell you that I spoke with them?"

Cosmas nodded. "He did."

"She told me there were changes she and my father planned to implement, but they died too early. They never had the chance. I...think they planned to create a system similar to what the Loyalists want."

"But that would be counterproductive to their rule."

"Not entirely. On the surface, we still had a President of the United States who oversaw the country. He wasn't all-powerful, and our people had a right to a vote. We don't have to end the monarchy, but we *can* give others rights."

His smile dwindled, features turning solemn. "Is this what you want to do?"

Anxiety formed a hard knot in the center of her stomach, occasionally tightening around her ribs, too. Of all the people she thought might oppose her, she prayed her friend wasn't one. "Yes."

Cosmas took her hand and squeezed it. "Then you have my aid, in whatever way I can give it. I'll support you."

Her shoulders sagged. "Thank you."

"You'll always have my support, Kai. But there's... a matter we must discuss now."

She canted her head. "What is it?"

"I think we should reconsider the engagement."

"*What?*" Aegaeon and Hipponax had made it clear she wouldn't be considered a true leader of Atlantis without a noble counterpart to assume the role of king. Of all the other eligible suitors, none had held a candle to Cosmas. "You're dumping me?"

"What? No, I'm not dumping you."

"Not sure if things work differently in Atlantis, but where I come from, if you tell someone you're rescinding your proposal, it's called dumping."

"Technically, you come from Atlantis, too."

She didn't answer, chest hurting too much to deal with sass.

"Come here."

"You're injured."

"Come here," he repeated. She considered resisting on principle, but tired and irritable and hurting, she went to him anyway, burrowing into the warmth of his arms. Even if he did smell like anti-septic and medicinal seaweed. "Honestly, Kai? I enjoy your company. I'm in awe of your spirit, your dedication to saving this kingdom, and so many other things that make you a wonderful merwoman."

"But?" she said, sensing the unspoken word on the tip of his tongue.

"Love never entered the equation when my uncle asked this of me. It's for Atlantis, but I like you enough that I don't want to force you to marry me."

"Oh." A few seconds passed while she digested the news. "I'm not doing this marriage for me. I'm doing it for Atlantis, too. You're not forcing me into anything, Cosmas. These people want to see a romance like my parents, and if that makes them trust me on the throne, I'll do it."

His heavy sigh ruffled her dark hair. "That kind of romance won't happen for as long as there's another mer who has your fancy. You and I both know I'm not the particular commander you want. I've *never* been the commander you want."

Kai jerked back and blinked at him. "Cosmas—"

"I'm not angry at you or him. Trust me. I get it."

Despite his assurance, the tips of her fingers prickled and tingled. "Did Manu tell you?"

He barked out a sudden laugh. "No. I saw it with my own eyes."

"Saw it?" she repeated, blinking slowly. "We were alone, and it was only the one kiss." Not that the temptation didn't come to her frequently, maddeningly, and there wasn't one thing she wanted more in all of Atlantis.

"I didn't have to see you kiss him to know there's affection between you, Kai. I saw the affection between you. Every day that you were together, I saw a man who would protect you with his life not because you are his future queen, but because he loves you."

"Loves me?" The prickling began in the tips of her fingers again. "Don't be crazy. Manu doesn't love me."

"He does. His eyes shine with love for you the moment you walk into a room. The rest of our world stops."

Her heart raced a little faster. "You're wrong."

"Trust me. I've known Manu since we were children. And I heard the words he spoke to you when you lay on your deathbed. He doesn't know that I heard them, but I stood on the opposite side of the door to your healing suite."

"Doesn't matter. Even if I were attracted to him, nothing could be done." Attracted? A fucking understatement. It wasn't just attraction she felt for him.

The moment Manu stepped into a room, she felt his presence before she even saw him.

"There's something," Cosmas said after a painfully awkward pause. "You can be with him, and I'll say nothing."

Her brow rose. "You're suggesting...?"

"That you either fuck him out of your thoughts and move on, or have him as a lover."

"But that's cheating—"

"It's only cheating if I'm unaware, or if we carry on with the engagement. We aren't. Neither of us planned for this to be a romantic involvement. I'd hoped in time we could feel something for each other, and I'd be lying if I said I haven't considered what it would be like to bed you, but honestly..." He tipped his head back. "My heart is with someone else as well."

"You're kidding."

His sad smile said otherwise. "No, Kai. I'm not. Which is why this was a purely selfless act for the kingdom and not for my own benefit. I could happily continue as Commander Cosmas without ever knowing what it would be like to rule as king alongside you, but the merwoman for me is also beyond reach."

"Who is she?"

"Doesn't matter. We are not of the same class."

Nothing could be stupider than the divisive class system of Atlantis. Her lips twisted into a deep frown, but she didn't push the matter. She hugged him instead and relaxed against his chest when he didn't draw away. "I'm sorry."

"So am I," he said after a moment. "As I said, love never entered the equation. I consider you a good friend, and there are worse fates than marrying one's friend."

"I consider you a friend, too." And there were definitely worse prospects when it came to playing roulette in the high mer marriage sweepstakes.

"But what are you going to do about your attraction to Manu?"

"There is no attraction to Manu."

Cosmas cocked a brow, staring her down. His mouth flattened into a tight line.

And she was not fooling this man. No matter how much she wanted to lie through her teeth, he saw through her as clear as glass. Sighing, Kai pushed her hair back from her brow. "I want him so badly it hurts."

"Thank you for being honest about it. At last." The corner of his mouth tipped up. "Misery loves company, after all."

34

BARED

With nothing else to lose, Kai knocked on the door to Manu's cottage.

Common sense told her to flee into the shadows before he answered.

Curiosity bid her stay.

She lingered, anxiety hammering in her chest every second she waited on the stoop under the pale glow of the porch lamp, its silver-blue light cool against her skin.

Pride told her she wasn't a coward to run from any man, no matter how much she craved him, regardless of how wet the sound of his name made her.

At last, the knob turned after what felt like hours instead of a few minutes. The door opened to frame him, showcasing a man with tousled hair and drowsy eyes, bare chest and sculpted abs a delicious torment she longed to touch so much her fingers tingled with as much desire as the rest of her body.

"Did I disturb your sleep?"

"No." He flashed a sincere but exhausted smile. "I crashed for a short while but couldn't remain asleep. Never can hours before an operation."

"Oh." Memories of the last time she'd visited his home danced through her mind, her body remembering too well the feel of his fingers on her bare ass, the taste of his tongue in her mouth. The sinful way it had moved and thrust past her lips, invoking fantasies of how talented it would feel between her thighs. *Now or never.* "May I come in?"

He moved aside. "As you wish."

Of all the men she'd ever felt attracted to throughout her life, Manu was the first to make her knees quake and body flush with heat simply by existing in the same space as her. She stepped inside, watching him shut and lock the door behind her.

"What can I do for you, Your Highness?"

Giving herself a little pep talk didn't alleviate the tension in her chest. Kai studied him, saw he was watching her with as much trepidation as she felt. "You picked out a shark for me."

"I did."

"Why?"

Manu said nothing, only gazing at her with those sad brown eyes that made her want to take his face between both hands and kiss away the blues.

"Tell me," she insisted.

"You want the truth?"

"The truth would be nice."

His shoulders rose and fell with his heavy breath.

"All right. The first time I saw Leilei, you were the last thing on my mind. I didn't go there looking explicitly for a mount to give you, but I've been friends with the stable's sharkmaster since I was a boy. The three of us grew up together. As Cosmas had another commitment that day, Anatolius asked me to come rate the newest batch of sharks with him." He looked boyish and vulnerable, gazing at her with unconcealed affection in his eyes. "We tested her for the program."

"But?"

"No one fit her. She was too green, too young and frisky. Anatolius decided she was incompatible with the needs of a Myrmidon, and I agreed."

"So you decided she was a fit for *me*?"

The richness of his low chuckle created a dull throb between her thighs. "Her beauty was what took me in first, her fins like the sky over Galveston the first evening I saw you. Purple and pink with twilight, a hundred stars above us. I hadn't seen a sunset in years, but all others paled in comparison to that night."

Listening to him made it difficult to breathe. She swallowed a few times, hating her dry mouth, how ineloquent she sounded whenever they spoke. "She *is* beautiful. I love her."

"I'm glad. Cosmas thought she'd be too much shark for you, but I had a feeling you'd both get on well."

Kai stepped closer and cupped her palm against his cheek. "Thank you for coming to our rescue."

"You're my future queen." He drew in a slow breath. Her other hand rested flat on his bare chest, stroking as it expanded with the deep inhale. "It will never be necessary to thank me for doing what's right by you."

"It is." Kai nudged forward with her hips and encountered only hardness encased by cloth, arousal unconcealed, trapped between their bodies. "I saw gliders crushed in the mouths of Gloombeast sharks and squeezed to death by octopuses. You're not invincible, Manu. My near-brush with death taught me something. None of us are immortal. We just live a long time, and death can come for us at any moment."

"Kai..."

"And I don't want to live with regret."

"Cosmas is my friend and I can't—"

"He knows. He gave his blessing." She wouldn't say what else Cosmas had told her. If Manu did love her, those words were for *him* to share. She wanted to hear them from his lips or not at all.

"His blessing?"

"We've decided to cancel the engagement." Mouth sandpaper dry, she licked her lips. "No one knows yet, but it seemed like the only appropriate step to take. I can't see him as more than a friend, and I also can't marry someone for the sake of Atlantis. I'm not that selfless, Manu. The kingdom will have to take me as I am. For who I am. I can't—"

The rest was lost, covered by a searing kiss.

Strong arms lifted Kai and carried her into an even smaller bedroom, most of its space occupied by the monster of a bed and an expansive aquagarden spanning the wall, the kind of marine setup she'd dreamed of having at home.

Funny. He'd mentioned liking fish, but she hadn't taken him to be an enthusiast.

Her back met a bed softer than clouds, then he placed one knee on the empty space between her spread thighs, bent above her. His long hair fell down over her bared shoulder, tickling her when she leaned up on her palms to kiss him again

"I didn't have to convince you this time. I'm afraid if I tease you, you'll kick me out again."

"Exaggeration. I didn't kick you out."

"Close to it. Still...what changed your mind?"

He leaned closer and kissed her neck, nipping hard enough to send a scintillating shiver through her body. "Let's just say I've learned not to turn down my blessings," he replied, chuckling low.

Wiggling her dress out from under her ass, she pulled it up and over her head, exposing every inch. For the second time in her life, she'd appeared on Manu's doorstep without a scrap on beneath her dress. Now that she'd bared her heart to him, it only made sense that her body would follow.

OUTSTANDING. No other word could sum the sight of his princess, sprawled nude across his bed while aiming a seductive smile up at him. From head to toe, her every inch was built for sin, designed for driving men wild with lust.

Manu drew in a long breath through his nose, though that was a mistake, as he could smell her arousal, practically taste it. He growled, gaze lingering on the dark tips of her breasts. He wanted both in his mouth.

His cock twitched hard, straining against the cotton. Before he had a chance to free himself, Kai reached and plucked the drawstring, freeing him again, exposing him to her bare hands. He thrust against her sliding grip and involuntarily moaned her name, much to her apparent delight because she *grinned* at him.

She knew exactly what she was doing.

The pants fell, pooling around his knees. He kicked them off and down to the floor.

From that moment, they were skin to skin, warm bodies and explorative touches trailing over defined limbs, him tracing her slender waist as her fingers caressed his broad shoulders. He kissed her throat and worshipped her breasts before claiming one perfect nipple with his mouth. Her satisfied moan was everything he'd needed and more.

Kai laced her fingers in his hair. "Amerin gave me a potion before I left the palace," she murmured. She raised her hips, pushing against him, grinding her slickness against his hard cock.

He chuckled, breath warm against her throat. "Eager?"

"I've been waiting weeks for this. Months."

"Months, huh?" His mouth traced a line across her jawline until he found her ear, delivering a delicious nibble that sent shivers down every inch of her body. "I want to taste you." He moved lower and nuzzled her stomach, kissing below her navel. She trembled as he traced her entrance. "That's not an answer, Kai."

"Manu," she said, a warning in her tone.

"Neither is that. I want you to tell me how much you want my tongue inside you. I want to hear how much you need it," he said, thrusting two fingers inside her. Kai was so ready they slid in to the last knuckle on the first stroke, her channel hot and tight and so wet it startled him. Her hips bucked against the slow rhythm he began, and then he withdrew them completely, denying her. "Touch yourself. Show me the way you want me to touch you. And then maybe I'll let you come on my mouth."

Her fingers flew between her thighs, and she shamelessly put on a show he couldn't look away from, captivating him. She alternated between squeezing and tweaking her nipples with one hand, plunging into herself with the other until he lost all control and practically dove between her thighs.

Kai fisted her hands in his hair, grasping handfuls of it and grinding against his mouth. He let her, turned on as much by her reaction as the taste of her. He found the sensitive bundle of nerves between her legs and decided to make it his, to ruin her for anyone else—positive from this night forward he'd murder any other mer who so much as looked at her with a hint of lust in his gaze, whether they were common, highborn, or royalty from Pacifica.

He didn't stop until she came first, gasping his name and tugging on his scalp.

His lovely princess was still in the throes of orgasm when he took her. In one thrust, Manu slipped into her tight, welcoming heat. "Kai," he breathed against her neck, unable to imagine ever loving anyone else. Ever needing anyone else. Ever wanting anyone else. Somehow, she'd captured his heart and become more than his princess; she was his queen.

35

ALL OR NOTHING

Nestling closer to Manu to press her face against his neck, Kai breathed him in and ran her fingers through his hair. It wasn't hard to develop an addiction to touching it when the strands were so silky and soft, a stark contrast to the rest of his body and the hard muscles beckoning her to begin stroking elsewhere.

Surrendering to the temptation, Kai's hand began a southward descent, caressing over chiseled abs and creeping lower until she reached his cock.

They'd already fucked twice like desperate bunnies, the first a failed attempt to go soft and sweet that ended with Manu absolutely wrecking her, taking her hard and deep, quaking her body on every thrust until months of sexual tension imploded. The second time, after she discovered he was an excellent cuddler, they teased each other until his willpower shattered. He'd rolled her onto her stomach, dragged her back by the hips, and hilted every inch inside her.

Then rest came. They slept...some, although Kai roused several times to peer at the digital readout glowing nearby, dreading the approach of morning.

With less than an hour before Manu was due to report for duty, Kai curled her fingers around his dick and delivered a lazy stroke. He firmed in an instant.

"I need to leave soon," he murmured.

"I know. Wish you didn't."

"As do I. The general requires the best of us for this operation if we're to retrieve the King's Treasure. We don't know if the Gloombeasts were drawn to it, or if they've taken it and we'll have to pursue them to retrieve it."

It struck Kai as sad that he never referred to Lago as his father. "Won't you have lost precious time, assuming they did take it?"

"Yes. But it couldn't be helped. If Lago is anything, it's thorough. The swarm there wasn't normal. Not within our borders, at least. It's amazing that you and Cosmas survived for as long as you did, to be honest. We're all in awe that you managed."

"You're not alone." Kai sighed, somewhat consoled by holding one impressive piece of masculinity in her hand. If Thalassa or any other deity of the sea had sculpted Manu, they would have had to break the mold afterward. Two of him would be too much sexiness for one realm, let alone a city. "I'm mad at myself for dropping it. I knew its importance, but I fucked up."

His hips rose, following the motion of her fist. "Shit happens in the heat of battle."

"What if it can't be recovered?"

"Then we keep seeking it. Our scouts combed through the area and detected some movement in the underground burrows, but they haven't found the gem."

"So Lago is assembling the army."

"He is. Finding it may not be easy, but the pearl belongs with Neptune's trident." He glanced at the scepter propped against his nightstand. "Just as the scepter belongs with you."

"I know. Doesn't change that I wish we had more time together. I..."

Didn't want to consider the possibility of the swarm assembling in force and growing even greater in strength, lying in wait for them. Instead of voicing her concerns, Kai straddled Manu's hips and spread her fingers over his broad chest, kneading firm muscle and bronze skin.

"Again?" He cocked a brow, and then a smug, satisfied smile curved his delectable mouth.

Kai shifted her weight and leaned closer, kissing him tenderly and savoring each stroke of tongue until she playfully nibbled his lower lip. "I can't send you into potential battle without a goodbye."

"Sound logic."

Aware that fate could rip them apart at any time, Kai slipped one hand between her thighs and guided him home.

Home. That felt right. Being with Manu was the next best thing to being at home in Galveston with her family. He didn't take her shit. He encouraged her. He made her feel cherished, and whether or not he ever uttered the word "love," she certainly felt it when he gazed up at her with wonder in his eyes, marveling at her like she was the goddess herself.

A languid rhythm carried her up and down, riding him gently and contrasting their frenzied first couplings together. What they'd done before had been fucking. This was the lovemaking she'd keep in her memory, no matter what happened.

Seeming to sense her intention, Manu didn't rush her. His hands glided over her hips, smoothed up and down her stomach before he cupped her breasts and squeezed. Then he leaned forward and captured one tight nipple between his lips, lavishing it with the affection she craved. As she clenched around him, he slipped two fingers between their bodies.

"Kai," he breathed against her skin, only to moan and tug her hair with his other hand, forcing a throat-baring arch to her spine. He nibbled, and she didn't care if he left marks behind or not, only that he didn't stop doing that wonderful thing with his fingers. He lay back again beneath her, gazing up at her with unfettered adoration, his eyes saying everything that remained unvoiced between them.

Does he love me?

Could he love her after so short a time?

He slammed deep, dragging her attention back to where it belonged, the crazy pulsing between her thighs winding the tension tighter with each pass of his fingertip. When Kai's orgasm slammed into her,

Manu was already gasping her name, emptying inside her.

They lay together like that until duty called him away. He slipped from beneath her and entered the shower. Silently, she debated joining him as the minutes ticked down, drawing ever closer to the unofficial moment when they would have to acknowledge what had transpired.

Kai thought of what Cosmas and Amerin had each told her regarding Manu's unshakable loyalty, his tenderness while holding vigil over her, and their shared defiance when facing down the leader of the Atlantian military.

They had no future together.

But they did. If she took her place as queen, they had a chance. As long as she fought for what was right, changing their world one outdated tradition at a time, they had a chance.

They *could* have a future. If only they had the chance to explore the depth of their affection and determine on their own if they belonged together.

Kai remained beneath the sheets until he returned, watching him dress in padded sharkskin and don armor. Long hair still damp around his shoulders, he idled at the foot of the bed and watched her.

"This isn't a one-night stand," she said, breaking the silence.

"The laws—"

"Can be remade. No law is set in stone." She crawled onto her knees and leaned up to embrace him, lacing her fingers behind his neck. "Do you trust me?"

Manu kissed the corner of her mouth and held her close, palm on the small of her back. "With all my heart."

"Then I promise, this won't be the end. Fight for Atlantis, and I'll fight for us."

KAI HAD COME to harbor certain expectations when it came to her Uncle Aegaeon. He had little social time for her, though he invited her to attend court beside him to learn the ins and outs of ruling a city, proving an adequate teacher when it came to Atlantian law. But that was the extent of their companionship; Aegaeon was unavailable beyond those meetings in his office, the throne room, or the occasional lunch together, during which he always appeared distracted, as if he would rather be anywhere but in the presence of his niece. His moods frequently ran hot and cold. He was either affectionate and friendly, or cool and indifferent toward her.

"Uncle?" Kai called, rapping on the door first before she nudged it inward.

Aegaeon was behind his desk as usual, looking ill-rested with his fingers steepled against his brow. He opened his eyes and straightened his back, putting on a genuine but fragile smile. "Kai, you should be resting. How are you feeling now?" He gestured to a seat.

"Better than I did before. Maybe I should be asking you the same. Have you slept at all?"

He chuckled. "No sleep for me. I spent much of the night communicating our plans with the archons of our other cities across the Atlantic. Lago wants more mers than we have available in the city to exterminate that massive horde. And since his crazy plan benefits every Atlantian, he wants units from every military installation, port, and city."

Kai frowned. "Do you think he'll be successful? You both made it clear that the Gloom can't be pushed back without *me*."

"We can only hope some progress can be made until you're ready. The discovery—*your* discovery of the King's Treasure is indicative of the changing tide. Not only was it exceptional for morale among the Myrmidons, who have fought against this sickness for centuries without improving our position, but it's a sure sign that the goddess hasn't forsaken us after all. We are no longer in a position to rest on our laurels while awaiting your transition to queen."

"I suppose. But I saw what happened out there when Commander Manu led his squad. He lost half of his men rescuing us."

"Ten. He lost ten. That assault annihilated all but Manu and a single pilot, and had reinforcements not arrived when they did, I suspect everyone would have perished."

Kai's vision blurred, eyes stinging with unshed tears creeping from beneath her lashes. No one had told her everyone was lost.

"There were six squads in the skiff led by Captain Leander, and of those seventy-two men, fifty-seven died as Cosmas and Manu bore you away."

Her airway became a pinhole-sized passage, barely allowing her to breathe. Sixty-seven men dead in a single battle, all because she'd left the city gates.

"You're wondering why I'm telling you this. Why I'm giving you numbers."

"Yes." She wasn't sure if she actually made a sound, or if her lips only formed the word.

"Because I've made decisions and approved military maneuvers for twenty-five years since taking the throne, sending thousands of mers to die in the name of Atlantis. As queen, you will become the authority sending mers to their death."

"I'll fight with them." She wouldn't sit in a safe office, handing down judgments from a throne room while others died for her.

"You will. When you're able. But you won't always be able to lead them, to battle alongside them. You can't divide yourself in two or three or even a dozen and attend every battle. To lead is to accept death is a part of our realm. To lead is to understand when one must do it from behind a desk, and when one must guide the charging line; to know when you are too *valuable* to risk, and when you are the inspiration the troops need. When it is time for you to enter the battlefield, Kai, they'll rally to you without question."

He'd read her mind. Seen straight through her. "But—"

"Despite the losses we suffered, I can't say it wasn't a worthwhile trade, given that you and Cosmas survived. You spoke of your mother's spirit telling you there are signs of Thalassa still in this world. You found the King's Treasure. It was waiting for you, and I believe that *is* a sign from Thalassa. Hipponax and I have discussed it at length. Lago may have lost his faith, but I haven't. The goddess herself sent you there. Those mers did not die in vain, Kai."

When a gravid silence settled between them, Aegaeon reached across the desk and took her hand. "But enough of that. Lack of sleep tends to diminish my verbal filter. This topic can wait until you've had time to recover from your harrowing experience. What did you come to discuss with me? I hope it's good news."

Her chest tightened. She definitely did not have good news. "No."

Proving to be more intuitive than she'd originally thought, Aegaeon's brittle smile faded. "Have a seat then. How badly is this going to ruin my day?"

"A fair bit."

"Ah. This calls for a drink then." He opened a desk drawer and removed a dark green bottle, two large round glasses following. He poured generously, nudged one of them toward Kai, and then leaned back in his seat to study her. "The betrothal is broken."

The cool liquid in the glass resembled melted

silver and reflected a million iridescent colors, smelling like honey and blossoms with an underlying savory hint that coated her tongue when she sipped it. Kai drank half before she found her voice. "Cosmas told you?"

Aegaeon topped her glass off. His was already empty. "No. *You* told me."

She blinked a few times. "I don't understand."

"Your behavior, dear one. And his behavior." He sipped and gazed out the window. "I may be a noble, but I'm not blind. It's none of my business, so I won't ask how long you've been sleeping with Commander Manu, and I also won't ask why Cosmas has stepped aside. It's never pleasant to be a merwoman's second choice."

He knew everything. Suppressing the urge to grab the wastebasket and puke into it, Kai swallowed a few times, trying to banish the sour taste creeping into her mouth. "Please don't punish him." All her hopes of confidently strutting into Aegaeon's office and declaring her intentions to change the under-water kingdom died, shriveling smaller than a dying anemone.

"Punish him?" Aegaeon swirled the contents of his glass, studying the reflective surface with bleary eyes. "I wouldn't dream of it. There would be no point. I do, however, want you to know the can of worms you'll be opening if your hopes are to change our laws and abolish the gap between the classes."

36

CHECKMATE

A DARK SENSE OF FOREBODING TIGHTENED Manu's gut as he piloted the coral glider from the western dock. The plan was simple. Lago wanted them to descend upon the fields in force to recover the King's Treasure, refusing to underestimate their enemy when Calypso's army had been fattened by a few thousand Helicians and Farers as shock troops.

Manu led a battery of five hundred gliders, half of them ordered to continue west beyond the fields to rendezvous with the three skiffs of gliders sent by Port Bermuda and the additional three sent from the northern colonies of the Labrador Sea. Their brothers to the south had long ago fallen to the Gloom, its vile darkness ever advancing from below the equator.

There were three whale thumpers in their company, each populated by two hundred infantrymen armed to the teeth with harpoon blasters and swords. One of those three would continue onward to join the patrol seeking the source of the recent invasion. They had to have come from somewhere.

Lago hoped to outnumber the potential ambush awaiting them, while also moving his mers into position.

Since Cosmas needed another two to three days to recuperate from his internal injuries and concussion, he assigned Captain Adelpha to lead the charge of three hundred riders in his stead. He devised their strategy from his sickbed and gave her orders via a comm channel when they set forth from the port.

Some of their Myrmidons rode armored battle sharks equipped with harpoons, others on fierce laomedons reserved for only the best in the cavalry. Those needed no ranged weapon, deadly enough without them, but often equipped with missile launchers just the same. Manu had been one of a small number trained to master the beasts prior to his lateral shift to the artillery forces. They'd needed him there more.

Manu didn't think his father ever forgave Aegaeon for that decision. He wanted his son's progression up the career ladder to be identical to his own down to the last rung, ending in acquiring the esteemed role of general when Lago retired in a few decades. The man rode at the forefront of their formation, a proud figure on a dragonfin shark. The beast shone vibrant red, scaled pectoral fins sharp enough to slice a Gloombeast in two.

Still, Manu couldn't shake the feeling that something was wrong, no matter how soundly his father had devised their plan. The plan gave them the numbers and strategy they needed but seemed to be lacking something he couldn't discern.

And it was fucking with him.

Manu grunted, still irritated after the scene in the Chamber of Heroes. While he agreed with the decision to decline Kai's offer to accompany them, the impudent remarks had been inexcusable. As far as he was concerned, Kai had earned not only their respect, but their loyalty as well. And if it came down to it, he wondered how many Myrmidons would choose her over Lago. If any would at all.

It won't come down to that, he thought, although it was more of a prayer and a wish.

"Ten minutes until we reach destination," Lago said over the comm.

On Manu's word, his gliders moved into formation, three skiffs of their battery breaking off into eighteen squads each. They drove past a bloated megalodon corpse, half-gutted but not taken by the Gloom.

Thank the gods.

As they were so large, their skin remarkably thick and difficult to penetrate, rarely did Calypso get her hands on one of those. He hadn't seen a mcg so close to Atlantis in years, unusual sight that it was. Uncommon, but not impossible.

Most mers dwelling in the rural sand beds developed the skill to steer away the greater predators. But once the Gloom took them, all bets were off, and even the wisest farmer or algae sharecropper found themselves trapped underground until Myrmidon forces arrived from the nearest outpost or city. If they survived the encounter at all.

Manu shuddered, still unable to shake the feeling that something was wrong.

Minutes later, they came upon the decimated expanse of ocean terrain once green with algae and glittering with starfish. Sickness permeated the eastern hill face, turning it slimy and brown with rot. Riders arrived, infantrymen deployed from the whale thumpers, and the search for the treasure began.

Coasting over the ruined fields, Manu spotted only the occasional gold star among the decay and refuse. Most of the surviving fauna had fallen into the sink holes, which their infantrymen searched with gloved hands, wearing filtration masks in addition to their helms. No one wanted to inhale essence of decaying Gloombeast or taste the foulness. It couldn't kill or corrupt, but it certainly made their kind ill and could take a mer out of commission for days.

The peace unnerved him, the lack of opposition raising the hairs on his nape. Their forces should have been up to their fins in monsters, vile creatures swarming everywhere.

"It was here that Princess Kailani believes she dropped the King's Treasure," Manu reported, marking the area with a light beam. Mers converged on the spot and began picking through the sand. "Be wary of the sandworm tunnels. There could be more abominations lying in wait."

"Copy that, Commander."

It didn't take long for reports to spill in over the comms of their mers finding action to the west and south, picking off opposition along the way, all easy targets with no direction.

It isn't like them to split off from the horde like this when they lack prey to hunt. What are they doing?

Cold prickles danced up and down his arms. A few of their swimmers entered battle, scarcely a fraction of the threat that slaughtered his squad.

Unable to bear any more, he patched into his father's direct communication channel. "General, we need to retreat. Something is wrong. It may be an ambush—"

"I'm well aware, Commander. We have the numbers to handle anything Calypso throws at us. This was the reason for the additional units coming from the north and west."

"General, what if we've been outplayed? What if the golden pearl was there for Kai to find? So we would return to do *this* maneuver? It's too convenient. It's too *quiet.*"

His father barked out a sharp laugh. "Calypso doesn't have the wit to—"

At that moment, the hill split like a canker and the ocean bottom cracked open, an enormous, terrifying fissure forming beneath them. The truest horror of the deep emerged from the hollowed swell.

In lieu of the horde they sought, Calypso rose above them, barnacles forming her armor, sea serpents a belt around her waist, her lower body a tangle of barbed cephalopod tentacles tapering to razor-thin points. Manu had never seen her, hearing only the occasional tale from a petrified survivor. None of those stories held up to the ghastly reality of the Gloom's progenitor.

"It's Calypso!" Leander cried over the communication channel. "Alert to all Atlantian channels. Calypso has been sighted. I repeat, Calypso has been sighted ten leagues west of Atlantis. Additional units needed."

Volleys of energy bolts and harpoons sliced through the water, though they did little good against her. Tentacles grasped their vessels and used them as shields, deflecting bolts off their own coral gliders. A salvo of harpoons pierced sharkriders and tore fist-sized holes through infantrymen. What few slipped past her defenses struck aberrant barnacles the color of night.

Something golden winked from among the tentacled mass, unmarred and shining against the black.

One of her slimy limbs held the King's Treasure.

"She has the pearl. It is vital we get it away from her no matter the cost," Lago barked.

Tentacles skewered sharks and lanced through laomedon flesh easier than a sharp knife through salmon roe. As she felled their mer, more moved into position. The numbers brought to battle the horde proved insufficient for taking on the corrupted nymph.

His father hadn't planned for that. Despite all his bluster and preparations, the one thing they hadn't foreseen was an appearance from Calypso herself so close to Atlantis. She'd last been sighted over a month ago near the coast of Georgetown, over 2000 miles away to the south, her whereabouts afterward a mystery.

It became a slaughter, and they were no closer to claiming the pearl.

General Lago rode in with the sharkriders, pulling off evasive maneuvers that reminded Manu of why his father had once served as the Commander of the Cavalry himself. When he hurled his trident, Manu followed through with a tight line of focused energy from the coral glider's blaster. Together, they burned a hole through her bloated trunk. The weapon flew back into Lago's hand.

"Fuck, yes!" Manu pumped a fist and cheered before returning both hands to the controls, thumbs on the triggers. They had this. They had numbers unlike anything they'd ever had before.

They could take her.

Others followed them, a combination of misses and precise shots, the next volley of spears from the infantry peppering her flank.

"Defense!" Lago shouted. "Locking shield formation."

A ripple of movement swept over the infantrymen in the front line, five hundred shields weaving together in rows and columns. When her tentacles bashed against them, they weathered the storm of her assault without a loss. The tide turned in their favor.

The man was a shitty father, but he knew how to lead, how to transform hopeless battle into guaranteed victory like alchemy performed with a trident. His orders came clear over the waves, executed flawlessly. They penned her, flanking from two sides with gliders, a third with sharkriders, from the fourth with laomedons. The pulse of battle sent adrenaline pounding through his veins. He piloted the glider like he never had before, weaving in and out and under, evasive maneuvers always beyond her reach.

And then the horde came.

"Shields out!" Lago roared above the din of battle.

Her behemoth size made her strong, but it also made her vulnerable to attack, giving them a larger target to focus their assault. Unfortunately, her skin was thick as steel, the rounds from their largest harpoon no better than stabbing a great white with a sewing needle. They needed every unit focused on her, though that was an impossibility once her monsters swarmed over their ranks.

"We have movement behind us on our six!" Leander shouted, his sharp cry tearing Manu's attention to his rear.

"Team Delta, fall back and cover our rear," Manu ordered a portion of his glider patrol.

"Urgent assistance needed approximately thirteen leagues south by southwest of the Fields of Gold!" a desperate cry came over the communication channel. "We are outnumbered and surrounded."

Similar cries came in from others, and a slow

understanding dawned over Manu when he looked at the situation. Looked at what was happening, at the numbers spilling over the field.

Thank fuck they'd had a backup plan.

"Now!" Lago cried.

The largest type of spear in their armory hurtled through the water, launched from the approaching whale thumper in the distance, its aim no longer obstructed by the hill Calypso had demolished. Thirty feet of steel plunged into her chest but didn't reach her heart. She ripped it out, polluting the water around her further.

Manu swore, as did his father.

When another whale thumper fired, their vile opponent batted it aside, each spear thereafter equally useless once her attention fixed on them.

"We need to distract her and give them the chance for a clear shot," Manu said.

"Any ideas, Commander?" Leander asked.

"Follow my lead. I'll go in from the front. Focus your assault on her flank where the barnacles have been removed. I'm going to distract her."

Gods, I'm sorry, Kai. So fucking sorry, he thought, flipping one switch then another, diverting every ounce of power to his thrusters. He couldn't ask one of his men to do what he himself wouldn't do.

Most of them had families. He didn't.

Leander had a wife. Most of his men had families.

And all Manu had was a father who wasn't a father. Bitterly, he gripped the accelerator and rolled it forward, praying Kai forgave him for not returning to the city.

His glider zipped through the blood-tinted water, a mechanical knife slicing toward her torso. The collision tossed him into the console, bounced him in the seat, and sent pain slamming into his forehead. Calypso shrieked her fury and her pain not once, but twice.

Through the network of cracks in his glider's viewscreen, Manu saw an enormous spear protruding from her chest. It had to have hit her heart.

Instead of flailing in death throes, a wicked grin split her mouth open wide, revealing rows upon rows of shark teeth. A tentacle wrapped around his craft and squeezed until the seals cracked and water flooded inside.

Calypso must have had more than one heart, which meant his risky maneuver had been in vain, all for nothing. Closing his eyes, he waited for death.

Sharply, without warning, the glider jerked again and popped free, falling to the ocean floor among their Atlantian dead, where it stirred flotsam and bits of Gloombeast. Above them, he saw his father's battleshark fiercely biting the same tentacle, its rider thrusting his trident into Calypso's rubbery flesh.

He also saw the moment his father died.

Calypso's barb rent Lago's cuirass like tissue paper and burrowed through him, emerging from his back in a red cloud. Helpless to do anything but shout, Manu's fingers froze over the controls, body rigid and unmoving. Reflexes failed him. There was nothing he could do.

As the hundred remaining gliders converged on the scene, Calypso rocketed away into the darkness, carrying with her the prize to top all prizes.

Her goal had never been to further weaken their army or storm Atlantis.

She had what she came for.

IN THE HOURS following their crushing failure, Kai listened to debates from the Council of Lords regarding the promotion of a new general. In an unanticipated display of empathy, her uncle dismissed Manu from duty for the evening.

Then he arranged for a memorial to honor Lago's sacrifice.

"Have you seen Commander Manu?"

The sentry skated his teeth against his lower lip. "I have, Princess. Saw him only a moment ago heading up the stairs toward General Lago's quarters. He will probably be gathering his father's personal effects for the memorial."

"Oh."

Kai hung back and reconsidered traipsing upstairs. Manu deserved a quiet moment.

But he also deserved someone there alongside him.

Torn between potentially sticking her nose where it didn't belong and leaving a friend—more than a friend, considering their last moments together—to suffer alone, she took the stairs and reached the general's personal chambers soon after. Each member of great importance to the monarchy, excluding High Priest Hipponax, who preferred his personal rooms in the Temple of Thalassa, received a suite on the uppermost floors.

At first, she didn't see him in the dimmed suite, the room cast in shadow. Manu sat on a bench positioned beside a floor-to-ceiling window overlooking the city below, his silhouette highlighted by the colors of a thousand lights.

She saw nothing but his stiff spine and downward tilted head, damp hair concealing his face. He'd already lost a mother. Now Calypso's viciousness had stolen his father. No platitudes from the mortal world seemed sufficient. And as no words could convey what was on her mind, Kai stepped closer and slipped her arms around him.

Manu said nothing, and time stood still. She waited for his rejection or for him to rebuke her, and when none came, she relaxed into him. His arms slid around her waist, and he tilted his brow against her middle.

Sometimes silence was better than words.

Fairy Tale Retellings

Beauty and the Beast

Red and the Wolf

Goldilocks and the Bear

Belle and the Pirate

Zarina and the Djinn

Rapunzel and the Griffin Prince

Sci-Fi Romance

Super Sexy Aliens, Cyborgs, Psychics.

Reverse Harem Romance

Three Greek gods, one reincarnated modern goddess

Divine Ambrosia

Paranormal University

College has never been this exciting. Or hot.

The Hidden Court

The Scary Godmother

Birds of a Feather

ABOUT THE AUTHOR

Domino Taylor is one-half of the pen name Vivienne Savage. *All That Glitters* was her first unassisted work. A video gamer by nature, she considers herself a horror movie aficionado and spends her evenings reading historical romance. She also enjoys the outdoors, jogging with her dog, riding horses, and going to renaissance fairs. Domino is a former correctional officer, registered nurse, and the mother of a brilliant son and daughter.

For more information
www.dominotaylor.com
author@dominotaylor.com

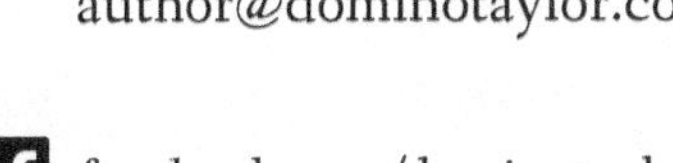
facebook.com/dominotaylor.books

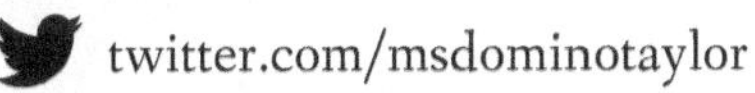
twitter.com/msdominotaylor

instagram.com/domino.taylor